GETTING WILDE

IMMORTAL VEGAS, BOOK 1

JENN STARK

The Immortal Vegas series by Jenn Stark

Getting Wilde

Wilde Card

Born To Be Wilde

Wicked And Wilde

Aces Wilde

Forever Wilde

Wilde Child

Call of the Wilde

Running Wilde

Wilde Fire

One Wilde Night (prequel novella)

For Elewyn

THE TOWER.

DEATH.

THE DEVIL.

CHAPTER ONE

The Devil was in the details. Again.

I leaned against the sticky countertop at Le Stube and glared down at the faded Tarot cards, the best Henri could scrounge up on short notice. The Devil trump looked particularly foul in this deck: all leering grin, fat belly, and clawed feet. Worse, it was the third time in as many days he'd shown up in my reading.

And this time, he'd brought along some friends. I'd turned up the Tower, Death, *and* the Magician card in quick succession. Heavy hitters of the Tarot who had no business being in my business, at least not tonight.

Tonight's transaction, while unpleasant, wasn't supposed to be complicated. It *wouldn't* be complicated, I'd decided. I'd had enough of complicated for one evening.

Le Stube's front door opened. I sensed Henri peering past me with his sorrowful bartender eyes— just as I caught a whiff of the guy coming in. I sat up a little, blinking rapidly. Dude was *pungent*. Even by Parisian standards.

I tapped the Prince of Pents card lying in the middle of all the Major Arcana cards. It was covered by the Five of Wands. Since pentacles equaled money, I was pretty sure this newcomer was my contact: some low-level knuckle dragger muling cash for his king, the buyer who'd commissioned this deal, here to relieve me of the artifact I had snugged up against my right kidney. Unfortunately, I was also pretty sure said contact was spoiling for a fight. Which might become an issue, since neither prince nor king was going to get his trinket tonight, if the payoff wasn't right.

Not my problem, though. I wasn't the one who'd lied.

"Un autre?" Henri sighed. Like most bartenders in the City of Light, Henri was a master of the resigned sigh.

I swept the cards into a stack, pocketing them as I nodded to him. It wasn't the prettiest deck, but it was trying, at least. I owed it a one-way ticket out of Paris. Henri plucked my glass from the counter, making a big production of concocting something way too involved to be my drink.

He set the mess down in front of me and scowled, gloomy concern evident in every line of his thin, hunched body. Which was more than I could say for the guy shuffling up to the bar, who stank of sour cheese and bad karma, and maybe...peanut butter? Didn't want to think too much about that.

I barely avoided a wince as he sat down. "You 'ave it?"

"You didn't tell me about the competition," I said, picking up my glass. "The price has gone up."

"You *do* 'ave it." My contact leaned toward me, his gun nudging into my side. Henri was applying his bar towel diligently to nonexistent dust at the far end of the bar. As if nothing that happened here would bother him, as long as I kept it tidy.

I could do tidy. The cards and their crazy were not the boss of me.

"If you have the money, we have a deal," I said, Miss Congeniality all the way. "Just at double our original price. What's more, I suspect you do have the money, honey, because you knew what I was walking into. Unlike me, for the record. Which, frankly, wasn't very neighborly of you."

His face didn't change expression. "You agreed to the terms."

I shook my head. With the mule this close, we could talk freely without being overheard. If only I could manage it without breathing. "No. I agreed to lift a minor, plate-sized relic off a clueless museum intern. You missed the bit where said flunky was also being targeted by the *Swiss Guard*, who, by the way, apparently don't wear pajamas when they're not at the Vatican. You also missed the part where the Swiss Guard had become ninjas. All that's a little out of my pay grade." I took a sip of my drink, wincing at the tang as I set the glass down again. *Horseradish.* Nice. If I had to use it on this guy, it was going to sting like a bitch.

"But you *'ave* it." Clearly the guy thought he could get what he wanted simply by boring me to death. I considered my options. He was powerfully built, with a thick jaw and a boxer's nose—but his curled upper lip shone with sweat, his beady eyes looked just a teensy bit feral, and his cheeks were flushed. Something wasn't right here. He was too nervous, too intent.

"The transaction was compromised." I spread my hands in a "what can you do?" gesture. "I wasn't given full information. With full information, I never would have taken the job. But, I can be reasonable. Which means your new price is merely double. So go talk to your boss, get the extra cash, and then we'll have something to discuss."

"No." Again with the gun. Harder this time.

Sharper. "You must give it to me *now*." The man practically vibrated with concentration, and my Spidey sense went taut. This definitely was too much reaction for the relic in question. We weren't talking the Ark of the Covenant here, no matter how much I was going to charge the guy.

I reclaimed my glass of horseradish whiskey and took in Henri. He remained at the far end of the bar, well out of the way of any untoward blood spatter. Very efficient, our Henri.

"Take it easy, my friend," I said, as casual as all hell. "We're just having a conversation." It wouldn't be long now, I thought, watching his nostrils flare. The golden seal of Ceres suddenly weighed a hundred pounds in its slender pouch against my body.

It was a pretty thing, really: a flat gold disk the size of a dessert plate, imprinted on one side with an image of the Roman goddess of fertility and grain. On the flip side, a half-dozen thick, raised, symmetrical ridges lined its surface at odd angles.

Not the most spectacular artifact I'd ever been asked to locate, but not the most mundane either. And with the help of the cards, I'd tracked it down easily enough.

Then again, I probably should have asked a few more questions before I headed out this evening. A third-century BC seal featuring a corn-festooned pagan goddess shouldn't have been entrusted to your average intern for a late-night museum transfer. And the guy had been really *young* too. Too young, too clueless.

Which might have caused me to stop and reconsider what I was doing, if I hadn't been so distracted by the ninja shadows of death who'd swarmed the Metro platform the moment I'd made the grab. I'd immediately thought the Swiss Guard had come to swipe the relic out from under me, but why? What had I seen to tip my mind that way?

And why would the Swiss Guard give a crap about such a minor artifact?

"Give it to me," my contact hissed, officially signaling the arrival of the next stage of our negotiation process: brute force. Then he lunged at me.

I moved just as fast. With a sharp, cutting jerk, I splashed the horseradish whiskey into the guy's eyes, then shattered the glass against the bar as his hands went to his face, his scream a guttural bellow. Henri was right beside me, ripping the man's gun away as I shoved my contact flat against the bar, the cut edge of the glass tight against his collarbone, pressing into his thick, sweaty neck.

"And now the price is triple." I glared at his clenched-shut eyes as tears rolled down his cheeks. "You want to pay, you know where to find me. You don't want to pay, I got plenty others who will."

"You wouldn't," he sputtered. He tried to open his eyes, but that wouldn't be happening anytime soon. "You were 'ired to—"

"You bet your crusty baguette I would. Tell your boss that if he's got the money, then he'll get the package. Otherwise, no deal." I stepped back as Henri and Le Stube's bouncer moved in. Henri whipped a spotless white towel off his shoulder to help my contact get cleaned up, while his muscle stood ready to hold the guy tight until I got out of there.

No wonder I liked this place so much.

Stepping into the warm, muggy night, I strode toward the Luxembourg Gardens without too much hurry, the popular tourist destination still illuminated despite the fact that it was nearing midnight. I angled my way through a dozen or so manicured plots, waiting for a tail to materialize. None did that I could see, so I changed course. I had that creepy crawly feeling of being followed, but there was nothing for it. I had more work to do.

Besides, all was not lost tonight. Not yet, anyway. Chances were good that the king of pents would cough up the money for his relic. Even at triple his original cost, it was probably a steal, if my contact's panic and the interest of the *freaking Swiss Guard* was any indication.

But, if the deal blew up, so be it. It wouldn't be the first time I'd been left holding the proverbial bag; it wouldn't be the last.

And I hadn't been lying back at Le Stube. The magical antiquities black market *had* been heating up for the past couple of years. If there were already two parties gunning for this chunk of gold — my buyer and, apparently, the pope — then someone else with money to burn was probably sniffing around too.

That cheered me up.

I left the Luxembourg Gardens and skirted the Odéon, turning onto the Rue de Tournon as I let my stride lengthen. Paris was drying out from a recent drizzle, and everything smelled like spring.

Father Jerome would be waiting for me, and though I'd wanted to be able to give him more cash tonight, I was not arriving empty-handed. It would be enough, I thought. It had to be enough.

I turned onto the Boulevard Saint-Germaine and scanned the long, wide street. As usual, the neighborhood was hopping, but that didn't concern me so much. As I approached the church, however, something about the tone and tenor of the large crowd milling around struck me as odd.

Specifically, that there was a tone and tenor.

Rollicking music blasted out from several venues, the partiers unusually raucous, while jazz, booze, and pot all hung heavy in the air. I finally caught sight of a large banner flapping in the evening breeze that explained all the crazy: Festival Jazz à Saint-Germaine-des-Prés!

Ah, Paris. City of Festivals.

I slipped into the throng, drifting toward the arched entryway to the church. With this many people, I could have been a gorilla in a tutu and no one would have noticed me. The main church entrance was locked at this hour, but, as expected, the side door opened easily into the cool quiet of the ancient church.

I'd barely stepped through before the bolt slid home, then the short, cloaked old priest was at my side. "Bienvenue, Sara." As always, his quiet greeting was as comforting as warm bread. "Is everything all right?" Though a native Parisian, Father Jerome's English was flawless, his words sounding richer and somehow more intelligent in his thick French accent.

I shrugged. "I had to cut short tonight's negotiations." We walked toward the nave of the church, where colorful frescoes gleamed in the gentle light of dim sconces, and I let myself relax a notch or two. Here in this sacred space, there was solace to be had. Even if just for a little while.

As we paused in front of the altar, where the light was highest, I reached into the left side of my jacket and pulled out the thick money pouch. I handed it to Jerome. "I'd wanted there to be more. The list grows longer."

"It will always be long." The priest's words were a quiet absolution I'd not realized I needed. He reached for the pouch but didn't take it from me immediately. Instead, his soft, papery hands enveloped mine, and he stared up at me. "You are *tired*, Sara. The need will always outstrip those who serve, and we cannot lose you too."

"You won't lose me." I pressed the money into his palms and turned away. "It's thirty thousand. That won't go very far." *It will hopefully be many times more than that, soon.* But I couldn't promise that to Father Jerome. I was done with promises I couldn't keep.

"It will go as far as it must." It was always this way with him — Father Jerome was careful, calm, and sure, even as he took risks that would have terrified a man half his age. Risks to protect the youngest and most defenseless members of the psychic community, whose very innocence made them coveted commodities on the arcane black market.

Standing in the half-light of the nave, he weighed the package in his hands. "We must make choices, though. The boy in Chartres shows promise — and with promise comes danger. He and his family currently live outside the village in relative safety, but small pilgrimages have begun to bring them food and gifts."

I grimaced. "What did he do?"

"The village's crops had failed two years running. A month ago, he blessed the soil in which they grew." Jerome chuckled. "Which ordinarily would have bought us more time, except the villagers have already gathered their first harvest, and it is barely spring."

A proven ability to hurry along the growing season? That wasn't good. "Then he's the priority. Chartres draws too much attention anyway with its ley line configuration. Someone will notice what's going on there. The family should be moved before there's trouble." I squinted at Jerome. "Only child?" He nodded. Single children were the norm in families like this. "Who else?"

"Two other families remain on the watch list," he said. "In Turin and San Sebastian. Those are established cities, with friends close at hand, and the children are young. So far, whispers of their abilities have been kept to close relatives. The château in Bencançon has received five more families in the last week, however, and yet another orphan. So whatever is not needed for the boy in Chartres will go there. And the search continues for others. " He sighed. "The young healer in Linz has not been recovered. The twin girls from Kavala, it has been nearly a month without word. The same with the child from Berlin. Fifteen remain at large, and those are merely the ones we know. "

"Pierre-Charles?" I couldn't keep the hope out of my voice, but I knew the answer before the old priest shook his head.

"He...was found in Nimes. His heart and eyes removed."

I glanced away, knowing the image would haunt me anyway, along with too many others. Pierre-Charles had been a blond, blue-eyed boy of fourteen, his features angelically perfect. But he had not been taken for his fair skin or sweet face.

He had been taken for what he saw.

Visions of holy fire and retribution, of a scourge of wings that would sweep the earth clean of its filth and degradation. Visions he'd been stupid enough to share with his fellow students at some backward Toulouse boarding school. Word had gotten out too fast for us to intervene. By the time we'd reached Toulouse, Pierre-Charles was gone.

Magic was a bloody business these days. True members of the Connected community had value as tools, yes. But also as donors for rituals. Their eyes, their organs, their limbs could all give power to a dark practitioner, or so it was said. And children with such abilities were considered to be especially precious.

It was always the children who paid.

"Bounty hunters?" I turned back to Father Jerome. "Or scared locals?"

"Hunters, we believe. The body was dumped outside the city, the surgery precise." He shifted in the half-light. "The dark Connected grow bold."

I nodded. "Something's bothering them."

I'd met Father Jerome on my second assignment, more than five years ago. He was an acknowledged expert in Roman antiquities. More importantly, he'd actually once seen the trinket I'd been commissioned to find on that particular job.

We'd worked well together, then Jerome had hired me to liberate some second-rate reliquary from a cesspool of dark magic. Back then, I didn't know how deep the underworld had become. Back then, I'd just been on the run, willing to hire out to everyone and anyone with money to spend and artifacts to find.

But I'd been lucky. Father Jerome had proven to be an able instructor.

I'd found other such instructors along the way. And with instruction had come awareness, then knowledge, then understanding. And, sure, the occasional betrayal. Eventually, I'd learned about the black market bounty hunters who were being paid top dollar to deliver not simply artifacts but real-live people as well, gifted psychics who could be used as arcane sacrifices — the younger and more untrained the better.

I tried to keep out of it, not get involved. I knew better than to make connections I couldn't easily walk away from. After that crisp, sunny morning in

Memphis ten years ago, when my whole world had gone up in a rush of fire and smoke and pain, I needed to stay as far off the grid as possible.

But I couldn't help myself in the end. Not when children were going missing.

Some things never changed.

"I should have more for you soon." A new thought struck me. Maybe Father Jerome would know what the big deal was about my current relic, why it'd suddenly been elevated to Rome's Most Wanted list. The old priest was an expert on antiquities, and I had a vague recollection that Saint-Germaine-des-Prés had been erected on a Roman shrine of some kind. I reached into my jacket. "Actually," I began—

"*A moment, Miss Wilde.*" The sensually familiar voice riffled through my mind, setting me on edge. "*I would rather you not do that.*"

"Yes?" Jerome frowned at me as I stiffened. "What is it, Sara?"

Dammit, Armaeus. "Just…Give me a minute."

I turned and strode down the long central corridor of the church, the world falling silent around me.

Then, as shockingly white light flashed through the soaring stained glass windows, the sky rained down with fire.

CHAPTER TWO

"Sara, it's only the fireworks! They're harmless!"

Father Jerome's words didn't slow me down. The lightshow outside was definitely fireworks, yes.

But harmless?

Not exactly.

With a shiver of premonition icing my skin, I exited the building and plunged back into the milling crowd of jazz fans before turning around to stare up at the sky along with everyone else. The night exploded once again, this time in an electric shower of blues and reds and greens. Starkly outlined against the night sky, the main tower of Saint-Germaine-Des-Prés was silhouetted by a burst of falling fire.

It looked *identical* to the Tower card I'd drawn at Le Stube not thirty minutes earlier.

Of course, I'd also drawn the Magician, the Devil, and Death in that reading. And now, here was the Magician standing not two feet from me, smelling of fire and heavy spices, of books and mystery and wonders untold, a genie uncorked from his bottle.

Man, he always smelled good. It was one of his finest attributes.

"What are you doing in Paris?" I asked, my gaze still pinned on the sky.

"I could ask you the same thing, but..." Armaeus

Bertrand's richly intoned words lingered in the air, leaving no doubt that he'd been following me this whole time. *Asshat.* I should have known better than to hook up with a guy who'd been around longer than the Arc de Triomphe.

Nevertheless, it was time for a refresher course on boundaries. "This isn't your job, Armaeus."

"I've taken an unexpected interest."

"Then I hope you've taken out an unexpected loan. Because if not, we're done here." I turned to him, praying that the newest talisman I'd purchased to blunt his effect on me would do its job.

Not even close.

Half-French, half-Egyptian, Armaeus Bertrand was a sleekly muscled male of rare and exceptional beauty. A male *what*, exactly, I still wasn't quite sure. He stood well over six feet, though I didn't think of him as tall so much as...overwhelming. Rich, ebony hair hung in thick waves to his shoulders, and his face was starkly beautiful, all bronzed skin and elegant eyebrows and sculpted cheekbones that angled down to that lushly sensual mouth.

For tonight's rendezvous, he'd paired a clearly expensive black suit with a royal blue silk shirt, open at the neck to reveal another swath of rich caramel skin. Everything about the man screamed money, power, and danger.

Most especially danger.

Now his pale gold eyes were more than a little amused as he watched me struggle to focus again. I randomly found two brain cells that remained firing and linked them together, rekindling my ability for speech. "So what kind of interest do you have in my relic?"

"An intensely...personal interest." He spread his

hands, his French blood ensuring that his merest shrug sparked carnal desires. Images suddenly scored through my mind: Armaeus naked and predatory, all that magnificent strength and intensity focused solely on me, his fingers sparking fire on my skin, his gaze locked on mine, his mouth —

I blinked rapidly, realizing that all the oxygen had somehow been sucked out of my lungs.

Which was, admittedly, making it tough to breathe.

"*Quit* that," I grated out, taking a sharp step back. Annoyed, I worked the hematite bracelet from my right wrist and let it fall to the cobblestones. Yet another charm that had failed the test.

Armaeus chuckled softly. "It is pointless to ward yourself against me, Miss Wilde. You will tire of this game long before I do."

"So you keep saying." I straightened, willing myself not to touch the one trinket that *had* worked against this man, an ornate knot on a long silver chain I'd purchased after consulting a carnie-level Connected on the south side of the Vegas Strip.

The Tyet had cost me half a year's wages, but it had been worth it. Sadly, Nikki the Seer had warned me straight up that the amulet's purpose was specifically to prevent actual sex. I didn't want to think about all the crazy that left up for grabs, especially not with someone old enough to have survived the plague.

"Cut to the chase, Armaeus," I said instead. "I've got work to do. What is this 'personal' interest? And how much are you willing to pay?"

His golden eyes regarded me steadily. "The seal is intact?"

"Of course it's intact." I didn't ask how he knew about the seal. I didn't need to. To the rest of the world, Armaeus Bertrand was a reclusive Vegas-based hotelier and casino owner. To me, and to other Connected who were, well, connected, he was the Magician. As in the Original Alchemist, the Trickster of the Tarot, the Cobbler...and the leader of the Arcana Council that was—quite naturally, I suppose—currently based in Las Vegas, Nevada. Keeping the world safe for all things magical.

I'd never heard of Armaeus Bertrand before he'd hired me for my first job with the Council about a year ago, after an epic night in Rio de Janeiro surrounding a highly coveted fertility idol. A new client materializing out of thin air hadn't fazed me so much at the time. I was used to anonymous players hitting the scene. And while my little knot of carnie psychics and magical artifact finders was chatty, we couldn't keep up with every flush nut job who trolled the circuit jonesing for some lost amulet or sacred tome.

So to me, Armaeus Bertrand had been no different, at least at first. And after the dust had cleared in Rio, he'd commissioned me to track down a dubious-sounding "Atlantean bowl" owned by an even more dubious-sounding Sicilian.

I'd found the bowl, of course, though it'd looked no more Atlantean than I did. The next day, a pile of cash had shown up in my account...along with Armaeus Bertrand's personal invitation to take on a second job.

At that point, of course, I *had* tried to do a background check on the guy. Sadly, my Google Fu was not strong. After I'd hit a few dozen sites listing the man's Vegas creds but no photos, no rap sheet, and no Facebook page, I'd gotten distracted by a before-and-after article on celebrity plastic surgery gone terribly wrong. And that was that. My usual sources had nothing on the guy, and my unusual sources weren't talking.

Either way, the man and his Council paid very well. Two jobs had led to three. Three to four.

Armaeus had insinuated himself into my dreams and more than his share of hallucinations from our very first contact, which had been a little intrusive, but it had its upsides. Eventually, he'd wanted more, I hadn't, and we'd adopted a grudging détente.

Unfortunately, he was a persistent pain in the ass. After my third job for the Council, he'd begun insisting I meet with him in person. By the fifth, he'd gotten me to show up in Vegas for longer than thirty minutes at a time.

By the seventh assignment, after a night of too much absinthe and too little sleep, I'd taken him to bed. Totally better than a gold pen, I'd thought at the time.

Fool me once.

Since then, Nikki's Tyet had kept my virtue intact, and for whatever reason, the Magician hadn't been super successful at crawling around in my mind. We could talk, but he couldn't compel me — usually.

But now Armaeus was here...and he wanted the seal?

I considered that. My contact back at Le Stube wasn't exactly going to be announcing his Mensa candidacy anytime soon, but he *had* figured out that I'd scored his Roman party favor. How pissed off would the king of pents be to find out I'd not merely flummoxed his flunky, but I'd pawned off said artifact not thirty minutes later?

Then again, I'd stated my new price, and Monkey-Boy hadn't been willing to pay. So how was this my fault?

"Is there a problem?" Armaeus hadn't seen fit to disappear into a puff of smoke during my mental gymnastics, but his attention wasn't solely on me, but on whatever was over my right shoulder. "Other than the fact that you are being followed?"

I scowled at the men I'd also just noticed — dark uniforms, black berets. Not *these* guys again.

"How'd you even see them? The guys I'm looking at are directly behind you. And what is *up* with the Swiss Guard tonight, anyway? Since when does the pope care this much about pagan gold?"

"Those men are not quite the Swiss Guard, Miss Wilde."

"I beg to differ," I differed, my gaze trained on the stylish soldiers of death. "Maybe you didn't see them? Tall, dark, enthusiastic? Snappy berets?" It certainly *was* the Swiss Guard.

True, they were all sporting black ninja gear, and their berets looked more special forces than ceremonial snap caps, but even at fifteen feet, I could see one of them had a papal seal tattoo right behind his ear: crossed keys, mantle, rope, pope hat. Vatican City all the way. That must have been what'd tipped me off when I'd seen them the first time, in the Paris Metro station — right before I'd swiped the golden seal from the museum courier, then nearly took my own life running along the tracks. Totally the same guys. Swiss Guard.

I glanced smugly at Armaeus, in case he'd missed my obvious smackdown. He stared back at me and shook his head. Some people just couldn't concede the point.

"I did note the presence of those men, yes. They are not your initial concern, however."

Then, without warning, Armaeus pulled me up against his body, *hard*. My pulse jacked, my sight dimmed, and everything froze up in shocked and shivering pleasure — except my mouth.

Naturally.

"Hey!" I hissed. "What are you—"

"Shh." Armaeus's whisper was right at my ear. "In addition to your not-quite Swiss Guard, the men to whom *I* am referring entered the crowd a few moments after you. They have since been joined by a fourth gentleman. They lost you when you entered the church, then regrouped once you stepped outside again. One of them has a newly-bandaged neck. Yes." Armaeus noted my flinch. "I suspected that was your doing. Give me the seal, Miss Wilde."

"But how'd they find me?" Without answering, Armaeus abruptly turned deeper into the crowd, towing me along with him. Then, with a movement so fast I had no hope of stopping it, he reached into my jacket and slid the Ceres seal free.

Something inside me deflated a little, as I realized I'd been violated without even getting dinner first. Pungent or not, my prince of pents back at Le Stube had been on the hook for at least eighty thousand euros for this little snatch and pitch. I really, *really* hated to see that money go. "You're paying for that, you know. And for the record, it's gotten really expensive."

"Keep moving." Without breaking stride, Armaeus opened the velvet bag and withdrew the heavy gold disk, slipping it into an interior pocket of his own jacket. He then tucked the seal's pouch into the pack of an oblivious passing tourist. I saw the young man plow energetically into the crowd, and didn't miss how half the Swiss Guards' heads swiveled to watch him go. The pouch had been bugged? By the *Guard*? How did that make any sense?

Armaeus steered me off the square, but it was too

late. The crush of tourists rapidly dwindled, and I could hear the boots of multiple men striding into the street behind us. Even if the Swiss had LoJacked the pouch, the prince of pents and his buddies were following us by sight alone. My brain bumped back online. "Hey," I protested. "Hang on a second. Those guys might actually be here to make good on this job. I need to talk with them."

"They are not interested in talking, Miss Wilde. Or in paying you."

Irritation flared, and I stopped short. "You don't know what you're talking about. And that money is import—*shit*!"

A sudden flare of semiautomatic rifle fire peppered the brick wall over our shoulders as Armaeus ducked low and pulled me into a side street that was little more than an alley, but at least it was heading in the right direction: away from the crazy men with guns.

"Three streets over," Armaeus said, his words unrushed over the clatter of my thrift-store boots and his million-dollar loafers. "A driver will transport us to safety." Behind us, I again detected the dulcet tones of my contact as he snarled something in French. Armaeus glanced back, his teeth glinting white as he grinned. Then I heard my contact's cry of confusion.

It was the last sound he ever made.

A second round of gunfire punctuated the night, the sound of the silenced weapons like the breathy popping of balloons, overtaken by the shouts of pain and the crunch of bodies falling to the ground. The Swiss Guard flowed into the street behind us, and Armaeus yanked me close. Every one of my nerve endings flared like a neon sign at his touch, but I knew better than to resist this time. The man could *move*. And sure enough, with each of his strides now, the pavement shot beneath us like a rushing torrent.

The Swiss Guards' angry Italian dwindled into the distance, and the buildings around us blurred. Trapped in that strange cocoon of movement, however, my mind refocused my cards. It always came back to the cards, and the cards had predicted Death. Sure enough, Death was all around me, shimmering in the night.

The cards had been right on the money, in fact — first the exploding Tower, then the Magician, then Death. All of them appearing in rapid succession, each more alarming than the last. The only card left was — the Devil.

What did the Devil card mean this night? More lies, more deceit? Or was its appearance simply a marker, a warning that I was about to head into the underbelly of society, down the well-trod rabbit hole of crime, prostitution, drugs, and death?

Maybe. Or maybe I'd soon be enjoying Devil's Food cake.

I voted for Option B.

Armaeus turned again, and he finally let me go, our racing footsteps slowing to a fast trot. I blew out a sharp breath, and forced myself to focus. No streetlamps cut the gloom of this dark street, but Armaeus had definitely relaxed.

Squinting into the darkness, I saw why.

A low, sleek limousine purred ahead of us in the shadows, double-parked on the street. Without speaking, Armaeus guided me to the car, but given that the danger was past, all the familiar panic alarms were going off inside me. Dealing with the Magician was hard enough when I could maintain my own personal space. Being stuck in the tight confines of a limousine with the guy was something else again. I honestly didn't know how far I could push my Tyet, and I wasn't in the mood to figure that out tonight.

"You know, I can pretty much disappear on my own," I said, taking a step back. "Just wire me the money for the seal as usual, and we're solid."

Armaeus scowled at me. "I have presented *distractions* to the men who follow you, not barriers, Miss Wilde. Get in the car."

"No, really, I'm good. Besides, they're not after me anymore. You've got what they want. So I head left, you head right, and all's well with the world. Easy peasy."

But Armaeus wasn't looking at me. He turned toward the darkened Parisian street behind us as if he could pierce the stone buildings, measuring the footfalls of our pursuers, gauging their beating hearts. Then he flicked his gaze back to me, and his golden eyes sent a chill right through my bones. "Oh no," I said, backing up. "No, no, no. Do *not* even think about it."

"*Nma*," the Magician whispered.

Blackness flowed around me and swallowed me whole.

CHAPTER THREE

"Miss Wilde."

Armaeus's words seemed to emanate from somewhere inside me, followed immediately by my brain's residual protest of *DANGER!* But it was all so far away, so insignificant, especially when all I wanted to do was curl up under the heavy blanket and sleep under the warm, softly muted amber lights.

Wait. *Amber?*

My world swerved precariously in a way that normal sleeping worlds do not move, and I shot upright, thrusting the sumptuously thick flannel blanket off me as I tried to lurch to my feet—only to practically bisect myself on a safety belt. I sucked in a deep breath and wrenched the thing off as I got my bearings, confirming what my sense of vertigo had already suggested. "Where the hell are we? Where are we going?"

Armaeus scowled at me. "To a friend's."

I scowled right back. "I didn't think you had friends."

"You would do well to know me better."

"I'll take my chances on that." I squinted out the tinted windows, watching the lights flicker by. We definitely weren't in downtown Paris anymore. The homes in this area were larger and spaced significantly far apart, and there were no blocklike housing communities. Probably right at the edge of Île-de-France, where the suburbs began to give way to charming cottages and overblown estates. "How long was I out?"

Armaeus didn't answer me at first. A flicker of movement caught my eye, and I glanced back at him. He sat across from me on a thickly padded leather seat, his legs crossed, his manner contemplative. A glint of silver hung from a chain in his hand. I froze.

"A Tyet," he mused. "It has been some time since I've seen one crafted so finely. Where did Nikki Dawes acquire it, do you know?"

I ignored the question. I also wasn't going to beg for my amulet. If anything, Armaeus's interest in it certainly confirmed its value to me. Now if I could just get the damn thing surgically implanted into my skin, I'd be fine. I sat back in my seat and scowled at him. "You want to keep working together, then you do *not* play mind tricks on me again, you got it? I have my limits, and you've definitely crossed them."

A faint gleam of amusement flared in the Magician's golden eyes. "I merely needed to get you to safety."

"Then you merely needed to *insist*. Or knock me out. But you don't *cheat*."

Armaeus's brows lifted in two graceful arcs. "Your outrage is misplaced, Miss Wilde. I have no interest in harming you. Most would not have noticed the projection." He nodded to me as if I should be proud of myself, like the horse that's figured out the purpose of the bit a second after the bridle has been strapped on.

"Not helping." I glared into his beautiful face, gratified to hold on to my fury, if only to distract myself from the way my fingertips kept twitching at the edges of my sleeves, as if taking off my clothes would be the most natural thing in the world for me to do next. My gaze slid to the Tyet swinging from Armaeus's fingers.

How much was my lack of control around him the result of me no longer wearing the amulet? And how much of it was just a simple lack of control?

Toss-up.

Armaeus smirked, demonstrating that he was still skulking around in my brain.

Asshat, I thought very clearly.

Unlike whatever pyrotechnics he'd thrown at my prince of pents and his goons, however, what Armaeus had used on me was *not* a magic spell, though it'd felt like it. The greatest of the Connected had utilized heightened vocal projection throughout antiquity, a manner of speaking that required both intense training and extreme force of intention, so that the words delivered with the chosen vibration practically resonated within the listener's bones. In the hands of a master, even stones and sea could be displaced.

But while I'd heard of abilities to compel at the level of Armaeus's, I'd never experienced it firsthand. From everything I had read, no one had in almost a thousand years.

Bully for him.

"You want to tell me what happened back at the church?" I asked, to keep my focus off my glittering pendant. Then my mind caught up with my words. *Oh no. The church.* I looked around the limo, locating my jacket next to Armaeus. "What did you do with my phone? I need to call Father Jerome."

Armaeus caught the Tyet in the palm of his hand, tucking it into his jacket pocket. Apparently, he was done teasing me with it for the moment. "Father

Jerome is unharmed. I have people watching him and the church. Those who are searching for the seal know he doesn't have it, however. They know you wouldn't have fled with such a prize inside, not with no one but a priest to protect it." His brows lifted in mock censure. "I could have warned you to stay out of the church altogether, and you would never have placed him in danger."

"Uh-huh. And to what do I owe your sudden burst of solicitude? Last we spoke, you weren't exactly part of my fan club."

"You didn't deliver the statue in the manner we discussed." Armaeus's face clouded over, and he straightened, his mood souring. Good. For the first time since I'd regained consciousness, the constriction in my chest eased and my pulse edged away from jackrabbit. "That caused me a great deal of trouble."

"Take it up with the union." Still, I had to be sure. "Is anyone hanging around the church I should worry about? Father Jerome made it home okay?"

"I have a guard assigned to him for the rest of the week. The priest won't be harmed." He grimaced. "It's not smart for you to work so obviously with him, however. Without protection, he could easily be taken when he travels to Chartres."

I narrowed my eyes. "Chartres is none of your business."

"*You* are my business, Miss Wilde, which makes your ill-advised attempts at playing crusader my business as well. If Father Jerome were to end up missing like one of the children you're so eager to protect, you would be of no use to me at all."

He had a point. I shrugged. "So?"

"So, I have dispatched a team to meet him and the young family you've identified in Chartres, to get them to a safe location."

"Awfully nice of you. You must need me pretty bad to put yourself out like that."

He didn't bother answering that one either, and I blew out a breath and stretched my legs, my scuffed boots jarringly out of place in the lush limo. "Okay, next topic. Why all the interest in this seal I grabbed tonight? From what I heard, it's been floating around Europe for the better part of the last three centuries in private but not particularly inspired collections, before the Louvre picked it up. And they haven't exactly been treating it special. What changed?"

"You said it yourself back at that unfortunate bar, Miss Wilde. The black market of magical artifacts is heating up. What was formerly of little interest now has a greater cachet."

"Which is fine, except that little Roman Frisbee you have in your pocket has no business being treasure of the year. The seals of Ceres were never coveted artifacts, and you know it. They couldn't enter a Roman temple without tripping over one."

He inclined his head to agree with that. "Perhaps the one you liberated was special?"

"Doubtful." I shook my head, though the idea of hiding a valuable artifact amidst a pile of worthless trinkets was exactly the kind of subterfuge the Romans would have enjoyed. "Because here's the thing. The Louvre assigned it to an *infant* to carry across the city. If that seal was actually worth something, the museum would have had stricter transport protocols in place. And for those keeping score, there were *two* parties after the thing. My client and the Swiss Guard, or whoever they were. Who somehow managed to bug the pouch." A bug which I'd missed in my careful inspection, so that was some Grade-A tech. "Why?"

26

Armaeus shot back a question of his own. "Why did your client say he wanted the seal? Or do you continue to insist on not asking even the most reasonable questions before you take on a job?"

Another sore point with us. "I ask the pertinent questions. Like what and for how much. I don't worry myself with the why, at least not through any official channels."

"And what did your unofficial channels say?"

His words were offhand, but his manner had sharpened ever so slightly. As the Magician, Armaeus didn't usually have to interrogate someone. He could simply rifle through their thoughts. With me, however, he could only go so far. I'd somehow thrown up barriers without realizing it. Which was a total bonus ninety-five percent of the time.

In this case, though, I didn't care enough to keep the information from him. "My client's family wanted it for leverage, is what I'd heard. Obviously, since they asked specifically for me, I figured there was some arcane connection, but I figured it was the typical goddess-veneration stuff. Lot of that going around these days."

"And you don't think that anymore?"

"Gee, I don't know. I've been playing hot potato with it for the past five hours, and now we're racing away toward your secret lair in the woods." I rolled my eyes. It's a particular skill of mine. "You say those ninjas weren't the Swiss Guard, but I think you're wrong. One of them definitely had the papal seal tatted on his neck, so they had something to do with the man upstairs."

Armaeus appeared unimpressed with my ocular gymnastics. "Your assumption about their provenance was not an unreasonable one," he said. "And not far off the mark. But I will leave that discussion for later this evening. The arrival of their squadron on scene is interesting, but not any more than your client's interest in the seal." His jaw twitched. "Who was it?"

I sensed the pressure of his touch against my mind, my own lips thinned. So he wasn't fooling around on this question. Once again, however, I didn't want to find out how good my blocks were, not for something so basic. "The Mercault family. Specifically the patriarch, Jean-Claude."

Armaeus leaned back in his seat. Not to be outdone, I leaned forward. "And for the record, the Council had better have restitution in mind, or you can kiss any further work from me good-bye. I could have gotten eighty thousand euros for that little hunk of gold, especially with the ninjas in the hunt."

He nodded. "That amount will be delivered to Father Jerome at Saint-Germaine-Des-Prés upon his return from Chartres. If"—he raised a finger as I perked up—"you take on a new assignment immediately. And reconsider my offer to permanently relocate to Las Vegas."

I hesitated, sensing a tidal wave of crazy coming my way. I was developing a sixth sense for it. There was no way I was going to dignify Armaeus's Vegas offer with a response, but the first part... "A new assignment doing what? And for how much?"

"Back to the pertinent questions, I see. You should take better care. If I hadn't been there tonight, you would have been trapped."

I resisted rolling my eyes a second time, but it was a close thing. "In case you haven't noticed, I was doing this for quite a few years before you showed up. I expect to be doing it for quite a few years after our little arrangement has ceased to provide any value."

Which was going to be sooner rather than later, if he didn't back off. "You want to keep me on retainer, you're going to have to put up a lot more cash than what you have been."

He lifted a long, lazy brow. "That's all it would take, Miss Wilde? Money?"

"It'd be a heck of a start."

"And with the money, you think you might have reached the young boy in Toulouse more quickly, I suspect?" His words dripped mockery, and I stiffened.

"You...knew about him? You knew about him and you didn't do anything to stop it?"

"If you took even the slightest amount of time to understand the Council's work—"

"Don't talk to me about your *work*, Armaeus. You've got more money than God. You apparently also know everything that's going on in the world, because it's not like the killers *advertised* the fact that they abducted an innocent little boy and gutted him for spare parts. How could you know that was happening and sit back and let it happen? What is *wrong* with you and your precious Council?"

The car abruptly slowed, swerving around a bend into a path flooded with bright lights. I barely caught a glimpse of enormous stone lions on either side of the drive as we plunged into a richer shade of darkness. Armaeus dismissed my concern with a flick of his fingers.

"Your crusade, laudable though it may be, is not the crusade of the Arcanans."

"Well, it should be! Kids are out there dying every day, which you apparently know with your all-seeing Eye of Sauron. All to give some shit-kicking dark priest a new spleen to stir into his cauldron. The whole underworld is going batshit crazy these days.

Everyone is hyped up—everyone is stressed. And finally your holier-than-God Council is choosing to take an interest, and all you care about is ridiculous gold seals and idols and trinkets? Why don't you start worrying about the people who are *collecting* these trinkets, Armaeus? That's where the real trouble lies."

Beside me, Armaeus's teeth glinted in the shadows.

"In that, I couldn't agree with you more, Miss Wilde."

CHAPTER FOUR

We swept up the driveway into a deep thicket of trees. Within a minute or so, however, I could see lights ahead. A lot of lights. "You're taking me to Disney World?"

Armaeus didn't respond. Rounding the last turn, the road opened onto a palatial estate that was lit from bedrock to rooftop. Beside me, the Magician eyed the house with a curious mix of emotions flitting across his face. Sadness. Regret. Pride. Affection.

Not for the first time, I wished I could crawl around inside *his* head. So much easier than the painful uncertainty of conversation. People could lie. Armaeus was about to, I knew before asking the question. "Um, who lives here, exactly?"

He drew his fingers together, steepling them in front of his nose. It was a movement that for anyone else would denote prayer, a petition to the heavens. But Armaeus *was* the heavens—and the earth. He prayed to no god that I knew of.

A second later, he drew his hands away, and I blinked. His face was completely devoid of any expression except pleasant affability. Gone were the deep lines of tension that had bracketed his mouth. Gone was the stern cast to his brow, the hard set of his jaw. In its place was the unlined, carefree face of a handsome man in his thirties who'd apparently just returned from a six-month vacation in Fiji.

"Whoa. That is so much better than Botox."

"Try to mind your manners while we're here. If it helps, imagine that you have taken on the identity of someone who is polite. Even charming."

"That'll cost extra."

"I have no doubt."

The car slowed, but before it came to a full stop, the front doors of the immense mansion swung open. An actual liveried butler stepped out along with an equally outfitted housekeeper, much more chatelaine than French maid, both of them completely ruining the Downton Abbey effect by beaming like they were little kids.

Bustling out between them was a tiny old woman wrapped in a shawl, her white hair glistening in the floodlights. Beside her strode a remarkably gorgeous man. He was tall, well built, with piercing eyes that stared out from a burnished bronze face, and lustrous black hair that edged past his collar. He was seriously stunning. And, more to the point, he could have been Armaeus's little brother.

I straightened. "Um…"

"Your manners."

With that, Armaeus's door was opened, and he stepped easily out of the car, then turned to hand me out. For the first time tonight, I was excruciatingly aware of my beat-up leather jacket, my three-day-straight leggings, my battered boots. Armaeus's hand twitched with annoyance, so I took it a little harder than necessary, practically ripping his fingers off as I hauled myself out of the car.

"Mon seigneur." A man I hadn't noticed was flanking the car now, but before he could fully get the words out, the old woman exclaimed with sheer delight. She dashed down the steps like she was eight, not eighty.

Armaeus turned as she flew into his arms, and he lifted her up and swirled her around. "Grand-père!" she squealed, laughing like a child.

I tried manfully not to faint. *Grand-père?*

"You are Miss Wilde?" I turned to see the gorgeous man from the top of the stairs looming over me. On close inspection, he wasn't exactly Armaeus's doppelgänger, but I made sure my perusal was very thorough, just to be certain.

Nope, he was shorter. And more slender.

More human too, with his watchful dark eyes appraising me, containing none of the otherworldly glitter that made Armaeus's eyes so unsettling. He nodded at whatever he saw on my face, which I seriously hoped wasn't naked lust, but it was probably a close thing. "I am Dante Bertrand, and it is my distinct pleasure to welcome you to Le Sri. Please forgive the bright lights. We do not often have the chance to entertain guests."

"Of course." I suppose the whole point of naming your house gave you permission not to invite people over. He placed a hand on my arm, which apparently set off an electrical pulse in Armaeus. He glanced over from the elderly woman, his gaze leaping from Dante to me.

"Mais, Grand-père! Elle est—" The old woman blinked rapidly, then beamed more brightly. "Of course, you are American, yes? How terrible of me to speak so in front of you. My name is Claire Bertrand." Though she was technically speaking English, her tongue turned every word into a trill, and I found myself trying to translate. She reached out both hands to me, and I obligingly put my hands in hers.

"I'm Sara. Nice to meet you."

"Mais, bien sûr!" As she gripped me with her delicate fingers, no thrill of awareness skittered along my palms, and I frowned. There hadn't been with Dante either. But there could be no doubt of the family connection here, given the last name and the resemblance.

The old woman chattered on, and I forced myself to concentrate. "You are hungry? Tired? How long can you stay? Please do not tell me you are leaving yet this night."

I caught the unguarded look of open affection on Armaeus's face as he watched his...granddaughter. Surely that couldn't be right. So far in our relationship, Armaeus's deep dark past had not fallen into the category of pertinent questions for me. Clearly, I was missing out.

Armaeus must have sensed my gaze, because his expression cleared. "Miss Wilde can spare only a few hours with us, regrettably. She'll be leaving at first light."

"You are *terrible*," the old woman clucked, saying the word with its proper French inflection. "But come in, come in. We have food and wine, and much to talk about from what I understand, yes?"

We climbed up the broad front stair to the château, moving into a wood-paneled foyer and on down a sweeping hallway. I half expected mail-bedecked knights to be standing at attention on either side of us, but there were only rather boring oil paintings framed in gold. Yawn.

After traversing roughly the length of a football field, we gathered in a room that looked like a set from *Game of Thrones*. Tapestries on the walls, a fire blazing in an enormous granite hearth. I was fully prepared to have an animal skin thrown over my shoulders, but instead I was led to a large, leather-stuffed chair. The servants bustled around us, setting up trays of food and drink, as Armaeus and his, um, *granddaughter* talked in hushed tones.

I took the opportunity to study the woman. She was tiny, with fine bones and large, clear eyes. She also had a fierce spirit about her that was currently being channeled into adoration, but I had no doubt that all her emotions were felt with equal intensity.

"You have questions." Dante had settled into a chair opposite me, his tone conversational but still managing to convey intimacy.

I felt another frisson of attention from Armaeus, but he had his own Frenchwoman to fry. I focused on Dante. "I assume you're family. Kind of a messed-up family at that."

He lifted a brow. "Armaeus is never one to share information that is not required, but I suspect you will get all the answers you require soon. He brought you here, which demonstrates his trust in you, no?"

"Right. You going to tell me the story, or do I have to guess?"

"My family history is not the reason why we're here." From across the room, Armaeus's words drew everyone to attention. The château's waitstaff turned to file out of the room, and I stared around curiously, because that's what I do. The moment the large door was shut, Armaeus moved to the wall and pressed a panel. The tapestry lifted, revealing a large flat-screen monitor, and I grinned despite myself.

I loved rich people. They always had the nicest toys.

Beside me, Dante had turned as well, and Claire

straightened in her chair expectantly, her face no longer wreathed in smiles, but watchful and intent. "What happened in the city?" she asked. "Dante would tell me nothing."

Armaeus's fingers flew over a small tablet apparently connected to the monitor. A line of code appeared on the screen, then winked out. "The information trail in Paris has validated our suspicions," he said. "We've successfully drawn out SANCTUS to show their hand. They are active in the city and have infiltrated the families. Their intelligence network tipped them off about the interest in the seal, and they were confident enough to attempt to take it in public."

"Wait, what?" I looked at him. "You're telling me the holy ninjas were tracking the *Mercaults*, not me?" I felt vaguely insulted.

"The Mercaults!" Claire drew her lips back in derision, a gargoyle with amazing hair. "They are filth."

I didn't dispute this. The Mercaults were filth who paid, however, and they didn't traffic in stolen kids. That made them okay by me. Still, something didn't add up. "I was at that Metro station alone. No one from the family there. Unless the Swiss Guard thought I was part of the family, in which case they're stupid." I shook my head. "And the papal office has hung around for an awfully long time to be that stupid."

Beside me, Dante snorted, but Armaeus held up a hand. "Despite your continued assertions, the men you saw this evening are *not* working for the Holy See. Not directly."

I opened my mouth to speak, but Armaeus turned to the screen. He hit a button on a little remote, and a map of Europe flared to life, glowing stark green against a black background. The major cities of each country glowed as green dots as well.

Overlaying many of those green dots were amber triangles — the largest of which was positioned directly over Rome. "They are agents of a quasi-military entity known as SANCTUS, a shadow cabal within the Vatican. Their director is rumored to be Cardinal Rene Ventre, one of the pope's closest confidants and a compatriot of the inspector general of Vatican security."

"Friends in high places," I murmured.

"Nevertheless, SANCTUS is not an official division of the Swiss Guard or of the Vatican corps. The pope can plausibly maintain complete deniability of their existence, as the office has maintained deniability of shadow security forces throughout its history. We first began tracking the organization's efforts in 1935, but their initial attention remained rather exclusively fixated on following the activities of Hitler and his compatriots, as the Nazis collected religious artifacts to add to the power of the Third Reich. SANCTUS's activity waned in the following decades but increased again at the turn of the century as interest in new age mysticism and ancient faiths experienced a renaissance. In the past decade, under the auspices of Cardinal Ventre, they have expanded operations dramatically. We have been monitoring talk for some time of their growing infiltration of the Connected community, especially as a new core mission has crystallized in recent months. For the moment, they appear to be dedicated to the cause of reclaiming false icons."

"False icons?" I frowned at him. "False to whom?"

"That appears to be a question adjudicated by Cardinal Ventre. To accomplish their mission, the agents of SANCTUS have been quietly gathering religious artifacts they believe to be critical to their cause. Some of the items they have acquired recently are...quite rare. And quite specific."

"And they're doing what with all these toys? Adding them to the papal collection?" The Catholic Church's treasure trove of artifacts was probably the largest assemblage of religious icons in the world, by several times over. "Seems a little grabby."

Armaeus shook his head. "No. While the Vatican continues its interest in preserving and cataloging *all* icons of ancient and pagan religions as symbols of man's imperfect faith, SANCTUS prescribes a far harsher approach. They seek to eradicate anything that is not of their god. They fear the power of such icons to sway a populace far too easily convinced by mystical prophecy or magical portents." He turned to me. "It appears the seal of Ceres would be included in that description."

"Uh-huh. And why would that be, do you suppose?"

Claire turned, her curiosity plain. "Did the Mercaults tell you nothing of the significance of the artifact?"

Dante also watched me as I considered the question. I was a big fan of a girl never spilling secrets, but the Mercaults hadn't warned me that Vatican ninjas were on my tail. Not very nice. "They said that they wanted it as leverage. Apparently they thought this particular seal was some sort of key. They didn't know to what, but they thought maybe that would become obvious once they had a chance to examine it."

"And did you have a chance to examine it?"

"Sure." I shrugged. "It definitely has energy, but not a lot of it. And it's not been boosted. I don't know how SANCTUS could've tracked it, honestly, unless they had a tip on the delivery boy. I couldn't find a bug."

"SANCTUS was summoned to the Louvre to take possession of the seal. They arrived several hours too late."

"To take possession..." I frowned. "But that makes no sense. If SANCTUS was on its way, why did the Louvre send the seal anywhere?" When his expression didn't change, I narrowed my eyes. "I thought you were big on not influencing events, O Great and Powerful Oz. Whose brain did you crawl inside to convince them to send that trinket across the city?"

"That's not important."

"Uh-huh. Kind of walking that 'no intervention' line a little close, wouldn't you say?"

Claire gasped, and Dante edged back in his seat a little bit. Wusses.

The Magician's next words were clipped. "The seal is vital to our interests, and by painting a target on it, we not only recovered it without drawing suspicion, we gained key information about the reach of the SANCTUS operatives. The news that the seal was a critical artifact only leaked in the last thirty-six hours."

"Painted a target." I considered that. "A target you knew I was going in after. That seems a little convenient. Were you the one who recommended me to Mercault too?"

"As you said, you were already in the city."

"Which you damned well knew." I was angrier than I should have been, but I didn't want to focus too much on why. I knew the Magician's stock-in-trade was manipulating people. He paid me a lot to put up with that. But the price was going up by the second. "So now you know that SANCTUS is willing to be drawn out with unverified information, to make mistakes. What about the reverse? You really don't think they suspect you're the one pulling their chain? And that it's you personally, or the Council?"

My words seemed to strike a chord in Claire. She turned to Armaeus with worried eyes. "You must be more careful, *Grand-père*," she said, her lilting voice a shade more resolute. "What we have learned about SANCTUS is not promising. They are amassing artifacts, but we have but limited understanding of what they are doing with them. They say they are destroying them…"

"They're not destroying them." Dante stood and went to the screen. "They plan to use them. As bait or as bribes, whatever works more quickly." As he passed his hand over several countries, their shading turned from black to various shades of blue—the pale ice of Ireland to the almost midnight black of Turkey and Armenia. "The activities of SANCTUS are concentrated in Eastern Europe, but they are spreading through the continent like a sickness. They have smaller operations in the New World, but those are growing."

I looked at him sharply, then at Armaeus. *New World?* Was Dante just being French, or was he drinking the same breakfast shakes the Council was? How old were these people?

Armaeus didn't notice my attention. He leaned forward, frowning at the map. "This information has changed since last we spoke."

"Significantly," Dante agreed. "Activity has been stepping up for a while, but it's spiked in the last few months. And there have been more public sightings of uniformed men giving the impression of Vatican authority outside of Vatican City. Places like Budapest, Ankara."

"Any violence?"

He shrugged. "None that ever shows up on official channels. The traffic of artifacts continues unabated. If anything, it has also stepped up. We're in the middle of an antiquities grab, it would seem, without the usual World War to serve as backdrop."

"Okay, well—not to put too fine a point on it, but so what?" I asked. The severity of my question seemed to catch them off guard, but I pushed on. "You said SANCTUS has been around since the 1930s, right? They've scaled up and eased back their operations several times since then. What's to say they won't ease off this time once they've collected enough toys?"

Armaeus shook his head. "Because artifacts are not all they're interested in this time around."

A chill chased up my spine as Dante hit another button at the base of the screen. In each of the nation states, small person-esque figures appeared, like bathroom symbols for "male" and "female." The darker the country, the more symbols filled it.

I blew out a low whistle. "SANCTUS is behind the missing Connected? They've kidnapped all those people? But why?"

"Not kidnapped, Miss Wilde," Dante said, frowning at the map. "Killed. They're committing genocide."

CHAPTER FIVE

"What?" I was on my feet now, moving toward the map. All those people. They marched across the page in silent testimony. "They're all Connected?" I shook my head, not needing an answer to my own questions. Of course they were all Connected, and of course they were being killed by religious nut jobs. It was almost too perfect. "The community hides in the shadows. They spend their entire lives trying not to be noticed. To prove that there's a trend of harassment, you have to admit that you're a member of a persecuted group, and this is not a club anyone's interested in advertising."

"It gets worse." Claire waved a hand from her chair, and the map dissolved again. How many remotes did these people own?

Still, the next screen was clearly the point of this little demonstration. The male/female figures were joined by smaller figures, unmistakably children. Once again, the countries in Eastern Europe were the hardest hit, but surprisingly, they were followed by India and China — countries that had had relatively low adult casualties on the previous map.

"Children? That doesn't make sense. They aren't trained. Half of them don't yet realize they have gifts, let alone know how to use them. They'd be useless to

SANCTUS."

"SANCTUS is honing its technique," Claire said, her focus on the screen. "The adults seemed like the reasonable place to start, but their loss was not felt so strongly. With the children being targeted, the game changes, and changes swiftly." Her glance shifted to me. "Half the atrocities suffered by the community in the past several months were authorized by SANCTUS. At least half."

I stared at her. "You're kidding me." All this time, I'd thought the uptick in child abductions was the result of the ignorant or the darkest of the dark practitioners. But even I had not been able to reconcile the incredible number of children taken, their bodies mangled and destroyed. "But their—what in God's name could SANCTUS want with body parts?"

"We've no information on that." Armaeus's voice remained, as always, unperturbed. "The abductions and deaths of the children could be swift, with the bodies left out to be scavenged, so as not to draw suspicion. Or they could be utilizing the children in the same sort of arcane experiments that the dark Connected are engaged in, to see if there is any truth to their claims. We simply don't know."

"But why leave any evidence at all? If SANCTUS is determined to eradicate magic in the world, you'd think they'd operate as quietly as possible. That doesn't include hanging out your trophies for your cronies to admire. No. There has to be something more."

"You're right, of course," Claire said. "The abduction of children serves a dual purpose. When the shock and outrage over the abduction of adults waned, naturally they needed to increase their impact. They found an unexpected benefit to their new strategy, as members of the Connected began to try rescuing the children."

My lips curled back at her words. "Bait," I said flatly, recalling Dante's earlier use of the term. "They're using the bodies of the stolen kids as bait, too. Every new abduction, every new death, draws out either someone willing to use the spoils, *or*, equally tantalizing, someone trying to stop the killing. They get both ends of the spectrum."

"And play them against each other along the way." Dante nodded. "SANCTUS doesn't care who kills whom. The fewer Connected, the easier their job will ultimately be. And once they infiltrated the community with information about potential children hitting the black market, they merely needed to watch who acted with intentions of exploitation and who with intentions of altruism, to adjust and refine their influence."

Fury roiled through me at my colossal miscalculation. How long had I been pouring money into the search and rescue of children? Three years? Five? It blurred together as I stared at the body count on the map. All the while, every one of my coordinated rescues, every infusion of money — it was like a big arrow pointing "Connected here." And I'd been standing there with a can of red paint, leading SANCTUS where they needed to go. I felt sick. "The boy," I managed. I glared at Armaeus's profile. "The boy in Toulouse. Was he one of SANCTUS's kills?"

"We have no way of knowing that."

"Then why are you showing me this?" Anger replaced violation with swift heat. "You let me walk into the middle of SANCTUS's little trap today not once but twice before stepping in, and then you bring me here for a game of map the dead kids? To what end?"

Armaeus eyed me coldly. "So that you will understand the stakes. This conflict goes beyond your little mercenary client runs for gold and ancient idols. When I suggest that you keep me apprised of your whereabouts, there's a reason for it. And when I suggest that my need for you on certain assignments is paramount, it would be wise for you to accept the job."

"Oh, right. Because you've suddenly become interested in the plight of the unfortunate Connected all of a sudden. You in your little cabin in the woods." I looked at Claire, who sat frozen in her chair. So much for politesse. "You *are* his family, right? Or what's left of it? Do you guys do anything other than compile slide shows?"

"Miss Wilde."

"How long?" I demanded, turning on Armaeus. "How long have you been involved with the Connected, because I sure as hell haven't seen you at any of the networking lunches. And if you're this knowledgeable about what's going down with these SANCTUS whack jobs, then why hasn't that information filtered down to the people who *are* in the trenches, the ones trying to save lives?" I stabbed a finger at the glittering map. "Even if it's a lost cause?"

"You have no right to talk to us that way!" Claire gasped. "We have been involved in the fight since the Fourth Crusade, and — "

"Claire, c'est assez." Armaeus's lifted a quelling hand. "Do not let her draw you out. She is overwrought."

"I'm way beyond overwrought. I'm well down the track to pissed." I glared at Dante, my anger ratcheting up a notch. "How many of you are there? And why aren't you doing more? Or do you buy into the same pacifistic rhetoric that Mr. Big here likes to favor?" I scowled at him, swiveling my gaze between him and Armaeus. "And why do you two *look* so damned much alike? You've got to be related, but how directly?"

"You honor me." Dante's grin was sardonic. "But alas, no. Le seigneur's direct bloodline ended with him. We are but—"

"That is *enough*." Armaeus passed a weary hand over his face. "Miss Wilde, I brought you here because of the intelligence that my family has compiled— without my direct order or intervention, I would add, as that is counter to my oath as a member of the Council. They can provide you with pictures of the organization's top operatives, a listing of names and likely locations, areas of influences and families most likely to already be infiltrated. You can do with that information whatever you need."

"Oh." I crossed my arms over my chest. "Well, why didn't you say so?"

"Because I thought you would allow them the courtesy of showing you themselves. Forgive me for the oversight."

"Hey, I've had a really bad day." Grudgingly, I turned to Dante and Claire. Dante still smiled at me. The old woman, not so much. "I apologize for my terrible manners. It's a constant failing."

Dante nodded and turned back to the map. "As le seigneur indicates, we have much we can show you about SANCTUS," he said. "You understand, we cannot send you this information electronically? You will have to memorize it."

"You all run out of minutes on your data plan or something?"

"Under no circumstances can this information be tracked back to my family, Miss Wilde." The Magician's tone brooked no argument. "If it ever is, I will lay that crime at your feet."

"Oh, give me a break," I muttered, squinting at the map, which was filling with images of surprisingly old men in dark robes. SANCTUS's leadership, I presumed. "Fine. Hit me."

It was over an hour later that Dante finally wound down, and by then I was swimming. I had a pretty good memory for faces and names, but the information the family had gathered was massive. And the overriding truth all the pictures carried was this: SANCTUS was well beyond some kind of nut job splinter group in the Vatican. These guys were well organized and well funded. Someone was bankrolling the war on magic. And if it wasn't the pope...

"Thank you," I said, realizing that Dante had stopped talking. "I will try to get this information into the ears of the right people who can do the most good."

"We would be very grateful." He glanced at Claire, who regarded me haughtily. She sniffed as I looked at her, and I fought the uncharitable desire to strangle her in her sleep. So I'd been a little testy. It'd been a long day!

Armaeus stirred from where he had been standing at the hearth. He'd been pointedly silent throughout the long speech, almost disassociated, as if he wasn't actually in this room, allowing members of his family to give me information that he, via some sort of pinkie-swear ceremony with the Council, had promised not to pursue. He also thanked Dante and helped his grandmother/granddaughter/whatever the hell she was to her feet. Without acknowledging me, he turned to the door with Claire on his arm. Her spirits, not surprisingly, now appeared fully restored. Armaeus could do that to a girl.

"Dante, if you can show Miss Wilde to the guest suite," Armaeus said. "We can continue our discussion there."

"Or, you know, I could just be on my way," I said brightly. Armaeus didn't honor that with a response, and Dante moved dutifully to my side.

"Claire does not sleep easily," he said. "If you would like to rest while you wait, you will find the guest accommodations most comfortable. We have prepared our finest set of rooms for you."

Finally, things were looking up.

The walk to the guest suites of the mansion was long enough to make me wish I'd packed a lunch. But with Armaeus distracted by his precious petite-fille who wasn't really his granddaughter at all, I figured this was the optimal time to strike. Unless he reached out and strangled his own family member, Dante should be safe. Or safe enough.

"So, the Fourth Crusade?" I asked as Dante stood aside to let me enter the guest room through the large doorway that looked like it had been carved out of a single block of wood. Show-offs. "Not really a great time to take up the banner for all things magical."

Dante laughed. It was a rich and rolling sound, and I realized I'd never heard the Magician laugh. In fact, the open affection with which he'd gazed at Claire was the closest he'd come to seeming like a human as opposed to some sort of demigod.

That wasn't entirely true, of course. I'd seen him in my dreams and in a few scattered hallucinations, which had generally occurred at the worst possible time for me. And I'd seen him once in his own bed. He'd definitely not appeared stoic then.

We walked into the spacious sitting room. I could see another door, closed, and assumed it led to an equally palatial bedchamber. This room was fancy enough, with its thick carpet over rough stone floors, its tapestry-hung walls — and the imposing chest that stood against the far wall, lined with crystal decanters and gleaming metal tankards. Apparently, the guests of Le Sri were heavy drinkers. Good to know.

Dante's words finally penetrated my brain. He was answering my question. "It is the lore of the family, but I am not surprised he has not told you. We do not often have the chance to share our tales with outsiders."

"And why is he letting you do so now?"

"I suspect so that he does not have to tell you himself."

I snorted. "Probably." Curiosity warred with irritation inside me. I should just wait and make Armaeus tell me, but I could be an old woman by the time he got around to it. Unless...

I smiled winningly at Dante; he looked more than willing to be won. "Tell me more about you, instead."

I could almost hear the warning bell sound, somewhere deep in the house. It was clear and light, but apparently on a frequency that wasn't audible to family members. Instead, Dante looked bemused. "Myself? There is nothing to tell."

"Oh, come on. Do you live full time in this maus — mansion? You and Claire."

"No, not at all. I live in Paris with my family. I only work at the mansion — Grand-mère as well — when we have work for le seigneur. Otherwise we both have our own homes, and the house is given over to other guests."

"Other guests?" The warning bell came more crisply now, urgent. Closer. "You mean, what, like victims of SANCTUS?"

"Mon Dieu, non," Dante said, his face aghast. His

surprise grated on me more than it should have, and of course he kept talking. "Le seigneur is adamant on that score. There must be no direct connection of aid or assault among the public. That is not within the purview of the Council, and he has worked too long for them to do anything that would run counter to his position there."

"Then who?"

"Members of the other families, Mademoiselle Wilde. Other Council members as the need arises, but mostly the families."

I frowned. "You mean families like the Mercaults?"

"*Miss Wilde.*" Armaeus sounded more irritated this time. It made my heart happy.

Dante shook his head. "Bien sûr, non. I mean the families of the Arcana Council. Each member has his or her trusted emissaries, who must travel in secret. We simply provide that secrecy as it is needed, the same that is provided to us whenever our need is great."

"Ah...emissaries." I tried to keep my eyes from flaring, my voice neutral, but this—I'd never heard of this. It was one thing to have a knot of half-baked demigods running around Las Vegas, declaring themselves the Guardians of the Galaxy. But an entire network of non-Connected relatives? "And how does that play with the non-fraternization-with-ordinary-people policy, exactly? That's got to be one hell of a loophole."

"The families have been a part of the process for thousands of years, perhaps before such rules were made," Dante said, supremely unconcerned. "And there certainly have been compensations." He gestured to the building that surrounded us, a veritable castle in the shadows. "When le seigneur committed himself to service, he was a foot soldier, and our family impoverished. Now he is arguably — "

Armaeus chose that moment to stride into the sitting room, his face dark with annoyance. "Thank you, Dante. You have been most hospitable."

"Of course, mon seigneur." Dante bowed, the gesture one of fierce pride more than servitude, then nodded to me. Without another word, he departed the guest suite, shutting the door definitively behind him.

"You never fail to surprise me, Miss Wilde."

"Twenty-two families?" I stared at him. "You mean to tell me there are twenty-two families like this one in service to the Council, and I didn't know they existed? Families whose entire *job* it is to help a sister out? You don't think I could have used that help down in Sierra Leone? Or that holding tank in Dubai?" I curled my lip in derision. "And don't even get me started about Budapest. Surely one of the Council Members had some extended roots of the family tree curled around that place. And you didn't breathe a word."

"You were quite convincing in your desire to express your independence."

"From you, yes. From normal people? Totally different story. Twenty-two families. I've probably tripped over a few of them without realizing it. And they never reached out, though I was openly working for you people." I tried to tamp down my outrage, but it was growing like a living thing inside me. Everything was suddenly too big, too awful. Why did it matter that there were families dedicated to assisting the Council? Why did anything with the Council matter at all?

Armaeus shrugged, apparently unfazed by how close I was to a meltdown. "We do not have the full Council intact, not anymore," he said. "And not everyone has a family, Miss Wilde. But if you are

51

finished with your outrage, we have much to discuss. Starting with your next assignment."

CHAPTER SIX

"You've got to be kidding me. You really think I have any interest in working for you right now, after learning all this? I have to get to Father Jerome, warn him. Hell, warn all of them about these crazy SANCTUS people. I don't see you guys putting out a bulletin anytime soon."

"Then I propose you think a little more broadly."

"Do you now?" I really hated it when Armaeus became sanctimonious.

He nodded. "Our interests are not mutually exclusive in this case. As it happens, the greatest amount of assistance you can provide Father Jerome and your compatriots is to assist me in recovering a particular lost item."

"Yeah, somehow I don't think—"

Armaeus continued as if I hadn't said a word. "One of SANCTUS's recent acquisitions is an item of great personal value to me, and necessary for the Council's continued work," he said. "I need you to recover it."

That did catch my attention. The members of the Council were collectors in their own right, and they were as avaricious as any client I'd ever had. But what the Arcana Council bought, it tended to keep. So far, I'd met the Magician, the Fool, and the High Priestess of their merry little band, though there were rumors of other Council members lurking in their hallowed halls. None of the ones I'd met, however, seemed too likely to give up their toys without a fight. "SANCTUS stole something from you? And you let them?"

"Not exactly. But the result is the same. The item is a very old gold-wrought box, a reliquary no larger than the size of your hand. It is unadorned except for the inscription on its seal, which is Aramaic and not important for your purposes. It will be heavy for its size and can grow heavier or lighter as you carry it. But it will not be unmanageable."

I nodded. The longer I was in this business, the less surprised I was by anything I learned. "Why turn to me?" I asked. "Why not tap one of these amazing family members you guys have apparently got scattered around the globe?"

"Understand this, and clearly." Armaeus's words were clipped with irritation, and I'm not going to lie: that made me feel good. "The families of Council members who are involved in our work do so at enormous personal risk, because they do not, in the main, possess any innate magical ability. The fact that one of their number rose to service in the Council does not at all mean that any of the remaining family members could do the same."

"Okay, fine. Then why didn't you go after this little box yourself?"

"My initial attempts to retrieve the reliquary have met with...failure," Armaeus said with a rare display of candor. "I had hoped not to involve you in this particular mission, but your presence in Paris made it an easy decision. It's time that we increased your work with the Council, and this is an ideal opportunity to do so."

"Increase, huh?" That sounded promising. Lying,

backstabbing asshats or not, the Council paid well. "So where is this little box? Here in Paris, or are you sending me somewhere more charming?"

"Rome," Armaeus said. "The relic has been temporarily stored in a holding cell for purification. I am given to understand that it will be moved again shortly, however, which makes its retrieval tonight necessary. It's located in the necropolis beneath Vatican City."

"Whoa, whoa, whoa." I held up a hand. "The *necropolis*. Under *Vatican City*. As in the home of those whack jobs back in Paris —"

"Your compensation will be the full amount for the seal of Ceres you were demanding from Monsieur Mercault, and more." His golden eyes were flat. "You will also cease any arrangement with the Mercault family, until we have identified who within their walls is providing information to SANCTUS."

"Or I could go tell Mercault he has a snitch and let him sniff it out." I tilted my head, considering my options, while Armaeus gave a disgusted snort.

If magic was a two-sided coin, Jean-Claude Mercault was on the dark side of the toss, one of the grittier adherents of the practices of the occult, rumored to specialize in unique drug concoctions that assisted with demonic possession. He wasn't yet involved with the trafficking of psychics, so he did have *some* standards, but still. He was one nasty customer. Which begged the question: "You mind telling me what this 'leverage' is that Mercault thought he had in getting the seal of Ceres? What's so special about that thing, anyway?"

Armaeus's mask of cool civility had slipped back into place. "In addition to the amount you intended to extort from Mercault, I will provide you with another fifty thousand euros. Payable to you—or directly to Father Jerome, as you wish."

I thinned my lips, suddenly catching on. I was good at what I did, and I was used to being paid well. But fifty thousand dollars for a few hours' work was not my standard day rate. It wasn't even my night rate. "What's the catch?"

Armaeus lifted a haughty brow. "There is no catch, Miss Wilde. If you take the job and return the reliquary to me within the next twenty-four hours, you will be paid handsomely. It is generous compensation for work quickly rendered, and, if I am not mistaken, timely payment is of the essence to you. I can have the money transferred to your account immediately upon delivery." His smile turned a shade more predatory. "In addition, I have information on two of the young psychics you are seeking."

A cold prickle iced my nerves, and I narrowed my eyes at him. "What information? And which two?"

Armaeus waved a lazy hand. "There is reason to believe two teenaged females of exceptional abilities have recently been transported to Las Vegas. Sisters, if my information is correct, from the Greek city of Kavala, who have been purchased as—"

"Sisters!" I straightened, my mind instantly ping-ponging back to my discussion with Father Jerome about the two girls who'd been taken weeks ago. "From Kavala. Where are they now, specifically? Who has them?" The rest of his words registered, and I frowned. "If they're in Vegas, why haven't you done anything about it?"

"the Council's role is not to dictate *how* magic is used." Armaeus shrugged. "Merely that it remains in balance. Where there is light, there must also be dark."

Anger flared within me. Not this again. *"That's*

what you call balance? Those girls were *abducted*, Armaeus. If they've been in Las Vegas for any length of time, they could already be dead. Or worse. You *know* that."

"Then it would appear you have urgent business in the city after all, Miss Wilde. And, additionally, the need for the funds and transportation I can provide you." The Magician's gaze flicked to mine, and I read nothing but calculation in them. "I will give you the young women's location and assist your efforts to extract them, once you've delivered my reliquary intact. And I will pay you well to help with their relocation. Do we have an agreement?"

I bit my tongue, pretending to consider the matter. Armaeus was certainly playing to all my weaknesses: greed, speed, and need. In the final analysis, I figured he'd get the better end of the deal, but still: my end was looking pretty good.

And, of course, the money wasn't the most important part of this transaction anymore. If the Kavala twins *were* in Vegas, they wouldn't last long. The practitioners of dark magic were not known for their restraint. The fact that the girls had been alive upon delivery to the city meant they weren't just being harvested for some low-level ritual, at least, but that was cold comfort. They'd be used as tools somehow. Vessels or conduits, their psychic gifts strained beyond endurance, their minds and bodies eventually broken in the process. If I wanted to get to Vegas fast enough to make a difference, I had to accept the Magician's offer.

"Fine," I said, nodding to him. I held out my hand. "Now give me back my Tyet."

Armaeus tossed the silver amulet to me. I caught it easily, feeling its cold reassurance in my hand. He hadn't switched it out for another piece. The necklace was definitely mine, and it felt the same as it ever did. I slipped it over my neck.

"All right," I said. "What else do I need to know about this little job of yours?"

The Magician's expression grew a bit darker, right along with the ambient lighting. I glanced around as the lamps dimmed in the room, and my fingers twitched, my heart rate picking up.

"Knock it out, Armaeus. What else do I need to know?"

"You have all the information you need about the assignment in Rome." Had Armaeus gotten closer? He *felt* closer. "But since you've replaced the Tyet, I confess there is something *I* have a burning need to know. Namely, whether or not that amulet can truly perform the task for which you purchased it."

"It's doing fine." I stepped back, knowing I needed to put distance between myself and Armaeus. It was warm in the sitting room now — too warm. Too close. The Tyet amulet lay against my chest like an oasis of ice, but around it, my skin was fairly blazing. "Did you do something to it?" I crossed to the bar and picked up a bottle of single malt scotch. Splashing some of it into a glass, I didn't miss the fact that my hands were shaking.

Armaeus didn't either.

I didn't hear him move, but a breath later, he was at my back, his arms reaching around me. He took the bottle from my right hand and steadied my left on the glass, encasing me in a cage of sensual heat. His mouth grazed my neck as he leaned forward to pour the scotch, the scent of fire and cinnamon drifting around me, heightening every one of my senses. "Miss Wilde," he murmured. "What precisely *were* you told the amulet could do?"

He let go, and I held the glass in both palms, willing it to stay steady as I raised it to my lips. Unfortunately, as the scorch of alcohol hit my tongue, Armaeus's hands lifted up to rest on either side of my waist, pressing beneath my open jacket to the thin material of my shirt, his heat searing through the fabric. "Because it does not appear to stop me from doing this—" He slid his hands up the sides of my torso until his fingers drifted along the curve of my breasts. "Or this," he breathed, bending his head down to draw his lips along my ear, the movement instantly reducing my brain cells to a quivering pulp.

"Armaeus," I said warningly. Or at least I'd intended it as a warning. The soft sigh that came out of me sounded distressingly like an invitation, even to my ears.

"I think I like this amulet of yours," the Magician said, the words vibrating against my neck. "I wonder if it will let me do...*this*."

CHAPTER SEVEN

Armaeus's body surrounded me suddenly, his hands reaching forward to take the full weight of my breasts in his palms. His whispered words were so quiet that only my subconscious heard them, and instantly the scene shifted in a slight but critically important way.

Namely, we were still in the sitting room, still standing in front of the large chest with its glittering crystal decanters, and Armaeus was still pressed up against me, his mouth at my neck, his fingers playing over my shivering skin.

Only now we were naked.

I glanced down, horrified and fascinated at once to see Armaeus's bronzed fingers flat against the swell of my breasts, with nothing but the glinting silver Tyet remaining to adorn my skin. In some distant part of my brain, I knew all this was an illusion...

But it was a very *effective* illusion.

The Magician's breath was hot, urgent, and his lips trailed in its wake, scorching a line of kisses over my completely bare shoulder.

"Armaeus." The word was half entreaty, half order, and his chuckle sent vibrations chasing down my arms.

"You can stop me at any time," he murmured. He tightened his fingers into my soft skin, and they trembled against me. That more than anything else—

the idea that Armaeus was somehow *affected* by touching me, was somehow as frantic as I was every time our bodies connected, skin against skin — made my knees buckle slightly, the fraying edge of my control tearing further.

I closed my eyes against the sheer sensual assault. I couldn't let myself give in to the swirl of doubts and need, the *want* that bubbled up inside me. My world worked because I stayed separate. Nobody got hurt, nobody died. I'd fallen in love once before, stopped paying attention as much as I should have, and that had ended with explosions and death. I was never going back to that girl, lost and alone, walking away from everything she'd ever known. I just — couldn't.

Sagging forward however, I suddenly didn't mind that my display of weakness turned Armaeus's chuckle into a dark laugh. Tugging me away from the bar, he didn't stop until my back was up against the nearest wall. He pulled my hands high, flat against the cold surface, then leaned down close to me, his golden eyes searching mine with an intensity that called to something deep inside me. An intensity that beckoned to me so forcefully, it was almost a physical pain. It demanded what I couldn't — wouldn't give.

Not yet. Not now.

"Armaeus —" I said again, but my words ended on a gasp as he pressed his body against mine, setting my blood on fire. The muscled planes of his legs braced themselves against my thighs with an achingly familiar intensity, as if we'd been born to this act. I tried to twist away from the contact, my actions feeble as need swamped me again and again, but Armaeus held me tight.

"I can feel your heat," he murmured, and his words once again didn't so much as brush against my ears as

61

resonate inside my mind.

"We can't do this," I moaned. He'd *been there*, dammit. The first time we'd tried to make love. He'd been lying right next to me when I'd blacked out before we even got to the interesting part of what, arguably, should have been the most incredible sexual experience of this lifetime or any other. And then my brain had deleted everything about that evening so forcefully from my memories that I could still almost hear that door slamming shut, warning me to *stay away*.

Armaeus didn't seem to care about any of that. He didn't ease the insane torment his body was wreaking on me even slightly. Instead, he leaned forward and brushed his lips against mine, the movement so needed, so perfect that I couldn't fight the whimper.

"We *can* do this, if you want it." And the fire grew higher within me as he kissed me, hard and sure. Somewhere in the dim recesses of my brain, I realized that his hands were moving down my body, ripping something open as if he was undressing me, before he pressed my arms high above my head again. Though I'd already *felt* naked under the influence of his illusion, this was something different, something more. Now I really *was* exposed.

"*Armaeus.*" I flared back toward reality with a burst of cognition, partially breaking free of the spell he'd wrapped around me. Which was good, because that was about all that was wrapped around me anymore, my pants and boots now tossed to the side, my jacket gone, nothing but my tank and amulet on my body. I should have been shocked, and yet...

"I...I do want this," I confessed, lifting my hands, placing them flat against his chest. "But how — ?"

"Stop thinking, Sara. Just feel," Armaeus said. He

stretched his body along the length of mine again, his fingers entwined in mine, his heavy arms flush against my forearms, my shoulders. He flattened himself against me, lifting me up with the force of his hips and chest, until I hung suspended against the wall, my breasts to his chest, my legs falling naturally around his hips. My eyes almost crossed at the intimate contact, but he held steady, staring into my face, his own expression racked with torment and wonder and—

With a guttural growl, he stepped back from me, and oxygen rushed back into my lungs as I fell forward, my collapse stopped harshly by the clamps on my wrists. In front of me, Armaeus had dropped to his knees, and I realized my entire body was trembling violently as he grasped my hips, his lips drifting against my thigh. Panic shot through me with violent strength—both panic that he would keep going and panic that he would stop. My heart was pounding so loudly in my ears that it almost unhinged my brain from the explosions of sensation at my thighs, my belly, while Armaeus held me hard, his lips plundering my body as if he sought to brand me with his mouth, to claim me for all time.

And…there went my knees again.

"Ahhh, what are you doing?" I swayed forward as Armaeus's harsh chuckle floated up around us.

"Research." As he spoke, he dragged his mouth against me, drifting ever closer to the vee between my legs as I fought against the restraints holding me high. "The Tyet is strong, and yet, I suspect it is…" His words broke off then, and he shuddered out a ragged breath before he could continue. "Quite specific. It cannot bar you from me, if you truly want me."

His lips finally reached the most sensitive point on

my body, and something gave way within me, something hot and primal that ached for Armaeus on the level of blood and bone. Was *this* what I had experienced before, a need so strong, so devastating, that my mind had discarded the memory of it rather than force my modern, mortal sensibilities to deal with the fallout?

I didn't know, and I was long past caring. As the wet heat of Armaeus's tongue slid out to meet my own surging reaction, I couldn't think, couldn't breathe. I threw my head back and cried out, sagging against the wall as Armaeus sent whorls of fresh panic and desire surging through me, my body shuddering against him as his fingers suddenly replaced his mouth to send me skittering out of control in an entirely different direction.

While my attention fractured, unsure where to focus, Armaeus kissed a northward arcing curve up over my belly, his body swaying into mine as he stood again. Then his free hand lifted to push my tank top out of the way of my straining, desperate breasts.

"Very specific," he murmured, words that meant nothing to me at this point as he caressed my left breast with a long, lingering kiss, taking the nipple between his teeth. All the while, his fingers stroked deep within me, curving and twisting, taking me fast and hard down the path to my release. I'd almost lost myself to the play of his hand again when he sucked the tip of my breast into his mouth, hard.

I rammed right up against the edge of orgasm, every nerve in my body ripped tight with tension. Then the pressure fell away, and I blinked my eyes open, barely able to focus, only to find that Armaeus's face was right before mine, his eyes shimmering with an unearthly intensity. His fingers twitched again, and their renewed insistence twisted me into a knot as primal and complex as the one hanging around my neck.

"Please," I managed brokenly, though I didn't know what I was asking of him. Did I want him to stop? To keep going? To rip off the amulet and —

No. A force so deep in me it seemed etched into my bones shot out, matching my carnal desire with its own desperate demands. *Stay away! Go back! You can't —*

And then something, just — shattered.

I didn't so much fall over the edge as crash off it, tumbling into Armaeus's arms, my body sprawling over his, all legs and arms and half-muffled screams. He caught me easily, crushing me in his grasp as if by strength alone he could keep my skin intact. I came apart anyway, my lungs heaving, my heart thundering, and a new and unholy need swamped me so hard that I nearly blacked out, just like last time. Armaeus murmured something to me in a foreign language that very well could have been English at that point, but all I could do was gasp and shake my head violently, tears of rage and panic threatening to surge forth.

"Make it *stop*," I groaned, realizing dimly that I was pounding his chest. "I can't *do* this."

"Of course. You needed only — "

"Stop talking!" I shoved him away as I felt the slender silver pendant shift on my chest, heat exploding from the amulet. I stumbled backward across the floor, landing on my ass near the pile of my discarded clothes. I snatched them up, then stumbled a few more feet away for good measure.

"Don't *touch* me," I practically snarled, the demand unreasonable even to me, given that he was now halfway across the room.

Armaeus nodded, but his eyes looked almost...

inhuman now. Lit with a fire I had never seen before, at least not that I could remember.

"This *sucks*," I bit out, wrenching my clothes on, reholstering my gun, pulling on my jacket as I patted pockets, sleeves, collar, reassuring myself that everything was still there. "This absolutely *sucks*."

"We could try it again if you were unsatisfied—"

"Ha. Thanks, no. I'm good." I drew in a long, staggering breath. I'd held firm. I'd stayed awake the whole time, anyway. That was definitely progress.

So why did I feel like crap?

Looking as if he'd done nothing but poured himself a drink, Armaeus leaned against the solid wooden chest, watching me with interest, but no longer the kind of interest that inspired such terrifying, blinding need inside me. Waddya know. Even more progress.

I straightened under his regard. "Was that why I blacked out the first time before we even...got this far?" I asked. "Why I lost my memories? It was all just—too much?"

The Magician shrugged, but he could not hide his own fascination with the question. "I can assure you, I do not know." His lips quirked into a dangerous smile. "Yet."

"Not going to happen." I shoved my hair back over my neck, resecuring my ponytail, no longer caring how he watched my every movement, no longer caring about anything except how glad I was that the Tyet had worked in the end, just as Nikki Dawes had said it would. I remembered *everything* that had happened between Armaeus and me this time, even if I couldn't understand it. Even if I didn't *ever* want to feel that horrible sense of panic, of urgency, that drive to have sex with Armaeus that was so strong it couldn't be right. This wasn't lust. It sure as hell wasn't love. It was a need that I couldn't merely classify as carnal, and it had come so close to burning through my defenses that I still could barely breathe.

What was wrong with me?

Armaeus, seeing the torrent of emotions no doubt plainly chasing their way across my face, took a step toward me, and I all but hissed, holding out a hand to stop him in his tracks.

"Has this ever happened to you...before?"

We'd never spoken about the first time we'd almost made love. As soon as Armaeus had realized that I'd truly lost all recall, he'd gotten very quiet and very intrigued and had just...watched me. Like he was staring at me now, in fact. I'd gotten out of his bedroom so fast, my feet had barely hit his insanely expensive marble floor. I'd found Nikki and her Tyet the next day. And the Tyet had held this night, after all. No matter what I'd asked of Armaeus, no matter how much I'd desired him, I hadn't given in to that unfathomable need.

Not completely. Not yet.

"Miss Wilde—"

I waved off his response. "Never mind," I said heavily, willing myself to put everything that didn't matter aside so I could focus on what did.

The job mattered. Only the job. That and putting one step in front of the other, walking and walking and walking until you knew no one was behind you. You knew no one was looking. You knew that no one cared.

So you couldn't hurt them.

I squared my shoulders. "Okay—what do I need to find this little gold box of yours? You have a map or something, or am I just going in with the cards?"

Armaeus looked as if he was going to say something else, then he nodded. "I suspect the cards will be helpful, particularly in this search. And you will also be needing this."

I frowned as he reached into his jacket, which still appeared perfectly pressed, and drew out the slender gold disk. "The seal of Ceres? So it does actually have a purpose?"

He shrugged. "The relic is not a necessary tool. Nevertheless, as it has graciously made itself available to us, we may as well take advantage of it." Armaeus's gave me the disk. "Beneath all of Rome lies the Mundus Cereris, or world of Ceres. It is a shallow vault of passageways that extends beneath the city, used by the goddess to search the uppermost levels of the underworld. For our purposes, it leads equally well to the Vatican necropolis."

"Underworld. As in catacombs." I stared at him. "Great. And this seal is supposed to do what for me?"

"The entry to the Mundus Cereris has been hidden since the times of antiquity. Although most historians agree it was housed somewhere in the Roman Forum, the opening, a stone lid known as the manalis lapis, has never been located."

"And this matters..."

But Armaeus was not to be denied his history lesson. "Ceres was the sister of Vesta, the two of them committed to the feminine concerns of hearth, home, family, fertility, and the harvesting of grain. It is not surprising that when Ceres began her search for her daughter, Proserpina, who had been taken into the underworld by Pluto, she turned to her sister, Vesta, for help. But to protect this passageway, which opened up an entire world beneath the city, she needed an entrance that no man would find and use for his own purposes."

"So she stuck it in her sister's temple, dedicated to

womanhood, home of the Vestal Virgins, guardians of the eternal flame. Got it," I said. Did he think I'd been working in the arcane artifact trade for the past five years for nothing? "And you're telling me this..."

"Because Ceres made several keys to her underground realm, one of which we happen to now have, thanks to you—and, of course, to me." As he broke his arm patting himself on the back, I turned the seal over in my hands. I noted the raised ridges on the back again, but frowned at him.

"If this is the *lid* to some secret passageway, we're in trouble, Armaeus. That'll be a pretty small opening."

"There is no lid, unfortunately. Not anymore." He shook his head. "But Ceres prepared for that contingency as well. Beneath the manalis lapis rested another entrance point, said to be etched into solid rock." He nodded at the gold seal. "I can give you the point at which it is located, but what lies beneath the temple is a world I have not seen for a very long time. Still, it begins with the seal—though I would caution you to be careful. When placed upon the bedrock of Rome itself, I am told it is a single-use key. And another thing, Miss Wilde." He smiled at me, amusement lacing his words. "Though your passage will be underground, you should not encounter any of the dead for the majority of your trip. Roman law forbade the burial of citizens within the city walls."

He had to remind me about the dead bodies. "Yeah, well, Rome started out kind of small," I grumbled. "That doesn't account for much terrain."

Nodding his acknowledgment of this point, Armaeus gestured to my chair and took his own seat. "You'll be leaving soon, and I must give you the rest of the instructions," he said. "You'll need to memorize them."

"Uh-huh. And where will you be while I'm off playing capture the flag?"

"I regret that business requires me to return immediately to Las Vegas. Where I look forward to you rejoining me late tomorrow, in fact, with the reliquary intact."

"Fair enough." I stowed the seal in my jacket. "So in preparation for that, why don't you go ahead and get your bank online as well. I'll want my money transferred the moment I toss you your pretty gold toy."

CHAPTER EIGHT

The driver Armaeus had hired to pick me up from Leonardo de Vinci Airport wasn't a local. It wasn't until I'd slung myself into the back seat of the dark blue sedan that I realized this important fact, as he started talking to me in a rich French accent. Just what I didn't need.

"Welcome to Rome, mademoiselle. Where are we off to?'

"The Forum," I said. "Anywhere close to the main entrance on Via dei Fori Imperiali."

"Mais non! It is far too early. Your boss, he is unreasonable."

I blinked at the man, catching his wide smile in the rearview mirror. "Excuse me?"

"It is Rome, at night under the stars. Sending you straight to a tourist trap, and not even one of the better tourist traps, is — pfft." His censure was more amusing than it should have been. Maybe I was tired. But he kept going. "Bien sûr, the Forum, it was quite grand back in its day, but its day is long past. It's not like it's the Colosseum or the Trevi Fountain. Mon Dieu, send you to the basilica at the very least, but the Forum? Please. The place, it is locked up tight!"

I couldn't help smiling as the driver kept up a nonstop stream of chatter. His banter, detailing the trials of being an on-command limo driver to the stars, kept me energized at least, and that, along with caffeine pills and some mumbo jumbo Armaeus had muttered at me when I'd left for the plane, was apparently all the rest I was going to get before this day was done. As we sped toward Rome, I went through the plan again. According to Armaeus, I would have to navigate through a mile of catacombs and underground passageways, one of them, notably, under water—before emerging into the subterranean underpinnings of the Vatican. The necropolis was relatively close to the surface but still deep enough that I shouldn't be disturbed at the hour I would be reaching it. I patted the pocket of my jacket, locating the deck I'd hijacked from Henri. This underground journey was going to be a series of yes-nos viewed by penlight, so I separated a few of the Major Arcana cards, sliding the rest back into the—

"Mademoiselle?"

"What!" I jumped about a foot, and the driver had the good grace to wince. We stopped at a light, and he turned around.

"Apologies," he said, his gaze falling to my hands. "Oh! You are a student of the Tarot. Excellent!"

"Ah, thanks." Several additional cards had fallen out of the deck, and I scooped them off the floor, keeping them separate from the pack along with my Majors. Cards didn't jump out of a deck for no reason, even if the reason was a bad one—like a driver who wouldn't shut up.

"I wanted to let you know we're almost there," the driver said, swinging back around to drive. "Is there anything you need before I leave? Mini bottled water? Tourist map?" He handed both items to me over the back of his seat, seemingly out of habit, his eyes never leaving the road once we started moving again. I took his offerings just as automatically, though I wasn't thirsty—and a map wasn't exactly going to get me where I needed to go tonight.

As I tucked the map into my jacket pocket along with the cards, the car slowed and angled over to the right. I peered out the window, taking in the uplit view of the Roman Forum. We were at one of the main entrances, as requested, some enormous old building half standing off to our left, its arched columns looming in silent testimony to a world gone by.

"Thanks," I said again, pulling out some folded euros. "Oh, and here—I appreciate you driving me this late."

"No problem at all, mademoiselle." The young man turned around, his eyes eerily black despite the brightly lit interior of the limo. With a boyish grin, he touched his fingers to his head in a smart salute. "And no tip needed, but my number's on the map. You need a ride out of here, call that line and ask for me by name." He winked at me. "I'm Max Bertrand."

Of course you are. "Bertrand of the French mausoleum Bertrands?"

His grin broadened. "The very same."

I watched as the dark sedan shot down the Via dei Fori Imperiali, waiting until it was well out of sight. It was a few hours before dawn, and the Forum's lights had been dimmed, throwing the ruins into shadow. Not even the most energetic of tourists was out at this hour, but I knew better than to waste any time.

Without hesitating, I hurried to the nearest fold in the imposing but ultimately harmless fence surrounding the long rectangular field of enormous ruined temples and scattered buildings. Where the structure dented inward, I paused, pulling on my gloves. I'd learned over time that sometimes, when it came to handling artifacts, it paid to cover your palms. The unexpected bonus was that for most modern climbing tasks, gloves came in quite handy.

The beautiful wrought iron gate proved easy to scale, and I was on the other side in less than a minute. Then it was off through the maze of ruins toward the Temple of Vesta, one of the few circular structures (or what was left of it) in the space. The temple had once been the home of the Palladium, the ancient statue of Athena carved of olive wood and said to have fallen from the heavens themselves. The piece had long since disappeared into the mists of history, but I was banking that the other great feature of the temple had not: its famed hearth, once kept constantly lit by an intrepid team of virgins.

I trotted the short distance through the Forum, past the Temple of Antonius and Faustina, and something called the Regia, which looked like a whole lot of nothing at all. When I reached my destination, however, my steps slowed, disappointment tightening my jaw. The hearth of the Temple of Vesta was intact, all right—mounted ornately on stacked slabs of rock in front of the temple.

What in the... I moved forward and circled the ancient building, still standing tall if somewhat tattered in her old age, a scant few of her columns remaining. I broke a few more city laws by clambering up onto the structure and skirting around its pillars, then dropped back onto the rubble that marked what had once been the interior of the shrine.

Not helping, not helping, not helping. Dirt lay in huge piles all around the space, and only a few areas of actual rock were cleared off completely. I squinted into the darkness, trying to get a fix on where the center point might be, but it was almost impossible to tell. What were they doing here? Some sort of latter-day excavation? I grimaced, dropping to my knees to where it seemed that the rock that had been unearthed was actual bedrock and not simply stones moved around for the hell of it. And then I started searching.

It took me a full half hour to find what I wanted — deep, tool-cut grooves etched into a stone just off the center of the temple, the rest of the surface worn down. The section was bordered on all sides by more rock, which also boded well. However, I saw no cut marks in the stone's surface to indicate that there was some sort of hatch I could unlock. Suddenly unnerved by the thick darkness around me, I pulled out the Ceres seal and considered Armaeus's words anew. How could this be a key?

No time like the present to find out.

Trying not to wince at the damage I was doing to the millennia-old seal, I turned the relic upside down and gingerly pressed it onto the stone.

Nothing happened.

I pressed harder. No dice.

"You have got to be kidding me." I forced all my weight onto the seal. Still nothing. I settled back on my heels, then shoved forward, forming my gloved hands into fists that I banged down on the seal like it was a square peg I was trying to hammer into a round hole. Nada. The rock stayed very rocklike. Very rocklike and solid. And hard, I realized belatedly, shaking out my hands.

"This isn't happening." I rolled up to my feet and scowled down at the stone. In the distance, I heard a police siren, and I jerked my head toward it, belatedly aware that I was, at a minimum, acting like a lunatic. At worst, I was doing my level best to deface state property with a stolen artifact.

"You know, I don't have time for this." I pitched my words calmly, quietly even. Never let it be said I didn't know how to negotiate with a chunk of metal. "I need to get to the Vatican, and you need to help me."

The seal remained stoic.

"There's got to be a way. That's how he works. You know that." I paced around the seal, then tentatively hopped onto the gold plate. Still nothing. "Totally not joking here." I hopped again. Then harder. And then I did a rat-a-tat march on it. I worked on my samba, my pogo-stick, even some Irish dancing.

Nada, nothing, zip.

And then, finally, there in the hushed corner of the Temple of Vesta, something deep within me sort of...snapped.

"Sweet Father Christmas on a tricycle, stop *messing* with me!" I stood off the edge of the seal, then raised my foot to stomp down on it with my heavy boot. "I have more!" *stomp*. "Money!" *stomp*. "Riding on this!" *stomp!* "Than I've ever seen!" *stomp stomp!* "In my *life*!" I backed up, launching myself forward again to execute a two-footed jump onto the now-battered seal. "DO SOMETHING!"

There wasn't even a crack, and I half stumbled to the side, turning around and staring into the distance as I desperately tried to work out another solution, my lungs heaving, my head filling with a bone-rattling roar that pounded through my brain and—

The whoosh of movement took me completely by surprise as a storm of smoke shot up around me and the rock surface suddenly gave way beneath my feet. I plummeted into darkness and smashed hard into a wall, bouncing off it into a shower of rocks and debris that chased me down to an equally hard floor, accompanied by a tumble of stones that clattered around me. I blinked for a moment, then an ominous creaking sound stretched overhead in the now-pitch darkness, motivating me to scramble to the side until I came up against another wall, spitting out rock dust as I pulled the penlight out of my jacket.

"One use only," I muttered, angling a narrow beam of light upward. I squinted at the completely blocked opening above me. Which meant—no exit either. So after I found the Magician's relic, I'd have to come up with some other way to get out of here.

Armaeus hadn't mentioned that part, of course.

I swung the penlight around as the rock dust cleared, relieved to see a darker opening cut into the rock opposite from where I was sitting—and only one said opening. This cut down on my possible options of which way to go, for sure. Even better, the dust seemed to be moving *into* that hole, versus hanging stagnant in the air, which meant somehow, somewhere, there was an opening up ahead.

Nevertheless, I put the penlight in my mouth and took the extra second to reach into my jacket and palm the cards, randomly flipping one upright into the thin stream of light.

The Devil stared back at me, grinning and fierce, rocking his evil badassery in the old-style illustration. I much preferred the more modern depictions of the horned beast, but either way, this wasn't helping. I reached for another card, focusing my question more specifically. Two cards came free in my hand, and I nodded when I saw them. *That's more like it.*

The Hierophant and the Eight of Cups—the Eight clearly one of the Minor Arcana cards that had tumbled out of the deck when the limo driver had startled me. So, apparently this road wouldn't be a yes-no journey after all. The Eight of Cups was a sign to get a move on, and the Hierophant was also known as the "Pope" card.

Couldn't get more literal than that.

I checked my watch's compass feature to reassure myself I was facing northwest. Then I got to my feet and headed out. Time suddenly seemed far too short. I had to get Armaeus's box and haul it to Vegas pronto, if he was right about the twin sisters from Kavala being shipped there. And I had no reason to doubt him. According to Father Jerome, the sisters were Greek girls of exceptional beauty, and from what the priest had been told, their gifts apparently extended to a kind of shared cognition—they could wield the Sight in tandem, piercing the veil of the future or the past simultaneously. In a world constantly searching for the next magical curiosity, they would be coveted treasures indeed.

I picked up the pace.

True to Armaeus's words, the world of Ceres made heavy use of ancient underground passageways hewn through the rock. The space remained blessedly empty of anything but stone and the occasional rat at first, but after the first quarter mile or so, bodies started showing up. I had clearly made it beyond the boundaries of the Old City. Some of the chambers were stacked with cloth-wrapped corpses as old as time itself, but others were filled with figures with a distressingly *fresher* feel. Holding my breath as much as I was able, I darted through the makeshift crypts, using the cards to guide me when I had a choice of more than one passageway. From time to time, I could sense the passages soaring above me and almost hear the distant traffic as the catacombs reached toward the streets of Rome. Other times, I could barely move, once shimmying on my stomach through a crevice carved into the rock, slick with running water. Apparently, I'd reached the Tiber River. I made pretty good time despite all that, covering the terrain in a little over an hour, before something decidedly different hung in the air around me.

It all started feeling…cleaner.

I slowed my steps, sweeping the penlight on the ground and up around the walls. Fewer cobwebs and dust, I decided. That was it. Someone had clearly strolled this way recently—at least within the last century or so. The air was lighter here as well, the narrow passageway between the stacked bodies seeming almost spacious.

I pulled another card, rolling my eyes as the Devil once again showed his ugly mug. The second proved more useful, however: the Sun.

I dimmed my light and advanced, realizing that the gloom of the space had lifted somewhat as well. Not enough for me to get away without using light of any sort, but enough to make me feel like I was no longer trudging through the bowels of hell. As I moved from one chamber to the next, I felt something else too.

The sudden sense of eyes on me.

"Hello, there."

I turned around quickly, sweeping the light.

"Who's that?"

Silence greeted me. "Armaeus?"

But no. And truth to tell, the voice in my head hadn't sounded like Armaeus. It was…younger. More carefree. Either way, "you're not invited, whoever you are." The silence continued, and I felt unreasonably satisfied about that. So there, imaginary friend. Go pound sand.

To make certain that no one was behind me, or

ahead of me either, I arced the beam around. Nope, nada. I shook it off. After having traveled through the graves of what felt like half the ancient Roman population, I should expect to be a little jumpy. I hit it again, moving through the passages with more determination. They had begun to tilt upward, and as I passed one cleft in the rock, I paused, something once more murmuring in the back of my mind, just out of reach.

I cycled up my penlight and flashed it over the surface to the right. Not stone at all here, but a metal door, deeply recessed into the wall and hung with shadows. I didn't need to pull the Hierophant card this time—the papal seal was boldly emblazoned on the metal, immediately above the door's old-style lock.

Transferring my penlight to my teeth, I reached up high inside my jacket and pulled my picklocks free. This would not be delicate work with a structure so old, but torque was important. I didn't want to lose my precious tools in the mouth of a stubborn iron lock.

The mechanism worked, though not without protest, my wrists easing the picks through their dance with steady pressure and a few choice swear words. Clearly this wasn't a common entrance or exit for the Vatican staff. That also boded well.

I pushed past the door and found more catacombs on the other side, along with a fair number of empty indentations in the wall. Too small for dead bodies, but clearly something had been placed here at one point—placed and then removed.

At length, the passage ended, and I was left in a room with no exit—just four stone walls and the entryway I'd come in. I flickered the penlight up over the stone surface overhead and frowned. A constellation had been etched into the chamber's ceiling, the earth at its center, the planets and sun revolving around that overlarge orb. I slid the light to the right of the earth, past the moon and to the large sun, its center pierced with a thick dot. A circumpunct, one of the oldest symbols of the sun — or of God — that existed. Peering up into it and remembering the last card I'd pulled, I flashed around the space at my feet until I found a big enough chunk of stone that was not so large I couldn't move it. I shoved it into place, then stood upon it, dimming my penlight again and flipping it over. I stuck the bottom of the flashlight into the groove created by the chiseled dot and pushed hard.

This time, I didn't have to wait for my reward. The penlight broke right through the thin layer of dirt, and shavings cascaded around me as a burst of light poured down over my face. The block moved easily enough at the push of my fingertips, stone scraping on stone, and with two hands, I was able to ease it up and to the side, revealing a hole large enough for me to climb through. Dim yellow light shone down from the chamber above, and I could see a tiny portion of its flaking ceiling.

I'd reached the Vatican necropolis.

CHAPTER NINE

I hauled myself up through the opening, trying to get my bearings. I was in an ancient room, but not as ancient as where I'd come from. It was one of the painted crypts of the necropolis, the sides layered in a rich terra-cotta orange, the floor decorated with an elaborate ornate mosaic. My entry square was in the center of a long line of similar squares, each with a hole in its center, and I was familiar with their function. The tiles had been used originally as food portals so that the ancient Romans could more easily deliver feasts to their dead relatives.

Very thoughtful, the Romans.

Now, the centers of most of the tiles were stuffed with dirt and clay, sealing them off. I swung my feet clear of the hole and scowled around, every sense on high alert, but no guards came pounding toward me, no alarmed cries went up. Nevertheless, I set the stone back in place and scattered rock dust over it for good measure. Wiping my gloved hands on my leggings, I reached the doorway of the ancient tomb and glanced back. From this vantage point, I couldn't tell the floor had been disturbed. Good.

I found myself in a long brick-and-stone corridor bathed in an eerie yellow glow coming from a line of recessed lights. I quickly made my way to the end, glancing into the empty crypts on either side of the passage, noting the ornate frescoes and striking images in some, the utter barrenness of others. At the end of the corridor, just as Armaeus had described, I found the original tomb of St. Peter, or whatever they were calling it these days. No way the guy's actual bones were still here, but the space itself had a strange feeling to it that made me slow down, the cards seeming to almost shift in my jacket as I poked my head into the narrow space.

Bingo.

I saw the gold box almost immediately, but it wasn't as if *that* took any special skill. It was lying right in the open, sitting in a sort of cut-out section of the wall, enshrined on purple and red vestments, candles lying around its base. A strip of red cloth lay crisscrossed over the relic, which, as Armaeus had suggested, was about the size of my hand from fingertip to wrist. There was no high-tech energy force field down here protecting the thing, just the cloth sash, and I frowned at the setup, inching closer. The light seemed particularly strange, surrounding the reliquary in a luminous glow. Was it a luminous *electrically charged* glow? That remained to be seen. I glanced around, listening, but no sound emanated from anywhere in the crypt except my own thundering heart.

Once again, I felt it. That strange sense of being watched.

I checked my watch. Four thirty a.m. The sun would be rising in less than two hours, and I had no idea how I'd get out of the catacombs anymore. I certainly wasn't going to be getting back out through the Forum. All of which meant I couldn't waste any more time here, not when I had a long flight into nowhere ahead of me.

Using one of the ceremonial candles lying to the left of the reliquary, I pushed the sashes off the box. There was a faint crackling noise, but God didn't cry out in holy fury. So far, so good. I squatted down, trying to eye the platform beneath the gold. No way to tell what was under it, and I stood again, weighing my options.

Just get it over with, I thought, feeling strangely inclined to laugh.

Sometimes, it really was that easy.

I reached out with my right hand and plucked the golden box off its pool of vestments. Something seemed to *shift*, and, frowning, I swept the vestments back — just as a green light on a technical-looking platform clicked to red. And started blinking.

"Crap!"

And sometimes, it wasn't. *Time to go.*

I shoved the box into my jacket, sparing a few extra, precious seconds to throw the vestments back over the blinking red light, as if that was going to have some meaningful effect on anything. Then I dashed into the long corridor leading away from St. Peter's tomb, moving fast. Sticking my hand in my pocket, I yanked out another card — *Chariot.*

I frowned, picking up my pace. *Chariot?* I'd expected the Sun again, dammit. Surely the best idea would be to go back to the room where I'd entered the necropolis.

The sudden crack of pounding boots on stone shot my attention toward the edge of the corridor as I skidded past a room dominated by an enormous mosaic of —

"Do *not* mess with me," I gritted out, swinging into the room and turning around, then around again. The chariot on the floor in black-and-white was unmistakable, and for added points, the scene it depicted was the freaking kidnap of Proserpina, daughter of Ceres — but there was *no* door out of this room, *no* big flashing arrow pointing anywhere, and I was out of time.

"Double Crap!" The box in my right pocket suddenly seemed to gain about a thousand pounds, and I hurtled forward, smacking facedown onto the floor. Just then, two guards ran past the crypt's doorway, their flashlights sweeping the space, but not stopping. Spitting out rock dust as quietly as I could beneath the tramp of their feet, I squinted up — and then I saw it. A grate at the base of the wall, maybe added after excavation to shore up splintering rock or to cover a dangerous hole, who knew. The important part was it was *there* — and darkness loomed behind it.

I scrambled for the grate and tested it quickly, realizing it wasn't attached. Seriously, who were these architects? Hadn't they heard of security systems? Not one to look a gift escape portal in the mouth, however, I yanked out the grate and stuck my penlight into the space, tossing more rock dust down. Nothing but open air lay beyond the hole, and then, *finally,* the pebbles struck bottom, loud enough to almost reassure me I wouldn't break every bone in my body trying to make the drop. Dare to dream.

As shouts erupted in St. Peter's tomb, I resecured my light and zipped up my jacket, then snagged the grate. I shimmied down into the hole, pulling the grate behind me until it clanked into place over the opening. Then I hung for another sickening moment in the open air.

And dropped.

The weight of the gold box eased up in flight, and I

landed with only the usual amount of pain, sprawling onto the chamber floor with a grunt, then rolling into a tight ball to condense the agony into as small a space as possible. The place was black as pitch, and I wrenched out my penlight again, flipping it around as I squinted into the darkness. The chamber held two doors, so, fine, two cards: Hanged Man and Sun. "Oh great, *now* you give me the Sun."

I'd take it, though. I was starting to feel a little claustrophobic. Being forty feet underground would do that to a person.

I headed back into the darkness through the east-facing door, the one indicated by the Sun, and prayed for a quick exit.

I didn't get one.

The cards started playing hard to get from that point forward, showing me the Devil at every turn as the weird half echo of spectral laughter dogged my steps. Finally I gave up and started jogging, taking whatever passageway seemed like it was leading up. My last intelligent card had been the Sun, after all. Well, the sun was in the sky, right? And the sky was up.

Finally, after what felt like hours but which my watch confirmed was only ninety minutes, I stumbled into a space that seemed ever so slightly newer than third century AD. A wide cistern of some sort had been cut into the floor, holding a deep well of murky water. I craned my neck upward, my penlight barely picking out a catwalk high upon the wall. And hanging down from that catwalk, bolted against the wall…

"Finally." I raced over to the side of the cavern, then stuck the penlight in my mouth again—never mind where else it'd been stuck during the last several hours—and attacked the ladder with newfound energy. Hand over hand, I climbed up the side of the sheer wall, not bothering to look down until I finally collapsed onto the landing of the catwalk far above, my lungs blowing hard. From there I could totally see where I was, if only I spoke Italian. The underside of an official-looking manhole lay above me not six more feet.

Pausing to ensure everything was going according to plan, I did one more check of the cards and got The Devil, which I was getting used to by now. Then the Five of Wands—another of the minors I'd already encountered this evening, and one I wasn't at all happy to see again. And then Justice.

I scowled. From my underground position, I had no way of determining what Justice meant. Was I going to crawl out in front of a police station or come face-to-face with the Super Friends? Justice was always a pain that way. You got what was coming to you, but every so often that was the boomerang of doom.

I glanced up at the manhole. Security forces were typically presented by knight cards, and knights were conspicuously not showing up to my card party so far. But if the enforcers for SANCTUS were waiting for me up there, for some reason, things were not going to end well for Armaeus's box.

Or for me, as it happened.

Getting to my feet, I pulled the dull yellow reliquary out of my pocket and held it under the gleam of the penlight. As Armaeus had instructed, there was nothing on the piece but the inscription, carved into the box in some unreadable language. Aramaic, he'd said, but it didn't matter. It could have been Alien and I wouldn't have known the difference. The box looked bug-free at least, so that was a bonus. Kept things from getting too crowded.

I fished around in one of my inside pockets until I

found the slender plastic disk. Squatting down, I placed the reliquary carefully on its side, then pulled the disk free from its backing. I stuck the wafer to the corner of the reliquary, where the metal was the smoothest. Once in place, the sensor was virtually invisible, a tiny disk, but through the miracle of plastic tech—and a very wise decision I'd made with an incredibly smart, incredibly hot circuitry genius a few years back—it would make sure I didn't end up empty-handed.

Satisfied, I stowed the reliquary in my jacket once more and slipped the safety off my gun in its shoulder holster. Then I hit the next ladder, picking up speed.

Just as the square slab of rock in the tomb had been easy to dislodge, the manhole cover above me proved equally accommodating, and I pushed up the circular slab of metal to see out. I was in the middle of some sort of side street, and though a few cars were visible lining the curb, no traffic stirred. I heaved the manhole off the opening, then crawled out of the shaft, pausing only long enough to drop the cover back over the hole. I'd finished that process, still on my knees, when I heard a car door open.

And then the lights came up.

Sweet Christmas, that's bright. I hunkered down in legitimate pain, practically blinded with the sudden glare after so many hours in darkness. Steps sounded loudly around me, official and precise, and I heard a gun cocking into place. My own weapon remained holstered tight to my side, but I needed to understand how many people I'd be shooting at before I went that route.

"The inscription."

"What?" I growled, turning around. Had someone said that aloud? And in English? No one spoke again for another moment, then the man closest to me started shouting at me in rapid-fire Italian.

"Scatola!" the man next to him cried out over his associate's words, and I understood what they wanted, despite my lousy Italian. Box. They wanted the reliquary.

Worked for me. To hit me, they'd have to go through the relic, and I figured they didn't want to risk damaging the thing. So with my left hand, I reached inside my jacket and pulled the box out, waving it in front of my chest as I turned, keeping my feet moving and the relic close.

"Read the inscription." The order was louder this time, more insistent. Definitely English. But I couldn't pinpoint where it was coming from.

"I can't!" I shouted back, finally getting a good look at the men surrounding me. A dozen guys ranged in a tight circle wearing black uniforms and berets, all of them with rifles trained on my twirling form. Oh, goodie. SANCTUS. *How did they find me so quickly? And what exactly* had *happened to Armaeus's other agents* —

Meanwhile, I sensed the press of otherworldly eyes upon me again as words were forming in my mind, words such as I had never heard before, ancient and melodic, hypnotic and strange. Running around and through and over and above the Italians who were edging closer, their shouts growing louder as the sun finally broke over the horizon and flooded the far-off street, its light not quite reaching into this side alley.

"The inscription!"

"Fine!" I bellowed. Waving the reliquary in my left hand, I squinted at it, then spoke the words that had come to me in a rush—all three lines, not truly knowing what I was saying as the sounds tumbled and crashed over themselves, my heart lightening as I neared the inscription's end.

Whatever I was saying, though, I wasn't saying it fast enough. I heard the cock of a pistol, sensed the gun aimed at me as I babbled out the last words. *Crap and double crap!*

Without warning, the box suddenly went from weighing about two pounds to two hundred. I dropped it, shocked, then instantly went for my gun, yanking it out as the box made contact with the asphalt—

And everything went sideways.

The reliquary bounced hard as an explosion ripped through the space with a percussive blast, though there was no sound, not even much light. I was knocked to the side, away from the manhole, but I had the easy end of it. The commandos standing around me all burst backward as well, like leaves caught in a strong wind, stumbling to the ground, smashing up against the alley's wall, while I was yanked to my feet, and—

Found myself staring into the face of the *second* most magnificent man I'd ever seen in my life.

"Second?" the impossibly beautiful vision in front of me said with a twist of his sensual lips. "How disappointing."

Innate recognition and outrage swept through me, flavored with a salty dash of fear that I stamped down with more outrage. "You've got to be freaking kidding me," I snapped. "Armaeus sent me after the actual *Devil*? As in the Prince of Darkness, Father of Lies, Enemy of Righteousness—*you're* what I just stole from the Vatican?"

The Adonis before me gave me a lazy grin.

"Speak of the Devil," he said, his voice as heart wrenchingly beautiful as his features. "And he shall appear."

CHAPTER TEN

With that, the Devil shot out his right hand toward the closest SANCTUS guard. "Besides," he continued, "they stole me first."

The guard screamed as his gun turned to flames, the fire jumping from his weapon to one held by a soldier across the alley so quickly I could barely follow it. Then it leapt again.

"Aleksander Kreios," the Devil said by way of introduction. He didn't let go of me as he stooped to pick up the golden box at his feet, examining it with marked distaste as the men around us erupted into screams. "I think we should be leaving. Where is the plane?"

"Ciampino Airport," I said, trying to process the carnage in front of me. Not very easy, given the smell of burning flesh on either side of us. "Just south of the city. Were you the one watching me in the catacombs, then?" I frowned more deeply. "And how did you get in that box?"

"It appears Armaeus did not expect us to meet. He always was a man of no manners, despite his protestations." He shrugged. "But it's time to go. As enjoyable as it would be to see these men suffer longer, there is work yet to be done." He turned, guiding me past a guard whose cries of torment only increased on seeing Aleksander Kreios standing over him. Kreios paused long enough to stop the man's screams — by kicking him savagely in the head. Then he turned back with a satisfied smile. "After you," he said, gesturing me on.

I glanced back as we strode down the alley. The fires dissolved into dirty smoke as I watched, but half the guards still seemed in abject pain, and the other half were held in some kind of thrall, none of them making a move.

"Um, are you doing that to them?"

"Not at all, Sara Wilde. They are doing it to themselves."

Breaking out onto a main street, Kreios walked right into traffic, moving ahead of me to flag down a sleek Alfa Romeo. The driver stopped, poleaxed with alarm, gaping at us as we approached his vehicle. Kreios put his hand on the hood appreciatively. "It is a fine car."

The man — a prosperous-looking businessman, judging by his suit and tie — promptly exited the vehicle with his briefcase in hand. His expression shifted to a decidedly enthralled look, and he stood by the driver's side while the few cars that were on the street pounded their horns and angled around us. Kreios nodded to him and spoke in musically fluent Italian, something about a Banco Credito. The man gestured magnanimously to his car. "È tutto tuo."

Then he walked off. Whistling.

"You see?" Kreios said, dropping my hand to open the passenger door for me. "Men of refinement yet walk this world."

I eyed the car, thinking only two words. "Flight" and "Risk."

"Um — you are planning to head back to Vegas

now, right?" I'd cuff the man to me, only the moment my brain contemplated that idea all other rational thought jumped ship. Besides, no handcuffs. Damned poor packing job.

Kreios smiled. "Have you any doubt?"

"Lots of them."

"Well, fret not on my account." His brows lifted as he studied me. "Now this is interesting. I have not been to Kavala in many years. Your desire to return those young women to their homes, it is a worthy goal."

Freaking Council mind-reading freaks. Still, I was more than happy to play phone a friend to get more information. "So they *are* in Vegas? They're still alive?"

"There is only one way to find out, it would seem." He moved to the driver's side of the Alfa Romeo. A chorus of police sirens suddenly screamed from a few streets over, and Kreios winked at me as he opened the vehicle's door. "Rome is always so invigorating."

He slid inside and I clambered into the passenger seat, barely getting the door shut before he slammed the car into gear.

"Buckle up, Sara Wilde." After the second turn, I did as he instructed, the belt the only thing keeping me from being plastered against the roof of the vehicle, the door, or the Devil himself. We raced through the streets, conversation impossible what with half the city roiling with lights and sirens, all of them seeming immediately behind us.

By the time I realized that the cars and noise had faded, I realized something else had disappeared too.

Namely, any signs referencing "Aeroporto".

"I'm pretty sure we're supposed to be heading to an airport." I eyed Kreios. "You know, a place with planes?"

"I regret that I will be unable to join you in that endeavor. But hopefully you'll agree that I did not leave you to fend for yourself alone in Rome, yes? I do not want to appear callous."

"How about you appear sensible and turn the car around now."

"I do hate to disappoint a woman of your undoubted skills." As if on cue, the car slowed, but that didn't make me feel any better. If anything, I tensed up further, sensing a trap as Kreios skidded the vehicle onto a side road, fishtailing. There were large warehouse-looking buildings along this stretch, and little else. "Yet it appears we are doomed to both be disappointed today."

He turned the wheel sharply and we flew into the parking lot of a large, flat-topped concrete building, which looked absolutely abandoned until another vehicle emerged from the far corner, heading toward us fast. Before I could react, Kreios gave me one last grin, then opened the door and jumped free of the car, wrenching the wheel as he went. The car shuddered and bucked, then suddenly we were rolling, as if Kreios had managed to flip the car with no more than a flick of his wrist.

Chaos rained down as I screamed, the car turning over once, twice. The concrete and the building and the sky became part of a kaleidoscope of light and terror and bone-wrenching fury as I caught sight of the asshole getting into the car that now idled at the opening of the drive, waiting patiently for me to stop rolling.

When the Alfa Romeo finally crumpled to a stop, with me strapped in and hanging upside down, it roared off.

"Asshat!"

I sucked in a tight breath and unhooked my seat belt, letting fly a litany of curses as I crunched to the ceiling of the car. The windows had shattered, and the door opened willingly enough on my side. I crawled out and lay on the ground, staring up at the sky, panting.

"Bastard." I liked that name better. My chest heaving, I rolled to my knees. My head had suddenly morphed into an overripe grapefruit, and I suspected I'd herniated myself on the safety belt. Otherwise, I was intact. Sweat poured off me, the adrenaline of the high-speed chase and the Devil's precipitous exit combining with the overdue reaction to the race out of the necropolis. I blew out a long breath, squinting across the sun-soaked pavement, then checked the sky again. He'd gone east, I was almost certain. Fair enough.

What wasn't fair? Not getting the freaking information I needed from the Cat in the Hat. Armaeus was going to pay for this. He'd sent me after a *box*, not Mr. Muscles. Aleksander Kreios. *The actual Devil. For the love of Kansas.*

Gritting my teeth, I hauled myself to my feet and reached into my jacket. My phone was there. So was something else. Something I hadn't expected to be needing again quite so soon: a map of the city.

My new favorite limo driver picked up on the second ring. "Maximilian Ber —"

"You have any knowledge of a warehouse under construction south of Rome? Maybe thirty miles out of the city, just off a main highway? Blue signage that's half-finished, begins with PRO?"

"Ah, yes I do, Miss. Very nice facility, construction halted due to permits, and —"

"How long till you get here?"

Max didn't pause. "Thirty minutes, give or take. You have shade? Water?"

I squinted back to the battered car. No way was I getting back in that thing. But beyond the vehicle, a line of trees stood at the far end of the parking lot. Just enough distance for me to stretch out my legs and maybe lose the throbbing headache. "Shade. No water."

There was the slightest hesitation then. "Are you hurt?"

"I'll manage. Get here as quick as you can, please."

"It will be my pleasure."

Twenty minutes later, the familiar sedan pulled up. By then I'd ditched my jacket and was sitting on it, hunched over my phone like an irritable gargoyle. Grinning like one too.

Max brought the car up to me and had barely slowed when I heard the sound of his door locks disengaging. I pulled open the passenger door before he came to a complete stop and slid into the back of his vehicle.

"There is water and a first aid kit in the case to your left," he said, replicating his cheerful patter from this morning. Had it only been this morning? "Where are we headed? I can assure you I know everything there is to know about Rome and southern Italy. It has become a sort of passion of mine."

I glanced down to my phone. After he'd popped out of the reliquary like a grumpy genie, Aleksander Kreios had pocketed the gold box, and apparently had not paid too much attention to it. My bug remained intact, and for the past twenty minutes, I'd been following it as it made its way southeast of Rome, trying to figure out where it was heading. "What's Sermoneta? What's its importance?"

"Sermoneta?" Max frowned from the front seat, but he bounced the car back onto the access road and headed east. "It is a very pretty medieval town, with a fine abbey and castle to boot."

What would the Devil want with an abbey? "Abbey as in still active?"

"Yes, indeed, though it's had a bit of a troubled past. It was founded by Greek Basilian monks in the eigth century AD, a very secretive order, and was home to the Templar knights for a time, right up until they were disbanded. It's somewhat famous for an unusual Sator Square on the grounds, impossible to be translated but rumored to be very powerful. The Cistercian monks work the place now, a very practical, somewhat boring lot. But it's a pretty enough abbey."

"Right." I'd had my fill of the religious for the day, but there had to be some reason Kreios was heading there. I reached into my jacket and thumbed free a few cards. A quick glance confirmed we were on the right track, so to the abbey we'd go.

"Who owns the castle?"

"The Caetani family. Very ancient, very rich. Well connected too." Max snorted. "One of Italy's most famous popes was a Caetani, actually, Boniface VIII. You might remember him from *Dante's Inferno* — made it all the way to the eighth circle of Hell."

"Nice."

He laughed. "The family remained consistently loyal to the church, though for a time their own castle was confiscated by a later pope, Alexander VI. One of the Borgias, not a nice character. But the Caetanis continued to thrive, producing more bishops and cardinals along the way. That line of the family died out in 1961, though. Very sad."

I frowned. "I thought you said they owned the

castle."

"Their descendants do, but they are no longer of the pure bloodline, eh? Times, they change."

"Yeah." I leaned back against the rich leather seat, watching the Italian countryside zip by. Max Bertrand had not asked about the car that I'd abandoned at the warehouse. He'd not asked a lot of things. "How much did Armaeus tell you about me?"

"Le seigneur? He said only that I must fetch you from the airport and deliver you safely to wherever you directed. He did not tell me why. He also did not tell me that I would have the pleasure of your company a second time."

I eyed him. "And have you reported in?"

"What am I to report? That a beautiful woman cannot last a day without me? That would be terrible hubris, no?" He flashed me another smile. "It is enough that I am able to serve you in my own small way."

"Got it." I thought about Armaeus. He'd said he was going to be called back to the States imminently. Was he across the pond yet? In flight? As long as there was a body of water in between us, as I'd learned quite by accident, he'd have no way of contacting me. I preferred having an ocean of distance between us for that very reason. That, and I no longer trusted the Tyet to keep me safe.

Nevertheless, while I had the Magician on mute, there was no use wasting a willing tour guide. "How connected are you with the Bertrands outside of Paris? How much do you know about their operation?"

"Not as connected as I once was," Max said with a little shake. "Why do you think I am here, so far from home? I've been assigned as a watchdog for the family, without knowing what it is I am watching."

I frowned at him. "You've learned nothing about SANCTUS?"

"Oh, but of a certainty. I merely don't know what the importance is of what I know. That is for wiser minds. I report on them coming and going from the Vatican, of attacks in the city. They wisely do not trouble much of the Connected in Rome proper, so as not to draw too much attention. But the whispers, they have been coming to us from other places. Budapest. Ankara. Cairo. Close enough for us to hear about, not so close that any are worried."

"But the family is worried?"

"Not for ourselves." His shrug was noncommittal, betraying his French origins. "We are not part of the Connected, exactly."

"Um, how is that possible?" I asked, thinking about Dante and Claire. "Don't *any* of you have psychic skills?

"It only takes one member per generation to retain the blood tie. Time marches on, the families do not practice the old ways, they weaken, they die. Much like the Caetani, we too will have our end if we do not rekindle that nascent force within us." He sighed and shook his head, a sigh not even Henri could have bettered. "I once thought I had the whisper of magic within me, but as a Bertrand, we do not take such things lightly. There was another of my generation who had already been chosen for that coveted spot, and his bid was not to be denied. He had the very cast of le seigneur."

I thought of Dante, back at the mansion. I'd not felt even a flicker of magical ability within him, though, and I frowned. "And how did that work out?"

"I assume well," Max said. "It is never spoken of. The chosen simply do the work they are called to do, and the rest do what we are told. I cannot help but wish though, eh? It is a weakness I cannot put behind me."

As he spoke, I put my hand inside my jacket, an instinctive move I didn't really think about until I felt the cool, crisp surface of my cards. I fanned through the deck, nudging out a card. I slipped it out as we angled off the main highway onto an exit.

"We're coming into Sermoneta now," Max said. "What are we looking for?"

I glanced down at my hand. The Six of Swords. A card of journeys over water, better times ahead and, the old books said, the voyage of an initiate toward psychic mastery. I grinned out the window as we passed over an ancient medieval bridge, a crystalline river snaking beneath us, flashing in the sunlight. "I think we're looking for trouble. And along the way, I suspect all your dreams might just come true."

CHAPTER ELEVEN

We left Max's car as close as possible to the edge of town, pointing outward, as if we would be able to dash back out and escape the city before the Saracens caught up to us. The place just had that kind of feel. We walked through tiny cobblestoned streets and almost passed as tourists. Max had ditched his cap and suit jacket, and strolled along in the heat wearing a shirt and tie like a businessman on lunch hour. I trudged along in my leather jacket, battered clothes, and boots like a biker who'd lost her ride. None of the natives paid any attention to us, and the tourists were too busy with their own selfies to notice anyone else.

As we walked, I kept my phone handy. I wasn't an idiot. I knew if I was able to track Kreios, someone could track me doing so. But I had a few things going in my favor. Thing One, Armaeus didn't know I'd lost his prize—at least not yet. Thing Two, my phone was the equivalent of a burn phone, though admittedly jacked up with a state-of-the-art international plan that included the latest bells and whistles in security along with its powerful tracker app.

Accordingly, I had a snowball's chance in hell of completing this search undetected, at least while Armaeus was in the air and not aware that I wasn't safely en route to Vegas as well. Either way, I had to act fast. Because I had a bad feeling about the Devil being here.

Which sounded ridiculous even in my own head.

Still, there was something important I needed to figure out here. If Kreios had merely wanted to dump me, he could have left me on the ground with the SANCTUS guards. Had he somehow been trying to protect me? If so, I didn't know if I should be charmed or irritated. Irritated was winning. And besides, his idea of protection needed work, given that he'd left me in a tumbling cage of Alfa Romeo.

"We seem to be heading directly for the abbey, not the castle." Max's words cut across my thoughts, his voice casual, as if we were discussing the merits of Italian street food. "Does that make sense for what you're seeking?"

I glanced at him. "Do you really not know why I'm here?" Another French shrug, and I shook my head. I'd been pissed when Armaeus had left me out of the loop, but Max was family. Surely that should count for something more. "I'm trying to find one of Armaeus's...fellow Council members. Embodiment of the Tarot Devil, maybe you know him?" At Max's blank stare, my irritation ratcheted up another notch. "Your little Council needs to get on Twitter or something. You guys are the worst."

"the Council has thrived because of its isolation. They won't be eager to change that."

"Well then, they'll be eager to fail. I don't know what the devil the Devil is up to, but he's totally gone off the reservation, coming out here. Armaeus wanted him collected and returned to the fold, not haring off on some field trip through Italy."

"Perhaps he had unfinished business?"

"Yeah, well, that's not..." I stopped. As in literally

stopped, standing stock-still in the street while Max continued forward a few more strides before turning around to glance at me.

"Miss Wilde?"

"You said the abbey had unusual Templar artwork here? Some sort of Sator Square, but different?" I took off at a brisk trot, and Max hurried to catch up with me.

"Yes, the Sator Square here is in a unique design. Normally the words make up an actual square—five words lined up, one beneath the other: SATOR AREPO TENET OPERA ROTAS. You can read them upwards, downwards, backwards—you'll always have the same order of words. There are other consistent repetitions as well. But the one in the abbey is different. Same words, but they are laid out in five concentric rings instead of a true square, with each of the five words flaring out from the center, like five points on a star— or a target. You can read the words edge to edge, or around the circle."

"Clockwise or counterclockwise?"

He thought about it. "Clockwise. Does it matter?"

"We'll find out."

We reached the abbey and edged into the back of the line, where two young lovers leaned into each other, the girl loosely holding her tickets as she sighed up at her paramour. I brushed by them with irritation, pushing to the front of the line, past a group of feral teens, a harried tour guide, and a stern-faced older woman holding a guidebook like it was the Holy Bible.

"Biglietti." A sweet-faced young girl held out her hand, and I gave her two tickets, Max's head swiveling to watch the transaction.

"The young Americans?"

"They'll get over it."

We entered the abbey and drew closer together, the hush of the ancient place demanding reverence.

"You've been here before, you said?"

Max bowed slightly. "I was a tour guide for five years. There is no rock in Italy I haven't peered under." Max took me by the arm, and I froze for half a second. "What is it?" he asked.

"Nothing. Lead on." I shook him off but didn't bother hiding my grin as he strode ahead of me. Had Armaeus known? Dante the golden child back in France didn't have one-tenth the kinetic power that Max's casual touch had betrayed, and yet Dante was the one holding court at Le Sri, while Max was playing tour guide. How long was Armaeus going to let that continue? Or did he care?

Or, more interestingly, was he doing it on purpose? From what I could see, being a member of the Council had its perks, and I would assume one of its ranking generals would have its benefits as well. But with perks generally came sacrifices. Armaeus could easily be trying to protect his extended family in his own misguided, megalomaniac way.

Max turned toward me. "It's just around the—"

"Stop." I pulled him into a long hallway hung with paintings that were not original to the abbey by any stretch. Behind and between the paintings, the walls were hung with carpenter cloths, pinned into place with low scaffolding. "What is this place?"

Max looked down the long gallery. "They removed the original frescoes for restoration, but this was once an entire room of beautiful artwork, commissioned over the years by the Holy See."

"Uh-huh. As in popes and bishops of the Caetani family?"

Max nodded. "Of course. Whenever they could

divert funds to Sermoneta, they did so. Enrico Caetani commissioned one of the more famous pieces, but it is no longer viewable by the public."

"And he lived…"

"Late 1500s."

"Right. And that fresco hung here, in this room. While the Templar Sator Square is in the next chamber. Do we have any other weird symbols close by, either for the Templars or the—"

Max cut me off excitedly. "You're looking for a line?"

"I'm looking for anything I can find. My phone says my guy is here, but—" I waved around. "Here is a little broad."

"Of course, of course." Max blew out a breath. "There is the Templar Cross in the rose window overlooking the nave, of course. And the symbols of Solomon's knot in the courtyard." He frowned, turning as if to stare through the walls. "That would be in a direct line from here. The knot, that is. With the Sator Square between us."

I nodded. I remembered the cards I'd pulled in the limo on the way here. The Two of Pents, with its infinity symbolism, equal sides balanced and intertwined. The Wheel. And the Hierophant. And here I was at the end of a line of artwork, starting with Solomon's knot, ending with a fresco commissioned by the pope. And in the center of us was the Wheel-like depiction of the Sator Square. It all made sense. Almost.

Max kept frowning, though. "But your quarry, this devil character, he cannot do anything here in the abbey. It's public. Hundreds of people see that symbol every day. There is doubtless a tour in front of it right now. He can't be next to it without being seen. It's not possible."

"He's not." I shook my head, flipping my phone around for him to see. "He's beneath it."

Max frowned. "There is no beneath—"

"Bullshit. Where's the nave where that window you mentioned is?"

We reached the stunning chapel quickly enough. It was nearly noon now, the sun pouring in the brilliant window, lighting the floor in a myriad of brilliant colors. This wasn't Indiana Jones, it wouldn't be that obvious, but the light was still going to point us the way. The four equal stems of the cross flared brilliantly on a panel on the floor. A panel that appeared like any other panel. Due to a trick of the light, however, the cross seemed to elongate slightly, its top stretching a bit almost to point...

I looked up. A confessional box stood at the far end of the chamber, ornate and unused. It gleamed with modern fittings. "Bingo."

"Bingo?" Max followed my gaze. "You wish to make your confession?"

"They lock those things?"

"Sometimes yes, sometimes no." Max followed me over to the booth, and I tried the doors. First, the side box. It opened. I poked my head inside, saw the placard. Part of the display, not used for actual confessions anymore except on special occasions. Even the Italians were embracing Vatican II, it seemed. It'd only been in play since the 1960s, but baby steps.

The main box was not quite so easy. The door didn't budge, and an old-style lockset gleamed beneath the handle. "Stand right there for a minute."

"It is a marvelous place, this abbey, is it not?" Max gazed upward, his voice reverential but not quite hushed. He nattered on as I pulled my picklocks from my jacket pocket. The second skeleton key worked, and I felt the door give way. Leaving the door slightly ajar, I leaned against Max, drawing him away as we caught the eyes of a passing tour guide, who smiled and nodded at us.

"Keep going along the side of the nave," I murmured. Fortunately, the day was a busy one. The room seemed to go through a full turnover every ten minutes or so.

We climbed the small steps to the public access area of the nave, at a safe and respectful distance from the high altar. As expected, the view was deeply moving. But it wasn't what I was looking for.

My own upbringing in Memphis had been sadly lacking in a number of ways, but I'd spent my fair share of time in Catholic churches. It was what had inspired in me a love of the arcane and magical, or so I'd always thought. So much beauty, so much symbolism wrapped up in extraordinary art and artifacts, all to celebrate the greater glory of God. And more to the point, so much consistency from one church to the other.

Without breaking stride, I stepped over the small velvet rope and moved into the sacristy. As I suspected, the small room was lined with closets. And in the closets were vestments. I pulled out a set I figured were close enough.

Max was right behind me. "What are you—" He pulled the vestments out of my hands. "No, you're too small. You'll never pass as a man."

I scowled at him, but I didn't have time to argue, especially because he was right. "There should be another door on the far side of the confessional box. Look for the cross, the square, the knot, use your imagination, something that matches up with the

Templar artwork. Tap on the door if you find it. If not, get the hell out. We'll have to wait until the Devil moves again to get his position. If you find it, though, go through and stay put. I'll be right on your heels. You've got five minutes before you're out of there."

It took him less than three.

When the telltale knock sounded, a group of school children was clustered around the nave, their eyes filled with admiration for the frescoes on either side of the altar and the lovely graceful archways of the ceiling. A schoolteacher spoke of the reasons behind creating such beautiful artwork in such a place, to encourage the faithful to gaze up outward and upward toward the heavens and remember there was something greater than themselves gazing back.

I was just happy not to have anyone gazing at me. I rose from my kneeling position and stepped quickly over to the confessional, then pressed inside, shutting the door quickly behind me. I heard the lock snick back into place and adjusted my eyes.

Max, of course, wasn't there. Given that the compartment was about the size of a Twinkie, I would have noticed him. Instead I noticed that a slender panel stood ajar against the back of the compartment, letting in a thin sliver of light. I pushed the panel open, stepping into a cool space smelling of age and rock dust, not unlike the chambers below the Vatican. "Thick walls," I whispered.

Max nodded but held a finger to his lips. He leaned to my ear as he pointed down the narrow passage, which quickly turned into a staircase leading down. "People. More than one."

We set off along the passageway, Max in his robes, his Ferragamo loafers silent on the stones. My boots did their job as well, and we moved silently, step by step, down the stair and along another passageway. Roughly, I knew we were heading back toward the main gallery we had seen before, but how many levels would we have to go?

And how would we get back up?

A loud rasping scrape reverberated from below us, the sound making my bones grind together. Beside me, Max grimaced as well, and I heard a choked gasp, then a flurry of gritted words, which, quite literally, were all Greek to me.

Beside me, Max's eyes were rounded. I checked my phone again. The Devil was definitely down there.

But I'd been expecting him to rule the day, not be ruled by it.

Max waved furiously for my phone, and I handed it over to him, frowning as he swiped it to the notes app. He typed furiously, then shoved the device back at me, and I squinted down at the screen to read his words. "One of the myths of the Sator Square: used as a demon ward by the Knights Templar. No one knows how."

The shirring sound started up again, that sound of bone-on-bone agony, but this time I realized it had a resonance, a cadence. It had words. The words of the Sator Square — spoken over and over again, backward, forward, upward, down. It was enough to drive me mad.

And apparently I wasn't the only one.

"I knew you would come, Aleksander Kreios." A dark voice floated out over the murmuring words. "And now we'll see if the dark legends of Sermoneta Sator Square are true."

By the sound the Devil made after that, I was betting they were.

CHAPTER TWELVE

The cry that tore up through the rocks was cut off short, but it served as enough cover for us to make our way fifty feet deeper into the passageway, down a second flight of stairs, this one far steeper, and along another passageway. The walls and ceiling pressed in on us, but we could manage—myself more so than Max, whose height was becoming a liability. Clearly, the passage had been carved at a time when everyone was built to a smaller scale.

Eventually the corridor widened again to become a kind of gallery—short, stubby columns stretched from the ceiling to a waist-high ledge, allowing a view into a chamber below, which was filled with light. The passage continued forward, but we slowed as the outline of a man became clear, standing at the top of the stairs.

This guard wore priest's robes, his gun equipped with a silencer. I frowned. If he had a gun and a silencer, and their point was to kill whoever was below, then why not get it over with? I had to assume it was the Devil down there making those unearthly guttural sounds, and I had to assume these people knew he'd already escaped once. Why mess around?

Then I peeked around one of the stone columns to the space below. Oh, of course. They wanted to play with their prey first.

Idiots.

But these weren't the minions of SANCTUS, as I'd originally expected. They didn't have the same air of military efficiency. The whole religious-motif thing, though, they had down.

Aleksander Kreios was strapped to a stone platform in the middle of the room, his chest bare, his fine trousers looking very much worse for the wear. He was alone, so whoever had driven him here had either betrayed him or wasn't along for this particular stop on the tour. He scowled at the men above him, but the effect was ruined somewhat by the helmet that encased his head, covering his ears. Even at this distance, I could hear the shirring noise that must be pretty much exploding his eardrums. The priestlike man standing at the base of his makeshift torture bed was adjusting an instrument panel, every turn of the knob making Kreios arc off the bed in misery.

I edged back, wincing, and Kreios's face turned, his eyes searching wildly. When they rested on me, though, I froze. There was fury and pain there, yes. But there wasn't any doubt. Not yet. If anything, the magnitude of whatever was pounding through his head seemed to make the Devil more exhilarated, like it was its own special kind of drug.

Note to self: Kreios is a whack job.

Our brief connection was summarily broken with another twist of the dial. I could hear the words again, the Sator Square's apparently meaningless babble repeating, switching back on itself, running forward again.

"Good, good." The man at the instrument panel nodded with apparent satisfaction, and only then did a second man emerge from the shadows. He spoke in

Greek, and Max fitted himself close to my ear, translating on the fly. "You will suffer now."

"I will kill you now," Kreios gritted out. "Betrayer."

"No, you won't." The man waved another hand, and the intensity of the volume picked up again. I winced along with Max. What was it about the combination of these words that pricked the senses of those with psychic abilities? "You have no power here. I'd almost given up on you escaping your little cage, but you always do manage to impress. You were foolish to come here, though, when I had already trapped you once." He gestured again, and my gaze followed the movement. The Devil's reliquary sat, open, on a bench against the far wall.

"What do you want, Barnabus? What is your game?" Exhilarated or not, the Devil's voice was ragged, vibrating with pain.

"No games." The man in the Templar robe smiled. "I'm not foolish enough to believe anything you might say now. Not until you're broken. But then!" He spread his hands. "Delivering you twice will elevate me to the highest levels of trust."

"You had *our* trust."

"I did!" Barnabus crowed. "And I used it to my advantage. Why do you think I was so eager to help you find your missing Connected in Hungary? And now, here you are once again. The words of the Sator Square burn, do they not? It is not just an old superstition after all." He paused, grinning down at Kreios. "You will be very useful to us, eventually."

Kreios moaned something then, but it was too low for me to hear. Barnabus still seemed pleased.

"We no longer need your help in that manner. Your order is lost, Kreios. There is only one order to follow now. One path to ultimate divinity. You will see this more quickly than most. You will see everything soon."

"Who?" The word was anguished now, and I tightened my hands into fists.

"Always so persistent in your pursuit of the knowledge. That was in your file too." He shook his head. "They know everything about you, Aleksander Kreios. From the beginning. They have always known about you. Your abilities were clear even when you were nothing more than another poor stiff working the docks for a day's ration of bread, laughing in the very face of the war that was brewing atop the sea you loved so much." The man's face twisted. "You should never have joined the Council. The death of your mentor was unavoidable. Yours was a choice."

That seemed to affect Kreios more than the pain. He went deadly still. "Don't speak of him."

"Still burns, does it? Seeing him gutted, then shut up in that reliquary, buried alive before your own eyes? The lore of that day has been etched into our history." He shook his head. "But now, it will be different. Now the Devil of the Arcana Council will be laid to rest, and he will not be replaced."

"Fool!" Kreios's eyes snapped open, and he glared at the robed man with enough ferocity that his tormenter stepped back, his hands stealing to the heavy cross that hung around his neck. A Templar cross, I realized. "The path you follow will betray you even as you betray the watchful gods of old. Balance will be kept, Barnabus. It has always been kept."

"Do not deceive me, Prince of Lies." The man made a sharp, cutting motion with his hand, and I felt rather than heard the surge of volume in the device. Pain wrenched through me. Max's hands now gripped my shoulders, whether for my benefit or his, I didn't know. "Who else now sits on the Council?" the man demanded. "Is it truly reassembling?"

Kreios's response was also in Greek, but Max didn't bother to translate it. Another turn of the dial, and I felt the tears on my face before I realized I'd shed them.

"Who?"

"All of them," Kreios spit the words. "The Fool. Magician. The Emperor and High Priestess and our very own pope. You want me to continue? You know the roster as well as I."

"You're lying," the man shot back. "You could never find all the stones to rebuild your unholy church."

"And you are led from darkness to greater darkness, scrabbling with your bones, your beads, and your unfounded hopes. Desperate for a savior who is *not coming*." Kreios practically pulsed with an internal fire, and I scowled down at him, remembering the golden reliquary into which he had been forced. Now, under this pain, with his focus so fixed on his tormenter, he almost seemed to be disintegrating. "He will never come, Barnabus. *We will not let him.*"

"You will stand in his way?" Barnabus stepped forward with new excitement. This apparently was something he hadn't expected. "None of you have the strength."

"Is that what you believe?" Kreios's voice had taken on an air of slippery danger, as if he were luring the robed man toward an open pit full of spikes. And, like the fool that he was, Barnabus took a step closer. Still, he wasn't a complete loss. With his right hand, he made a twisting motion, and the stooge at the dials twisted the notch again, once more making Kreios writhe.

"Tell me, Aleksander. For the family you have sacrificed, whose cries torment you at night. For the children you have lost to perdition. Tell me and absolve yourself of all your many sins."

"You dare!" Kreios's eyes blazed with rage and something else, something not right. They burned too brightly not to eventually explode.

I did a recon of the chamber, because showtime was clearly close.

Two men guarded the reliquary, both of them masked. Another pair of guards stood at the second entrance to the room, and I assumed a final guard stood at the bottom of the stairs to this gallery. Six men against Max and myself, and the Devil who even now was starting to look a little too incorporeal for comfort.

I couldn't afford for him to up and disappear on me. I didn't know if he'd get sucked back into his box or go poof for good. Or for bad, as it happened.

I reached into my jacket. Beside me, Max already had his gun out. Neither of us had silencers. Hopefully the tours above had moved along.

Wait, I mouthed, as Max's eyes were trained on my face. *Wait.*

Barnabus gestured another time.

Kreios cried out in fury one final time and I shoved myself half over the banister of the gallery, shooting at the guards at the far wall before dropping all the way through. I hit the ground and rolled, gunfire skittering off the floor as I ducked behind Kreios's platform.

"Finish it!" Barnabus snapped the order, and the man at the controls dived forward. I launched myself at the cart, shoving it out of the way as I took him down at the knees. I coldcocked him with my pistol once, twice, before looking up to see Max at the bottom of the stairs. He cracked the soldier's neck against the stone, the skull crunching into the rock, then let the man fall. His quick, efficient shooting took out the remaining guard. Barnabus was already running, and I gestured Max after him while I turned to Kreios.

The Devil was barely breathing. The screech of noise from his helmet reverberated through the room, and I pulled a knife out of my pocket, ripping at the wires that held the helmet affixed to the sprawling cart. It seemed permanently attached to the platform, so they had to have somehow gotten Kreios into it without protest. Which would have meant he'd been knocked out. But how?

With the severing of the last wire, a spray of sparks flew across the room, and merciful silence blanketed us. I slumped forward over Kreios's body, my ears ringing, the abrupt cessation of pain like a benediction. Beneath me, the Devil's chest was slick with sweat, his own lungs heaving beneath his thickly corded pecs.

As I steadied myself against him, soft words floated down around my ears.

"As pleasant as I'm sure this experience would be for both of us, we may want to wait until we are completely alone, Sara Wilde."

I jerked back upright as Max appeared in the doorway again, his face grim.

"Gone?" I asked.

"Dead." He shook his head at my startled expression. "Some sort of suicide pill, frothing at the mouth before I got to him. Stuck in an oubliette, no way out." Max tossed me a set of keys. "These might be helpful."

"Don't count on him being dead," Kreios gritted out as I grabbed the ring, turning first to the ankle manacles until I found the right one. "Go back for him.

Guard the body."

"Go," I nodded. I had the second ankle manacle off and was on the left wrist when the chest bar snapped. I narrowed my eyes at Kreios. "You could do that the whole time?"

"Not all of them. And not with that infernal noise. Besides, I rather enjoy you doing it." He reached up with his right hand as soon as I freed it and used the leverage to push himself down, out of the fixed helmet. I blinked—his head had been shaved bald. It gave him a savage ferocity that, combined with his glittering eyes, made me wonder if he was fully sane any longer. "Accursed Sator Square. Knew this place had one, but shaped like a wheel..." He shook his head like a bear coming out of hibernation. "Wasn't prepared for that."

Max's curse floated back to us, and Kreios hauled himself off his platform. A quick step, and he collapsed against me heavily. I groaned at the weight, which was several times more than what I'd expected. "What in God's name did you have for breakfast?"

Kreios ignored me. "Where's Barnabus?" he asked instead. "The body."

"Now he's gone." Max came back through the doorway and willingly took Kreios's weight as I moved to the side of the room for the reliquary. After snapping it shut, I shoved it inside my jacket and zipped the pocket closed, then returned to Kreios's side.

"So, what?" I asked. "Fake arsenic pill? I hear they sell those on the Internet now."

"Not fake," Kreios managed. He kept trying to get his feet under himself, and skidded and slipped instead. "Built up a tolerance. Simply one of an arsenal of tricks."

"Stop fighting us," I bit out when he practically

horse-collared me again. He was drenched in sweat, but his skin was ice-cold. "What the hell was that helmet?"

"Variation on an old theme, I'm afraid." Kreios coughed. Blood dripped from his mouth and he wobbled again before leaning heavily on both of us. "A very effective variation. Someone's been doing their homework."

"We're coming up on a door." Max warned. "It's open. Gotta be where Barnabus went out."

"Check it," I said. "If he's left us a welcome party, it's going to get messy."

But he hadn't. Barnabus was nowhere to be found in the basement. The door at the far end was locked, of course, but I'd been target practicing on locks for a long time. With a few rounds, it swung open easily. Max went forward several steps before giving the all clear.

"Looks like the storage room for the abbey gift shop," he said. "Hope they don't pick us up for shoplifting."

I eyed Kreios. "He's not going to be able to make it all the way to the car."

"Agreed," Max said. "And he's going to need some clothes."

Between us, Kreios sighed heavily. "I'll be all right in another minute. The glamour is not a difficult effect to reconstruct."

"I've got a better idea," I said.

CHAPTER THIRTEEN

Coming up out from the depths of the abbey into the gift shop a few minutes after Max slipped up the stairs, I kept my head bowed, my eyes on the shuffling form that preceded me down the narrow aisle. The irony of the Devil wrapped up in clerical clothes wasn't lost on me. Fortunately, the woman at the cash register wasn't paying attention to us but to the elderly couple buying postcards, so we got out into the sunshine without incident.

"There's a bench to the right, three — well, maybe five paces, the way you're walking now."

"Always so critical." For all his bravado, the Devil wasn't looking so good. He sank down on the bench like a man fifty years past dead. I perched beside him, arranging his elbows on his knees, lacing his fingers together so that he almost gave the appearance of being lost in contemplative prayer.

"Wanna tell me how you ended up in Barnabus's bed?"

His chuckle was his only response for a moment, and I stared diligently at the side of his head, willing his secrets to spring forth.

Who was this guy, really?

Aleksander Kreios appeared foreign born, just as the Magician was, but their similarities ended there. As golden as the Magician was dark, Kreios's large, sensuous eyes were jade green, his body sleekly built. The combination of high cheekbones and sculpted lips looked almost too perfect on a man, but the sexual aggression that lay barely restrained in the guy's every move transcended everything as his defining characteristic. Even if he was practically dead at this point.

Which begged the question, why hadn't Armaeus warned me that I'd be carrying around canned Master-of-Darkness?

I hit him up with the obvious question. "Why'd you come here?"

"That's not necessary for you to know."

"Uh-huh. You want me to include this little side trip in my report to Armaeus?"

"Only if you want to risk my annoyance."

I eyed him. "Not gonna lie, that doesn't seem like too much of a threat right now."

The laugh seemed dredged up out of Kreios's stomach, a rasping huff. "I can see why Armaeus never bothered to arrange an introduction between us. Where have you been all of my lives, Sara Wilde?"

"Just focus on breathing, big boy." I squinted down the long cobbled street, praying for Max to hurry it up. "So walk me through this. Who picked you up at the Alfa Romeo dumping ground? Why did you come here?"

"Those were my associates." Full stop.

"You're not very good at this, you know. Where'd they go?"

Kreios lifted a hand to wave me off, but I batted it away. "Tell me, or I'll call the Magician on the Batphone. I have to assume he's got more family out here than Max."

The Devil sighed heavily. "I did not bring my friends into the city. This is only partially their fight."

"Yet they handed you over, gift wrapped, to Barnabus? Because it sure seemed like he was expecting you."

I could see Kreios's smile in profile. It was not a particularly good smile.

"'Cowards die many deaths.'" He gestured to the street. "This place—it belongs to an extension of his family. He considers its inner workings his own. It was reasonable that this was where he would go to ground."

"Yeah, well, he was wearing a *Templar robe*, Kreios, and it looked like the real deal. I thought that order died out, oh, about eight hundred years ago."

"The Templars still have a robust following."

"Yeah, well, so do skinheads. Doesn't make it cool." I waited a beat. "So you came here because he was the one who'd stuck you in that box in the first place, and you knew this was where he'd gone to ground. Did you also know he'd have the helmet of doom waiting for you?"

Kreios coughed again. More blood trickled from his lips. He ignored it. "That was an underestimation on my part."

"How'd he get you in the helmet?"

"The moment I entered the abbey, he piped the noise at a frequency higher than human hearing. I wasn't prepared." He straightened with obvious effort. "I will be henceforth." He lifted a hand to forestall my next question. "Budapest was also a miscalculation. It's been a long time since I faced a worthy opponent." His smile flashed. "Rest assured, I've had sufficient time beneath the basilica to contemplate my sins."

"Okay." I blew out a long breath. "You go to

Budapest, get ambushed by SANCTUS. How'd they get you in the box?" The answer flickered in my subcortex as I asked it. "It's the pain, isn't it? With enough pain, you wink out." He didn't answer, and I grinned. "I'm totally going to force you to binge-watch the Kardashians, to see if we can try this at home."

His coughing spasm got worse, but I forged ahead. "Why the Templars, though? What beef do they have with the Council? I thought they were good guys."

The Devil's snort was derisive. "There is no mortal who is purely good, Sara Wilde. But the Templars are not the only group trying to find a balance with the members of SANCTUS. The entire Connected community is on edge. The Templars merely acted first. Unwisely, as now they will be persecuted. Again."

"Right." I patted him on the back, allowing him his bravado even as he wheezed. At length, Max drove up, once more in his spiffy uniform and hat. I was a big fan of the hat. I was yet more of a fan of the way he hopped out of the car and hustled around, hoisting up Kreios's gravity-defying weight as I struggled on the other side. Together, we got the Devil into the back of the car, and I scooted around to enter the vehicle as well.

"Destination?"

"Ciampino Airport." I frowned. "Has your car been LoJacked by Mr. Mephistopheles?"

"It was." Max smiled. "Then I moved the monitor to one of the limo service's other vehicles. This one is clean."

"I knew I liked you."

Kreios sighed beside me. "If we could start moving, that would be ideal."

The Devil was slumped back in his seat, but he

wasn't the Devil I'd hauled out of the abbey like a refugee from a Filene's Basement sale. "So what was the point of Barnabus shaving you?"

Kreios shrugged. His hair had already grown an inch, and somewhere along the line he'd either stolen or manifested sunglasses. Still in his cassock, he looked like some kind of rock-star priest, the poster child for Catholic cool. "It gave him something to do that didn't actually cause me pain, so I was happy to oblige him." He straightened a little in his seat, wincing against the movement.

"You're kind of freaking me out right now with all the pain emoting," I said. "I didn't know you guys could get hurt."

"If by 'you guys' you mean the Council, then once again I am sorry to disappoint you. We can be hurt. We can be killed. Why do you think we need to keep tabs on the Connected? When we have to replenish our ranks, we are generally not in the mood for that process to take a great deal of time."

"Fair enough." I knew Max was listening avidly from the front of the car, but I didn't care. If this much crazy was coming after the Connected, we needed to be prepared. All of us. No matter who we had in our family tree. "We going to be followed?"

"Doubtful. Barnabus won't want to advertise his failure, and without his leverage," Kreios tapped his head, "he won't try again. Better to keep the blame for losing me firmly on SANCTUS's military force."

"What about his Templar den mates?"

"I doubt their leadership knew of his plan. Certainly not the execution of it. We..." He winced again, shifting in his seat. "We go back a long way."

Oh? "Are they, ah...affiliated with the Council?"

"When they have reason to be." Kreios lifted a

hand. "Silence, Sara Wilde. I am afraid the sonic attacks leveled upon me were more robust than I would have given them credit for. I will need time to address the damage."

I scooted back to my side of the car. "No sweat. I'll just play Candy Crush over here."

My phone jangled in my pocket. Which was a problem, since it was set to silent.

Pulling it out, I scowled down. A text from Armaeus. Apparently, he'd reached an altitude where the combination of water and distance wasn't screwing with his senses anymore...or he'd asked someone to check in with air traffic control.

Why aren't you en route?

I shrugged and nudged Kreios's arm, lifting the phone so that it reflected off his mirrored sunglasses. "You want to answer that?"

"It will be my pleasure."

Dutifully, I punched in Armaeus's digits. The call rang through, and, as usual, Armaeus didn't keep me waiting. As the call was picked up, my phone slipped out of my hand, leaving nothing behind but a shiver of promise, like a mild electrical charge against my fingertips. Kreios was clearly on his way to finding his happy place once more.

"*Armaeus,*" Kreios said in his luxuriously sensual voice, his eyes steady on me as I shook out my hand. "*Look* what you have brought me."

I rolled my eyes as he settled back in his seat. "We are on our way to the airport now." More listening. "I was in slightly worse than anticipated shape. It's taken a while for me to recover." More listening. "But of course." He glanced back at me, his eyes unreadable behind the reflective lenses of his glasses, his smile wolfish. "She has been with me the whole time. She has proven most useful. You were right to send her." I could hear the sharpness of Armaeus's retort, then Kreios slipped into a language I had no knowledge of — something that didn't sound remotely European.

I shook my head, irritated, but more with myself than the Council. My laissez-faire attitude about information gathering wasn't going to work with this crew. I couldn't deal with Armaeus, not if there were twenty one other potential demigods lurking in the shadows, whether current or planned. As it was, I barely knew a few of the Council members.

The Fool was a reasonable enough sort, kind of like Loki's nerdy younger cousin, with an affinity for fast cars and faster tech. I'd met him once when the Magician had been too busy to track me down himself. He'd sent his message via the Fool without warning me. The Fool had delivered it to me, catching up with me in LA right after I'd delivered another job, but he hadn't come clean about his purpose until we'd shared a very expensive bottle of tequila and had ended up poolside of a celebutante who kept calling him Luscious. I still wasn't sure about the provenance of the name Luscious, but anyone who can keep down half a fifth of hundred-dollar reposado was okay by me.

The High Priestess was completely on the other end of the spectrum, haughty and lovely, with long black hair, flashing dark eyes, and an ability to whine that was almost a superpower unto itself. She had joined the Council fairly recently, I got the feeling. But with these guys, that could mean any time after 1950.

And that was, well, it. I had a vague sense of the Emperor and Empress skulking about in Sin City, but I'd never picked up a clue about the Devil. How could I have missed someone so…unmissable?

I stared out the window as the landscape whipped by. At length, Kreios ended his call and tossed the phone on the seat between us. I left it there. I didn't feel like touching the guy again, and something about this entire operation sat wrong with me. I was beginning to think it had been Armaeus's plan all along to con me into getting sucked into the Council's business. And I really wasn't in the mood.

We reached Ciampino Airport and turned onto the private airstrip. A gleaming white jet rested alone at the head of it, pointed out toward the far horizon. On its tail, a corporate-looking logo of a blue dragon bracketed by two arching red flames was the only marking I could see. Kreios, in a burst of newfound energy, was out of the car before Max had even fully parked it. A second later, I realized why. In his hand he held the reliquary. How had he…

I shook my head. I needed to pay closer attention to these freaks.

"He looks like he's going to be okay."

"Yep." I eyed Max's reflection. "What about you? You gonna get in trouble for your little side trip?"

"Doubtful. Bottom line, you were attacked, and your cargo was taken from you. Since you were honor bound to go after it, I was honor bound to protect you while you did so. In the end, I safely returned you to the airstrip that had been your original destination, and waited around until you were safely on your way. Mission Complêt."

"Right." Together we watched Kreios disappear around the back of the plane, holding the gold box aloft as if trying to examine it from all angles. I wasn't feeling too good about that box's chances of making it to Vegas in one piece. I clicked on my phone and was relieved to find the tracking device secure. I was pretty sure Armaeus wanted to examine the reliquary, but I suspected that Kreios wasn't too keen on keeping it around. I'd let them figure that out.

I returned my attention to Max. "So, where will you go from here? Back to the limo service?"

"I think no. I've been shuttling around guests of le seigneur for the past five years. Never has it been more interesting than today, and today is not yet done. This man called Barnabus, he disappeared on my watch. He was hurt, at a minimum." Max gave a long, heartfelt sigh, then winked at me. "I feel badly about that. He may need a ride somewhere safe."

I lifted my brows. "Uh-huh. And you're just the guy to help him with that?"

He grinned. "I live to serve. At the very least, I can pick up his trail and see where he goes from here. Who knows? Maybe he'll let me join his secret club."

"Or maybe he'll kill you. Which wouldn't be nearly as fun."

"It would certainly make for a diverting afternoon, though." Max patted his steering wheel. "It's time I broadened my horizons."

I blew out a long breath. I couldn't let this guy just hare off after a nutcase, but it was clear he needed to do something. And driving tourists around in his limo wasn't going to cut it, not after today. "So what's your kink, Max? What psy power do you actually possess?"

He frowned. "I don't. I told you—"

"Riiight." Armaeus was going to be pissed, but the Connected had to stick together. And if there was ever a man gifted at discerning the talents of an untutored psy... "I tell you what. Why don't you go to Paris instead—no, not to your family, though if you do, give Claire my love. We're besties. But I really would rather you go to the Cathedral of Saint-Germaine-des-Prés.

There's a priest named Father Jerome. Tell him I sent you."

Max's eyes lit up. "And what is the reason I should give?"

"Tell him you're ready to join the team."

CHAPTER FOURTEEN

We said our good-byes, then I exited the limo, patting its flank like it was a good pony as Max drove off. Then I turned toward the sleek aircraft that awaited me. Kreios was nowhere to be seen, but I climbed the long stairway alone, nodding toward the woman who stood at its top. She was perhaps the most attractive flight attendant in the history of aviation. Figured.

The jet Armaeus had commissioned for this jaunt was sleek and well equipped, and apparently came with enough money to expedite minor inconveniences such as identity checks and customs management. The attendant followed me into the cabin and began to describe the plane to me in a silken, heavily accented voice. Then Kreios appeared, and the woman's head completely separated from her body.

Oh, boy. This might take a while.

While the attendant tried to recover her capacity for speech, I wandered over to the bar, pulling out a bottle of water and listening to the captain crackling instructions over the intercom. Taking one of the overstuffed captain's chairs, I watched Kreios discuss the upcoming flight with his newest convert.

Eventually, of course, she had to go back and do her actual job. Kreios ambled over, looking entirely too smug as he sprawled in his own seat. I'd sat across from the Magician just the day before in almost identical positions, of course. But while Armaeus had breathed refinement and control, the quintessential European aristocrat, the Devil was like a half-drunk frat boy, lounging with one leg over the arm of the plush leather seat, his body canted back, his gaze several shades too contented.

"How long is the flight?"

"Twelve hours, give or take," he said. "Armaeus has a several-hour head start on us, but I'm sure he'll be eager to see you again."

I looked at him, my curiosity finally getting its moment in the sun. "So, before we go further: you're not the *actual* devil, right?"

"A matter of semantics, I suspect."

"Uh-huh. And what exactly was SANCTUS hoping to do with you—or Barnabus, for that matter? Because they had to keep you alive for some reason, and I don't think it's because of your sterling personality."

"So quickly does the rose turn to thorn." Kreios shrugged. "But it is a worthy story, and since Armaeus did not see fit to share it with you, I shall. I was heading to Hungary quite some time ago, if it is truly now late spring...?"

I nodded, and he continued. "On very good information from a man who, while not a friend, precisely, had certainly never been my enemy before now."

"Barnabus."

"No. I'd contacted Barnabus after receiving the information about Hungary. He was to help facilitate my meetings there. Barnabus was also, up to this point, someone I did not consider an enemy. It seems my trust has been very misplaced of late."

"Yeah, you might want to work on that." I

considered his words. Hungary had become a hotbed for the underground antiquities market over the past few years, but I'd managed to avoid the place so far. And the country was too far east for its lost children to find their way onto Father Jerome's list. Though based on the map I'd seen at Armaeus's family homestead, we should be paying more attention to those children, and pronto. Their value was definitely heating up. "What's in Hungary?"

"A family of mystics, as it happens. Very old, very well respected. They had gone to ground around the turn of the last century, and there was some indication that perhaps they had resurfaced with the recent...global rekindling of interest in the magical arts. A member of their line had once upon a time been part of the Council, and a very strong part at that."

"I take it you didn't find this family?"

He shook his head. "Regrettably, no. I no sooner landed in Budapest than I was met by a group of very earnest young soldiers who, apparently, Barnabus had directed toward me."

"They trapped you in the box?"

"A charming thing, no?" He leaned back as if imagining it in his mind's eye. "Diaboli Reliquiarum Thecam. The Devil's Reliquary. The last time I saw it was in Consta— No!" He snapped his fingers. "It was Istanbul by then. Ah, how things change with the passage of time." He regarded me with his heavy-lidded gaze. "A dear friend of mine, my mentor, if you will, had drawn the attention of some very unfortunate men, rigid adherents to a code of religious practice that we found tedious at best, despicable at worst. My friend, he had grown to become a person of prominence by this time, and to see him brought down by such unfortunate parasites was, as you might imagine, quite affecting."

I watched him, tracking the danger in his tone. Though his manner remained easy, the edge in his words was unmistakable. "And how long was *he* in there?"

The Devil shrugged. "As far as I know, they cleaned his ashes out of that accursed box in order to put mine in. And to that *we should drink*!" These last words were shouted, and the beautiful attendant materialized in the doorway to the cabin, hastening to his side.

"Do you have a preference, Monsieur Kreios?"

"Scotch," he said, glancing at me. "It's what the lady likes."

I stiffened. I was a fan of scotch, yes, but there was no way that I had said as much to Kreios in the few words we had shared—I certainly hadn't been thinking it. And I could not imagine that my beverage preferences had come up in the conversation between Armaeus and Kreios on the phone. Nevertheless, as the attendant looked over to me for confirmation, I nodded. "Glenmorangie."

Kreios raised his brows. "You seem quite confident that it's in stock."

"And you seemed quite confident of my drink of choice. Why is that?"

"One of my many charms." He spread his hands, anticipating the return of the attendant with the glass at his side. She smoothly handed him the drink, then presented me with a cut-crystal tumbler as well. When she'd withdrawn to whatever antechamber served as her holding cell, Kreios lifted his glass high. "To Marcus, long of life," he said robustly, the lilt in his voice breaking through, betraying his Greek heritage. "That he did not die in vain."

"To Marcus." I nodded. The scotch was as smooth as I had come to expect, but it burned a fiery trail down my throat. "That he had not died at all."

"Well, I'm not sure I would go that far," Kreios said, angling his glass to me. "After all, without his death, there would have been no becoming for me. And then, my dear Sara Wilde, we would not have met. That *would* have been a pity."

I tried to stifle my chuckle, but Kreios peered at me, his eyes missing nothing. "You have not worked with the Council long, but there is no excuse for Armaeus not to have introduced us."

"I'm not in the city much."

"Of course you aren't." Kreios's smile was far too knowing. "Still, something could have been arranged, before my unfortunate excursion, don't you think? It is a curiosity that we have not met. And curiosities interest me."

I shifted uneasily in my seat. "I can't see how it matters."

"Perhaps you are right," Kreios conceded. "One evening of carnal pleasure with Armaeus, no matter how intriguing, does not a relationship make."

I scowled at him, knowing he was baiting me but unable to resist the challenge. "As you say."

His smile broadened, and he leaned forward, his entire being focused on me. The effect was heady, dangerous. "Well then. Since the Magician does not *now* share your bed, perhaps you can tell me how I might be of service."

"And perhaps," I said, leaning forward as well, my gaze lingering on his eyes, the curve of his jaw, his sensual lips, "you could tell me *specifically* why SANCTUS stuck you in that box. Or why Barnabus suddenly hates you so much that he wanted to turn

133

your brain to rice pudding."

Kreios's laugh was a thing of raw, primal beauty and did nothing to ease the tension in the cabin. He took another sip of scotch, regarding me more closely over the rim of the glass. "Old prejudices die hard, Sara Wilde," he said as he tipped the tumbler toward me. "The men who captured me are not the exact caste of the priests who incarcerated Marcus, but their desires are the same, as are their needs." He rolled the glass in his hand. "As it happens, needs and desires are my stock-in-trade."

"What, the damning of souls lost its shine for you?"

His smile was wicked. "That depends. Do you have a soul you'd like to be damned?" His gaze rested on my mouth again, stoking an alarming response until he settled back in his chair again. "I assure you, my role on this earth is nothing so tedious. How much do you—ah!" His beautifully arched brows lifted high, as if he'd had a flash of inspiration. "Has Armaeus told you so little, then?"

I rolled my eyes. "Do you do that all the time, answering your own questions?"

"Forgive me." He inclined his head. "You will find that as cloaked as our dear Armaeus can be, I am his opposite. In this as in so many things. He uses deception and illusion to gain his ends. I find that the truth can be far quicker—and, when skillfully applied, far more devastating." He set his glass beside him, then clasped his hands together. "But I was telling you of my unfortunate altercation with SANCTUS." He said the name with a delicate twist of his lips, making it sound like an epithet. "What do you know of them?"

He had the grace to allow me to actually answer this time. "Evil minions of some cardinal, dedicated to destroying all the Connected in the world, starting with their icons, statuary, and twenty-sided dice."

Kreios nodded. "The role of the Arcana Council since time was born has been to maintain the balance of all magic. 'All magic,' of course, presupposes that there will be dark to counter the light. Dark, as it happens, is my specialty." He ducked his head, the soul of modesty.

"The rest of it—the worship of an anti-God, fire and brimstone, eternal torment—that is not a construct of mine, nor of any of my predecessors, but the Catholic church does not see things in quite the same light, nor have they for centuries." He shrugged. "I cannot blame them. Their zealotry has served them well. But—I, and Marcus before me, and all who came before him—we mean to *enjoy* this world, not bathe it in screams of terror." He lifted his brows. "Which is not to say the occasional scream isn't quite satisfying, in the right context."

He grinned as I rolled my eyes. "But the ruination of the teeming masses is not, nor has it ever been, our purpose. It would be quite tedious, in fact, when there are so many pleasures to be had."

"Uh-huh. So if you're not truly the enemy of the Church, then why—"

"Well." Kreios spread his hands once more. "I never quite said I wasn't an *enemy* of the Church. That would be a lie, and as I have told you—"

"Right. Champion of truth, defender of honesty, got that."

He nodded. "Whatever you would know, I can tell you. Especially, as I have mentioned, your deepest needs, Sara Wilde. Your darkest desires."

I considered that. My darkest desires had taken a turn of late. I wasn't too comfortable with that going out on the psychic network. "My worst fears too, I suppose?"

"Never that." He shook his head, shrugging off my surprise. "That, I must be told. You would be amazed, however, at the number of people who cannot help but share their worst nightmares aloud, as if begging for them to be unleashed in their midst. But do not evade the question." He steepled graceful fingers beneath his chin. "What truths do you seek?"

"Are the young women from Kavala in Las Vegas? Are they alive?"

"Too easy," Kreios said. "But yes, and yes. Armaeus has told you this already. He would not lure you to a city you despise only to show you corpses. And why do you despise Las Vegas, Sara Wilde?"

So not going there. I refocused him on the more important question. "Where are they?"

"The young women? You cannot help them until we land." He tilted his head, his green eyes searching mine. "But there are other questions you should be asking, and well you know it."

I felt the challenge in his words and knew the opportunity he presented. The opportunity, and also its unstated truth. *What else has Armaeus been keeping from me?* "Who else is on the Council that I don't know about?" I asked. "Are there actually the full twenty-two Major Arcana represented?"

"Too safe." Kreios dismissed the question, his lush lips turning down in a pout. "And our current number is far less than twenty two, I assure you. The Fool and High Priestess are in the city now. I suspect you have met them. They are well in the public eye. The Empress and Emperor are present as well, but remain uncommitted to the war that Armaeus would wage. The rest—scattered. Some of the positions remain unfilled. And the houses are all in ruins."

I lifted my brows. "Houses? This is different from the families?"

"Of course. The minor houses that have always served the Council." He waved casually. "Swords, pents, wands, cups. They have not been mobilized since the reign of Charlemagne, though. No need, really. The world's use of magic has risen and fallen with the tides of money and power." He shrugged. "It might do so again, without our intercession, despite the current threat."

I put aside the mind boggle of yet *more* minions of the Council I knew nothing about. These people had their fingers in way too many pies. "Is SANCTUS really all that powerful?"

"A year ago, I would have said no. But we have gotten lax, it would appear. We have seen, too long, solely what we want to see. It is why there are so few of us to hold the line as it is. Or to dance over it, from time to time." His gaze flickered back to my face. "And speaking of the dance, that's not all you want to know, is it?" he prompted. "I can see it in your face, hear it in your blood."

I grimaced. "My blood?"

"It *sings* to me," he said, leaning close. "And it tells me you have much to learn, that you are on the precipice of knowledge, on the very verge of slipping over, never to return." His smile deepened, drawing me into his spell with his eyes, his voice, his words. "So tell me, Sara Wilde. What truths do you truly yearn to know?"

CHAPTER FIFTEEN

Kreios's chuckle brought me back to my senses, and I stiffened. How long had I been sitting there, staring at him? Enthralled like a rabbit by the wolf? "Quit that," I muttered, wishing there was more scotch in my glass. I felt like I could down the whole bottle.

What did I truly yearn to know, he'd asked, and too many options lodged themselves in my brain. Why is this happening, why now, why to me? And will it all end so horribly as it had before, with everyone I knew just…gone?

Unaccountably, my heart turned over, thumping painfully as my life stretched out before me. My ragtag childhood, my mother's boozy laughter — her love too impossible to predict, too ephemeral to hold onto. The emerging of my own abilities out of nowhere, and Mom's delight in showing me off to her friends, her neighbors and, finally, to the impossibly perfect cop who'd looked down at me without flinching and asked if I could help find a missing kid.

Don't go there. Don't ever go there. He's dead to you.

But he wasn't dead, not really. I felt his sharp presence every time I touched down in Las Vegas. He'd transferred there. Of course he'd transferred there, the one city I needed him not to be. He'd risen to the rank of detective now, and if he ever saw me… If he ever realized that I was alive, and that his frenzied search to find me after that horrifying day in Memphis had all been for naught, that the moment he'd given up on me and acknowledged I was dead, I'd been five states away singing show tunes at an RV campsite… I couldn't imagine how much he'd hate me then. But I'd had to do it. I'd had to. No one else could die because of me.

They're all dead to you.

"You should never resist your desires, Sara," Kreios purred, and in my hand, my glass was suddenly more than half-filled with the glittering dark liquid.

I swirled it, the aroma of the aged spirits rising around me. "And this is real," I said flatly, forcing my memories down to focus on the Devil and his tricks. "I could drink this, and it would affect me as much as any drink would. The flames burning those men — those were real too."

He shrugged. "Did they seem real to you? Does the scotch taste real?"

I tilted the glass and took a sip, savoring the familiar burn once more. "Yes. But that's not what I asked."

"What is reality?" Kreios stood and stretched luxuriously, sweeping his hand around the space. I was drawn by the movement of his hand, watching it like it was the pendulum at the end of a hypnotist's chain. "Is this airplane that Armaeus so generously provided us real?" he asked, strolling a few steps toward the bar before turning to me. "Is the air we breathe and the skin we inhabit real? Am I real?"

"Any of me?" A second voice sounded, and my gaze jerked back to Kreios's chair. Sitting there was a second Kreios, his smile wry as he took in my startled glance. "Armaeus really *has* fallen short on your training, it appears. I could assist you with that."

"It's all illusion," I said, swiveling my gaze from one of him to the other. "Which one is —"

"Which one would you like to be real?"

I nearly dropped my drink as the words fanned across my ear, lips grazing along my neck. A third Kreios had taken up residence in the chair beside mine. He leaned into my space as I sat rigidly, his laughter setting whorls of sensation skittering along my skin. "The entire point of an illusion is for you to see what you most want to see, what your mind can allow you to see. And taste." Kreios part three reached over and slipped the glass of scotch out of my fingers, taking a slow drink before letting his fingers go lax, the glass and scotch dropping out of his hand. Reflexively, I grabbed for it, even as it winked out of existence, and he caught up my hand in his strong, warm grasp, pulling it to his mouth.

"And touch," he murmured.

I stared at him as he pressed his lips against my fingertips, the responding reaction deep in the center of my being swift and absolute. The ache of my own memories flipped to an unexpected heat that pooled within me, flooding me with need.

"This is an illusion," I tried again, though my words sounded shaky to my own ears.

"If you wish it to be," he said, and his grip on my hand firmed. With a ruthless yank, he pulled me over the short distance between our chairs, then turned and tossed me from him, half hurling me backward across the room. I barely kept my feet as I heard the attendant's concerned voice, then the sound of a slamming door as I skidded to a stop against the far wall. My vision swam back into focus.

Kreios stood in front of me, too close, too real.

"You are an *illusion*," I gritted out, my words ending on a moan as Kreios suddenly leaned in, taking my mouth in a hard, searching kiss, tasting, demanding — and my body felt like it was going to go up in fire, the heat so intense that I desperately feared he'd cast off my clothes as easily as Armaeus had done, and then we would be positioned body against body, need against need, with nothing between us except my own fraying control.

"Perhaps. But I think you *like* this illusion," Kreios said, his words tight and almost angry as he shifted his mouth up next to my ear. "I think you have yourself and your abilities, so locked up inside a cell of your own making that you are afraid to truly feel, Sara Wilde. Afraid to truly own the gifts you were brought into this world to share. And more than that," he said, lifting his head again. "I think you *like* the way I make you feel, trapped in my —"

"*No!*" Summoning strength from the depths of my being, I cracked my head against Kreios's chin, the shock of the movement forcing him to back away. "I told you *no*."

The Devil's laugh drifted down over my ears.

"You did. And that's all you will ever have to do." He blew me a kiss that I could feel against my burning cheek. "Something for you to remember."

A blink later and he was across the room again, seated in his chair.

Kreios regarded me with amusement, his drink still in his hand. Mine sat waiting for me next to my chair, its level indicating that I'd had a few healthy swigs, no more.

"An illusion," I managed shakily, straightening my clothes. Not a stitch had come off my body. Even my Tyet had remained firmly in place, not reacting cold or hot to the Devil's assault. "That…was all an illusion."

Kreios shrugged. "Did it feel like an illusion?"

I gingerly flexed my fingers, wincing at the pain. "But—"

"Come here," he said, his voice echoing in my bones. Ignoring him, I walked over to the bar where the Glenmorangie still sat, and pulled another crystal tumbler from the rack. Kreios's chuckle was rich and full behind me.

"You see? You *can* choose that which you prefer to take as real, versus what you choose to see as illusion. Which makes me wonder why you allow yourself to live with the illusions you do."

I turned and scowled at him. "I'm aware of the Council's abilities of manipulation, Kreios. And I appreciate the reminder. But don't treat me like a fool."

"Then stop *acting* like one." Just like that, Kreios was in front of me again, his impossibly beautiful eyes staring down at me, his lush lips bare inches from mine, sending my body into another spasm of need. "You, more than most in this world, have the ability to see beyond your fears, your desires. To recognize them merely as tools that serve to unlock a greater truth. You should learn to trust yourself."

"I can't trust myself!" I shoved him, and he fell back easily, which only served to piss me off more. "You of all people should know that. I can't—"

"Ah-ah-ah," He raised a finger, the danger shimmering between us almost like a living thing. "Have a care with sharing your fears, sweet Sara Wilde. Remember, I cannot know them without your tacit permission."

I broke off, staring at him, my heart thundering, the entire history of my horrible choices parading in front of my eyes, mocking me for *ever* having trusted myself.

"Then what can you see?" I asked carefully.

"I can see a woman so powerful that she blocks what she cannot endure," Kreios said. I shifted my gaze to him, and his mouth teased into a smile. "Imagine that. All the horrors that are clearly dancing in your mind are held back from me as if they never happened. Imagine, if these are the things you *see*, what you have *forgotten*. How deep must your terror be for something to just"—he fluttered long, elegant fingers—"disappear?"

I frowned at him, confused, then understanding dawned. "You mean with Armaeus. The fact that parts of...our time together, I can no longer remember."

"I do not blame you, of course. As tedious as the Magician is when standing upright, he must be an absolute trial in bed."

Heat scored my cheeks, but I managed to regard Kreios with a more or less steady gaze. "And you know *why* I blocked those memories, I take it?"

"Of course. I know your innermost needs and desires, Sara." He grinned. "And this blockage was born of those, not of any *true* fear. So yes, I know why you did it." He took another step toward me, leaning down. I was too busy wrapping my brain around his words to fully take in his movements—his arms reaching out to gather me close, his body fitting itself to mine, his head bending down, his mouth nuzzling against my lips, setting a thousand fires aflame along every filament of my nervous system. "Would you like me to tell you?" he asked, tasting me, teasing me, his hands sliding down my back. "Would you like to tell me why your need with Armaeus is so great that you must shutter it from your own mind?"

I didn't hesitate. "Nope," I said, my voice solid and sure. I could go another six or seven lifetimes without dipping my toe back into that murky water.

Kreios drew back, his eyes bright with delight, his grin unabashed.

"Excellent. Then I shall look forward to our next dance, Sara Wilde. You will learn, in time, that when there is no one else who will tell you the truth, that I will be there for you. And when you come to me, I will tell you everything. If you pay the price."

Then he dissolved in front of me, leaving me alone in the cabin—except for the last and final form of Aleksander Kreios far across from me, sprawled out on his chair in deep, snoring slumber, a contented expression wreathing his face.

"Asshat," I muttered.

His lips quirked up in a smile."

CHAPTER SIXTEEN

The sun poured in mercilessly from all sides when I finally stirred, disoriented, only to realize I was still in my chair, the unit cranked all the way back.

"I was wondering if you'd ever awaken," Kreios drawled. He looked freshly showered, his cassock changed to a linen shirt, open at the collar down to his chest, paired with buttery soft khakis. On his feet, he wore sandals, and it took great fortitude for me not to stare. Even the man's feet were beautiful.

"Yes, well," he said, though I hadn't spoken. "I tried to get you to share my cabin or to avail yourself of your own. But you were quite insistent about remaining where you slept. I have spoken to Armaeus," he said, holding up a phone I didn't recognize. "He is awaiting us both at that god-awful fortress of his."

"As opposed to where? I don't suppose you simply take out a suite at the Bellagio when you're in Vegas?"

"Why?" He grinned at me. "Are you considering paying me a visit after all?"

"Yeah. No." His words from earlier haunted me. What truths was he hinting at...and what price? Or was this simply how Kreios worked—getting his marks to believe he could give them something they didn't have, something they eventually believed they needed more than life itself, for a price they would never otherwise consider paying? I didn't know. And right now, I didn't want to know.

But I couldn't deny my curiosity about his home in Sin City. Because, seriously. One of the best charms of the Arcana Council had to be their digs.

The first time I'd seen the spectacle, I'd been caught completely off guard. I'd just rounded the Strip at the turn of the Venetian Hotel, steamed that I'd even agreed to come to Crazytown in the first place. Then I'd looked up and had almost been run over by the horde of chain-smoking senior citizens, raucous college guys, and giggling bachelorette parties the city seemed to aspirate with every rum-soaked breath.

Nothing could have prepared me for the Arcanan shadow realm, though. Hidden beyond the typical tourist's sight line, an entire candy land of enormous gleaming casinos soared above the boulevard, each one larger than the last. A stone fortress crested above Caesar's Palace, bleak and imposing as a mighty medieval castle. A glittering nightclub surmounted the Flamingo, with the word SCANDAL in brilliant neon along its roofline, and a lighting effect that made it seem like fire was crawling up the side of the building.

Then there was the massive castle billowing majestically over and around the Bellagio, a fairy tale palace wrought in pure rose marble and shimmering leaded glass. And above Paris shot a sheer black column in perfect counterpoint to the White Tower that had suddenly erupted beside me, rising above Treasure Island, both of them stark and cold.

Finally, in the far distance, topping Luxor Casino's pyramid and glowering sphinx, was an extraordinary gothic fortress of steel and stone, glass and fire.

Somehow, I'd known that that was where Armaeus

lived. But at first, none of the others made sense.

"Scandal," I said now. "That's your place, isn't it?" I held up a hand to stop his reply. "Because when I saw it last, it was lit up like a fire show and seemed to be doing just fine without you. Who took care of it while you were on your little forced sabbatical?"

Kreios quirked an irritated glance at me, but once more I felt like I'd displayed my ignorance, that this was information I should have known. *Would* have known, if Armaeus didn't constantly play his cards so close to the vest. Fortunately, the sudden *chunk* of the descending wheels of the aircraft cut off our conversation, and the plane touched down a few minutes later, the private airstrip one I'd come to know well enough in the past few months. We emerged from the jet only to be knocked almost level by the oppressive Nevada heat, which had to be pushing ninety-five degrees with the sun high in the sky.

A jet-black town car rested just off the runway, with a familiar figure standing beside it, holding a little white placard. As if there could possibly be anyone else arriving at this location at this time.

I grinned despite myself as Nikki Dawes saluted smartly, stunning in a chauffeur's uniform, complete with a snap cap, tight-fitting black jacket that barely contained her ample breasts, a pencil skirt that made the most of her mile-long legs, and towering, size-thirteen platform pumps. No hosiery touched her well-muscled calves, but the concession was a practical one — this *was* Vegas in May, after all. And besides, she had amazing legs.

Kreios trotted easily down the stairway behind me, admiring the scenery as well. "Armaeus is improving in his taste in drivers."

I smirked. "That's right, you two haven't met, have

you? She came on the scene after your incarceration."

"Your continual reminders do you no favors, Sara Wilde."

"And one day I might possibly care."

I'd gotten Nikki as a driver and general gopher for the Council once she'd hooked me up with the Tyet, since I'd quickly realized I needed all the friends I could get in Oz. At first she hadn't been able to see the more elaborate elements of the Arcanan world, since it didn't technically exist in this plane. But she was an advanced psychic in her own right, and it didn't take her long to catch on.

Now, as we approached her, her eyes widened under her heavy mascara, her face blanking with unfeigned awe. "I really, *really* like the souvenirs you bring home to me, babe," she said in her marginally feminine voice. Then she smiled widely at Kreios as she clasped her hands behind her back, tucking her placard out of sight to give him unrestricted access to the full glorious view of her. "To the Strip, sir? And where have you been all my life?"

For his part, Aleksander Kreios tilted his head, studying Nikki from the tips of her streaked brown wig to the toes of her sharp-pointed shoes, pausing notably to study her impressive — and very expensive — assets. He held up a hand, a card having materialized in it, which he slid into the plunging vee of Nikki's cleavage. "Please stop by my club anytime, Miss Dawes," he drawled as Nikki's eyes dilated despite the brilliant sun beating down on us.

She issued a sound that might have been a whimper, but, ever the professional, she dutifully opened the door for us. We slid into the cool comfort of the limousine, and I found myself relaxing for one precious moment.

Just one—but damned if it wasn't a good one.

"Straight to the man in black?" Nikki asked again once she'd taken her position behind the wheel, her composure firmly back in place as she flicked a glance in the rearview mirror. I hadn't seen if she'd palmed the card out of her bra or not, but knowing Nikki, probably not.

"It's a pity we don't have time to stop at Fremont Street." Kreios sighed. "So much unfinished business there."

"On Fremont?" I met Nikki's eyes, and just like that, my moment had passed. So that was where the girls from Kavala were.

Fremont Street was the home of the Las Vegas of yesteryear, where the city had really gotten its start before the heyday of the Strip had taken over with its ever-growing casinos and entertainment complexes. Though the Arcanans preferred the wide-open Strip for their immense personal dwellings, the older part of the city still drew its share of magic.

But it was the *darker* side of magic. As in pitch-black. Nikki and her fellow carnies who worked the Strip had their hands full keeping the young and the newly arrived in Vegas from straying into that hellhole, but it wasn't an easy battle. And each year, from what little she'd told me so far, it was getting a bit more difficult.

"Yes," Kreios sighed languorously. "The gentleman who gave me such poor information on my contacts in Hungary makes his living in the back of Binion's, as it happens. I shall have to pay him a visit soon."

"Not the nicest casino anymore," Nikki observed, and I turned to see Kreios's smile grow craftier.

"It suits him that way, I suspect," he said. "The fewer respectable people in the front of the house, the easier it is to get his business done in the back."

"The back? You mean Vato's?" Nikki regarded the Devil. "Nothing there but a highly questionable collection of stogies."

I cut short the inevitable conversation on cigars as I saw Kreios's interest being piqued. "And what sort of business would your one-time friend carry on in such an illustrious location?" I knew what Kreios was doing, but I also remembered his promise from the airplane. His penchant for the truth carried an eerie sort of excitement with it. He would speak honestly, I was sure, but that didn't mean he wouldn't be deceiving us.

"His newest venture is the recreation of the Oracle of Delphi, as it happens," Kreios said. "He was very excited about it—so much potential. He spoke of his search to find perfect young women for his masterpiece, lovely, pure psychics who would feast upon the mix of gasses once available only on the mountain of—"

"Cut the crap, Kreios," I snapped, staring at him. "I know what he's using them for. Where specifically is he keeping them?"

Kreios's eyes flared, and he tilted his head, almost as if he was scenting the air for corruption. "They are deep in the center of his holding. To get to them, you must go through a raft of other young women, all psychics, all blindfolded and in most pitiable condition, I'm afraid. One who is missing an ear."

"Hold the phone." Nikki's voice erupted from the front seat, startling me, though Kreios seemed unaffected. With a quick jerk of the wheel, she knifed the limo into a bus stop space, then turned in her seat. "What are you—"

She dropped off sharply. Kreios had vanished.

Her gaze swung to me. "Those girls he

mentioned—not the oracles, but the blindfolded ones. We've lost six girls from Dixie's in the last three months, Sara. *Six.* All of them too damned dumb to live, but Dixie was doing her level best to keep them safe, like she does every pitiful soul that crosses her shadow. One of them"—she punched a long, lacquered nail to where Kreios had been sitting—"had had an ear removed when she was six years old." Nikki's lips curled into a snarl. "Because of the things she *heard.*"

I tightened my own lips. Dixie Quinn was one of Nikki's friends. Given my penchant for leaving the city as soon as I'd arrived, we'd never met, of course. Nikki talked about her like she was some kind of Vegas institution, though—always on the lookout for wayward Connected. "I never did like Binion's," I said. "But given that we've lost our fare…"

"Maybe we should give it another shot," she agreed. "Hang on."

Nikki wheeled the car around into traffic, and we bounced back onto Paradise Road a minute later, weaving our way through the heavy knot of tourists. "Where'd pretty boy go, anyway?" she asked over her shoulder. "The Magician gonna be all hot and bothered you didn't deliver him?"

"I suspect they'll find each other eventually." And Kreios would have some explaining to do when they did. I took out my phone and checked my locator wafer on the reliquary—nada. Had Kreios strapped it into one of the exhaust pipes of Armaeus's private jet, conducting his own personal cremation ceremony? If so, I had a bad feeling that would reflect poorly in my compensation for this little adventure, but given that the thing had been turned into Kreios's prison, I could hardly blame the guy for wanting it destroyed. Now I wondered if he had actually entered the limo with us, or if he'd taken his leave after depositing his card into Nikki's bra. "You have his card, right?"

"Are you kidding? It's been keeping my altogether warm for the past twenty minutes. Which one is he? Not that I'm planning to pay him a visit, but—"

"The Devil."

Nikki's mouth clapped shut. Her fingers stuttered out a rapid rat-a-tat on the steering wheel for another full minute, then she flipped on her blinker and got into the right lane. "I think we're gonna need a detour, doll."

"No detour." I frowned at her. "If those women are really at Binion's, they're not going to be in great shape. The Devil's been out of commission for a long time. I don't know where he got his data, but that could be outdated too. We might already be too late."

"If they're in Binion's, they're not alone. You heard him yourself. Apparently they've also roped in some of the local girls, and the one he was talking about with no ear? She doesn't speak English, and I sure as hell don't speak Romanian. But Dixie does."

I stared at her as she whipped into a turn. We streaked away from the Strip, into a warren of squat houses and scorched plots of land, as most of the Las Vegas residents varied between decorating decisions that involved rocks, cactus, and sand. Another turn and the houses got ever so slightly seedier, and then a final turn and we were back close to the Strip, in the near-but-not-quite-overflow area where the cut-rate casinos, strip clubs, and taquerias flourished.

It was where the carnie-level Connected of the Strip flourished too, I knew. The hole-in-the-wall psychics who weren't quite up to the main stage at Caesar's Palace, the dime-store palm readers and sidewalk channelers who could stare at you for thirty seconds and bring back your Great-Aunt Betty.

But Nikki didn't stop at any of those places. In fact, she didn't stop at all until she cut into a wide parking lot bracketed by a mini strip mall and a free-standing building, a giant white monstrosity fronted by a glittering billboard that proclaimed it as the Chapel of Everlasting Love in the Stars.

I stared. I couldn't help myself. "What the hell *is* this?"

"This," Nikki said triumphantly as she jammed the car into a parking space, "is Dixie Quinn."

CHAPTER SEVENTEEN

Apparently, my expression was enough to convince Nikki to take it down a notch. Or six. She used story time to check her lipstick as she spoke, her mouth going a mile a minute the way it always did when sharing her debriefs.

"Okay, what you need to know about Dixie Quinn isn't that she's an astrologer for a wedding chapel, though she is, and she's not half-bad. More importantly, beyond serving as the city's Welcome Wagon, she's sort of Vegas Homeland Security for the Connected community—she knows everyone and everything, what their skills are and where they live. She goes all out, even keeps records of this stuff, in the quintessential office black book. She's a little too Goody Two-shoes for my taste, just between us girls, but we've come to an understanding because I also like keeping up on who's coming into the city." She winked at me. "Only newcomer she hasn't drawn a bead on was you. But you didn't actually stay long enough to lay down a shadow, let alone a root."

I frowned up at the enormous chapel sign. "And you think she'll have information on these girls?"

"Oh, I know she will. She's the one who introduced them to me. You ready?"

"I want to get back to Binion's."

"Smart trumps fast in this case, dollface. Trust me on this."

She hauled herself out of the limo, and I followed suit, blinking around in the harsh sunlight.

The chapel reared up in front of us, a beacon of eternal love facing a liquor store and a tattoo parlor, its entryway surmounted by a second neon sign announcing "Drive-Thru Weddings." An incongruously dainty traditional church-style front door beckoned the love struck from beneath a bedazzled white stucco star-topped steeple, looking impossibly tacky at noon. I suspected the place got most of its business at two in the morning, though.

The chapel's landscaping consisted of a series of topiaries cut to resemble bow-wielding cherubs nestled in cutoff Roman columns that now doubled as flowerpots. A gaggle of stone geese bedecked in wedding attire waddled up the red-carpeted front walk. Based on the spotlights mounted every three feet or so, at night the entire place would be lit up with the kind of wattage usually reserved for used-car lots and crime scenes.

Both the liquor store and tattoo parlor were open, of course, and I made out the form of a thin ball-cap-wearing man leaning in the doorway of the tattoo shop, the trail of his cigarette smoke floating up to dissipate in the arid heat. He nodded to me as we passed. I glanced up to the battered sign atop the shop: *DarkWorks Ink.* Artwork lined the windows, along with a single flickering neon TATTOOS sign. One of the prints caught my eye: a faded poster of an armored warrior on a white horse, carrying a black flag with a white rose in its center.

I frowned. "Um, Nikki?"

Nikki's sharp curse covered my words as she

squinted ahead toward the chapel. "Son of a biscuit, not Henry again. He will *not* give up."

I swung my gaze forward then jerked to a halt beside Nikki, gaping at a tiny Barbie doll of a woman dressed almost all in white, crouching in the alcove of the chapel. Despite the fact that it was barely noon, she was rocking four-inch platform white leather boots that nudged up against a shimmering white miniskirt, which bared enough skin to show off an impressive swath of white fishnet stockings. And she was trying to rouse an older, pudgy but remarkably well-dressed man curled up at the base of a large cupid-themed topiary vase.

"Henry, honey, don't make me tase you." The woman's voice was soothing as she pulled at the man, revealing a white sequined leotard beneath her equally white leather bolero jacket, and sending a tumble of blonde curls free from beneath her snow-white cowboy hat. Yes. Cowboy hat.

"Please tell me that's not Dixie," I murmured.

"Henry, I'm telling you, you have to quit doing this to yourself," the bombshell cooed. "You have to stick to Libras and Pisces, if you're going to have any shot at all. Why do you do this to me, honey? You tryin' to kill me?"

"Owwuarggummafluevian!" the man on the ground protested, and the woman clucked in gentle rebuke.

"You won't say that to Bobby-Frank when he takes you home, promise? He's got feelings, you know. He's fragile." She poked the poor guy with a rapier-like nail. "Promise me, Henry."

"Iwufffliann."

"That's better. You'll be yourself in no time. I'll have those nice people at the Bellagio arrange a massage for you." She leaned forward and kissed him on the forehead. "And stay away from Scorpios, okay? You know they make you crazier than a bedbug."

The old fellow assented with a long, baritone mumble, and the woman rocked back from him, waving as if to the sky. Within fifteen seconds, a kind-eyed man who had to be Bobby-Frank ambled up, built like a fire hydrant and wearing a rumpled brown suit. He hunkered there with a sigh, eyeing poor Henry as the woman uncoiled herself and stood.

Or sort of stood. She couldn't have been more than five feet high, even in the boots.

"A Scorpio?" Bobby-Frank asked.

"Gets him every time."

Bobby-Frank leaned over and lifted Henry off the ground, settling the man on his feet with barely a twitch of muscle. A cab had magically appeared at the entryway to the chapel's drive, and Bobby-Frank folded Henry inside with a gentleness that belied his bulk. I glanced back at the tattoo parlor, but the thin man was gone and the place looked deserted.

"Well, Nikki, as I live and breathe — what are you doing here?" The bombshell's words, all sweet tea and Southern Comfort, whipped my attention back to her. "And who is this?"

"Sara, allow me to introduce Dixie Quinn. And Dixie, *this*," Nikki said with a flourish, indicating me, "is Sara Wilde, aka how we're going to get back Marta, Mary, and whoever else has gone missing you haven't told me about." Nikki popped a hip and settled her mitts on her sleek chauffeur's uniform. "I know, I'm impressive. It's okay to stare."

"Oh!" Dixie blinked perfectly mascaraed eyes at Nikki, then at me. "Well, gracious, come on in, the both of you. It's hot enough to fry cactus out here."

I didn't argue as Dixie led us inside to a cute little sitting room done up in bubblegum-pink walls, gold-framed wedding photos, and yards of white carpet. Dixie settled us into white overstuffed couches that looked like they'd been sold alongside their matching brass-and-glass side tables at a blowout sale at Big Lots. Several brass keepsake boxes were stacked artfully on the tables, with a small price card tented beside them. "So." Dixie smiled at me with a perfect cupid bow's mouth. "You're new in the city?"

"New enough," Nikki answered for me. "She's been working for the Magician. But we're on the clock here. We need to know about the girls. Languages, skill sets. Last known whereabouts. How many we might run into at Binion's."

"They're at Binion's?" Dixie frowned, then swiveled her gaze to me. "Not a good place. You go there to get your questions answered, for a price, when you don't like the answers you get on the Strip. Nasty place to do business, but the rumors of its accuracy are steady and sure." She nodded. "Come back to the office. I have everything you need there."

The office was little more than a closet, the walls lined by low file cabinets and literally dozens of hand-drawn cartoons of couples in various states of wedded bliss, apparently a "caricature with purchase" promotion the chapel must be running. But it was the file cabinets that intrigued me. I frowned, looking around. "You don't believe in the cloud?"

"I believe too much in the cloud." Dixie's manner was pure Southern charm, but there was no mistaking the steel underneath. "I wouldn't store anything there, not when it's so easy to hack. These cabinets are lined with lead, hematite, and more than a few charms to keep out prying eyes. It's the only way I've kept the information safe." She smiled ruefully. "And we're pulling in more information all the time." Somehow, I didn't think she was talking about wedding RSVPs.

She went to her desk, where a ledger sat, closed. She touched the front, and locks audibly clicked, rendering the notebook a grown-up secret diary. As she paged through its contents, she kept talking. "I'm sure Nikki has already filled you in, but I'm sort of the first stop, you could say, for the city's Connected — astrologers, palm readers, fortune tellers, hypnotists — the works. We make sure everyone is settled in, finds work, learns their way around the city. Ah." She reached an entry, then glanced up at both of us. "And when they go missing, we notice. Because someone needs to."

Her last sentence was loaded with a bitterness that seemed years in the making. "You have people go missing a lot?"

"Even a handful is too many, and it's happening more and more." She refocused on Nikki. "Which girls do you think he has?"

"Marta — that's the one missing her ear, right?" Nikki waved a hand past her own shiny mane. "And the entire group that came with her. No clue what their skills were, but there was a knot of them, remember? Maybe all sisters?"

"Oh, yes. Psychic attunement. They weren't sisters but close friends. *Are* close friends." Dixie pursed her perfect lips, reading in her book. "One moved, they all moved. One had a thought, they all had a thought. You could whisper something in the ear of one of them at the back of the audience, and the friend on stage would speak it purely, plainly, and without prompting. You could touch one of the girls, and the others would know that too. More faintly, an echo, but she'd know it." She looked up, her eyes fierce. "I do not want to imagine what's being done with them at Binion's. The girls arrived in the city two months ago, and they've been gone for three weeks now. Three *weeks*. I thought—I'd assumed they'd been taken out of the city. To think they've been here this whole—"

"Focus, Dix. You said they could speak anything spoken to them. So they know English? They can communicate?"

She shook her head. "They didn't have to know English to perform. They're mimics. Their own language was nothing I could figure out, some sort of pidgin Slavic that didn't match up to anything we understood. But we'd begun teaching them. They'd barely escaped detection getting here, and we lost them in less than two months." She looked at Dixie. "They won't respond to reason, only orders. You bark at them loud enough, they'll move. Their leader is tall, with long hair, so blonde it's almost white. I don't know if they'll have cut her hair, but I doubt it's shaved off. It's too beautiful."

Nikki considered that, nodded. "I can work with that.'

"There are two other girls there too, we think," I said, drawing Dixie's attention back. "Psychics from eastern Europe. Kavala. You have any record of them? When they might have come into the city, how long they've been locked up at the club?"

She frowned, shooting a glance at Nikki, who shrugged. "Her information is solid. I trust her."

Beautiful brown eyes swung back to me. "What's your interest, here?"

"The two girls from Kavala," I said, my nerves ratcheted up. "You got information on them, then give it to me. Otherwise, we're out of here."

Dixie bristled, and even that looked good on her, but she didn't glance down at her book. "Those girls weren't free when they got here. I don't keep such records in the main directory. That doesn't help them."

"Then what do you—"

Dixie cut off my words with a wave of her hand, gesturing to the drawings on the wall. They were carnie-level art—caricature artist renderings almost, but instead of being cartoonish, they looked almost poignant, beautiful young girls and dashing young men in their wedding finery, bridesmaids posing in front of a silhouetted kissing couple, best men mugging for the artist. Then I looked closer. "You've got to be kidding me."

"It's the easiest way to get their pictures around the city. I hear about men, women, kids being taken, I get their descriptions and meditate a bit on them, then provide as complete a picture as I can to the cartoonists. Their rendered images go up on artists' walls and in cafés and coffee shops up and down the Strip. I get a whisper of someone seeing a back-alley act where the players aren't all looking so healthy, same deal. Someone sees a girl who looks like his sister, his daughter... Someone sees a guy who might be the stripper she saw the night before... It all helps." She shrugged daintily. "The cops don't always listen, but when they do—"

I schooled my features to be even, my breathing to stay steady. "Cops?"

"Won't be any cops at Binion's today," Nikki said firmly, more to me than Dixie. She was scanning the pictures as well. "You think you have the girls up here? The ones from Kavala?"

"I'm afraid so." Dixie moved out from around her desk and strode over to the far wall. Her cowgirl getup should have looked ridiculous, but I was already getting used to it. Welcome to Fabulous Las Vegas.

She reached up and pulled one of the crisp drawings down from its clip on the wall, then turned and handed it to me. "These your girls?"

I scowled at the image. It was clearly a reprint, but the likeness of the girls was unmistakable, though I'd only seen one picture of them. Two beautiful young women, their long hair tied in thick, gleaming braids that hung to their waists. They were holding hands and gazing out at the viewer with wide eyes, their perfect Cupid's bow mouths smiling with bridesmaidenly bliss. Only, their bridesmaid's gowns were decidedly unique. "Togas."

"I remember that description when it came in. Someone had seen them at a private party — no connection to Binion's, I can tell you that. But they thought they were on drugs of some sort. They were almost in a trance, lying on each other, stroking each other's hair, murmuring nonsense. 'Beautiful and tragic,' my informant said."

"There's a lot of beautiful and tragic going on in the city," Nikki pointed out, her keen eyes on the drawing as well. "Why'd they stand out?"

Dixie tapped the picture with a long pink fingernail. "Something he saw them do. They were pulled up to meet someone and immediately started crying, pulling at their clothes, their hair. They got hustled right out, but the guy they had done the demonstration for was all outraged. Big spender, apparently, who was looking for some sugar, not some kind of fit."

I handed the drawing back to her. "Let me guess. He's dead."

"Found floating in Lake Mead not twelve hours

later. Spooked my contact good, but that's the first and last I heard of the girls, and that was a month ago and more."

I nodded. I'd seen the date inscribed at the bottom of the drawing. They'd been in Vegas five weeks and were now out of public view. There was very little chance they were still alive.

Nikki placed a large hand on my shoulder. "We'll get them." She glanced at Dixie. "There may be others."

"Well, darlin', I didn't think you came all the way over here for my apple pie." She reached languorously over her desk and scooped up her petal-pink cell phone. "You just run along. We'll be there whenever you need us."

We turned to go, and I stopped, looking back.

"Question for you. That guy by the tattoo parlor. What's he about?"

"Jimmy?" Dixie grinned. "Honey, he's been here longer than I have. Master with a needle and ink, not so much with his love life. Keeps to himself mostly, 'less you're his client. His shop may not look like much, but he draws in some pretty high rollers."

"Right." I frowned, thinking about the image I'd seen in his window. I would have sworn it was... "He's not part of the Council, right?"

"Oh Lord, no." She looked at me, startled. "He's not even a... I mean..." She frowned. "Bless my soul, I've never really spoken with the man. He could be a Connected, but if so, he's got to be a minor one. All his magic's done with his needle, nothing more."

"Thanks." We walked out into the bright sunshine again, and I stared over at the shop. Now the sign read CLOSED, but that wasn't the only thing that had changed.

The large print of the horseman and flag were gone.

Death had left the building.

CHAPTER EIGHTEEN

I mulled over the image the entire way to Binion's. Seeing figures from the cards in places I didn't expect them was kind of a thing for me. An ad for Red Devil pizza, a statue of Justice and her scales in the middle of nowhere. The image of a Hanged Man painted on the wall of an Italian bistro. For Death to show up in a tattoo parlor wasn't completely unusual, but given the givens, I couldn't help thinking there was a hidden message in its appearance.

What could it mean, though? Most of the time, Death meant extraordinary transformation.

Sometimes, however, it just meant a whole lot of Death.

We parked a quarter mile from Binion's. The "Fremont Street experience" included many things, but quick access to your vehicle generally wasn't one of them. Nikki changed out of her chauffeur getup into her usual street wear and lounged in a rare stretch of shade as I pulled a few cards. Seven of Swords, Pope, High Priestess. Since the Seven cautioned of trickery and the High Priestess could reference the girls' oracular powers, those made sense. The Pope, not so much. But I had a bad feeling about it.

"We good?" Nikki asked. Shed of her uniform and cap, her perfect brown mane of hair was pulled into an all-business ponytail, and her statuesque figure made the most of shiny black tights above her black stilettos. Her silky fuchsia halter top had a death grip on her chest, but her tiny bolero jacket was not exactly functional. When I nodded, she looked down at herself in sudden concern. "How in the hell am I going to pack a gun in this?"

"You're not," I said, reaching into my boot and tossing her the switchblade I kept there for special occasions. Because I'm festive like that.

She grimaced as she slid the blade out of sight between her breasts. "I'm better with a gun."

"I'll keep that in mind."

We headed off. Vegas being Vegas, we didn't draw much attention as we strode down Fremont Street. We reached the old casino in a few minutes. The stench of the place—cigarette smoke embedded into the very walls—greeted us almost before we entered the door, but it didn't take long to get used to the gloom inside.

Binion's was an old-style casino, and by old-style, I meant broke down and wheezing, with the barest glimmer of its old glory days shimmering beneath the worn façade. We pushed our way toward the cigar purveyor at the back of the building, and I slid my hand in my jacket, fanning through the cards. I pulled another one from the center of the deck.

"I love it when you do that," Nikki murmured beside me. "What's tricks?"

"Miss Wilde, what is it you think you're doing?"

"Wheel," I said, ignoring Armaeus. Apparently, our detour to Dixie's had given him the time he needed to get his bearings again. He'd figured out that we were no longer on our way to his fortress with the Devil in tow, and I somehow suspected Kreios wasn't breaking any land-speed records to get back to HQ.

Why couldn't Vegas have been built on a lake? "That's not especially helpful, though. It's not like we haven't already passed a half-dozen roulette tables in this place."

"True. Then again, none of those were hanging at eye level, pretty much like a big red X marks the spot." Nikki smirked. The dark, stained-paneled corridor led down toward ominous-looking restrooms at the far end, but what Nikki was eyeing was an old clipping pasted to the paneled wall with a roulette wheel prominently featured. She scanned down the panel for a doorknob, but there wasn't any in evidence. Still, the place had the *feel* of a door. "You think—" Nikki began.

"You ladies lost?" A gruff voice at my side drew me up short, and Nikki stiffened as well.

Her voice, when it sounded next, was a study in tremulous fear.

"We...we have *questions* that no one can answer. Not right, not the way we need them to be," Nikki said, her words barely a mumble, as if she'd mixed the wrong pills and downed the combination with a tumbler of vodka. "We were sent here for help. Please, honey—we have money. Lots of money."

I kept my head down, doing my level best to scuff my boots on the ground. I never could pull off feminine, so I did better with desperate and ragtag.

"*You're* looking for answers?" The man leered, sticking his face into Nikki's chest. "You come back up front when you're done, and I'll give you all the answers you need." He laughed at his own joke, then banged on the wall. The panel behind the roulette wheel image pulled back, clearly a one-way door, and red light poured out of the opening. "That way." The bouncer jerked his thumb toward the ominous hallway.

"No, do not — "

The Magician's warning was cut short as the bouncer shoved us forward, apparently either not expecting us to be armed or not caring. Stupid, but not surprising in the community of dark practitioners. It was as if the weapons of this earth somehow took a backseat to true mystical powers. We walked down the shadowy hallway, peering through the murky red light. The place stank so badly, it was a miracle anyone ever came back here on purpose.

Then we were dumped into a much larger room with pounding music and the acrid smell of burning flesh heavy in the air. When my eyes finally adjusted, I revised my opinion. Based on what I was seeing, it was a miracle anyone made it out alive.

The place was a demon hole.

A favorite construct of the practitioners of the dark arts, demon holes were half club, half rave, all illegal. Bodies were packed into the tight space, writhing and churning, partiers of every shape and size, all of them clearly transported by any of a dozen synthetic cocktails mixing drugs, hallucinogenics, and magical stimulants. Music blasted from every direction, so loud the bass practically jumped the floor. How had we not heard this outside? Then screams of delight went up, and we saw the central attraction as we passed along its outskirts.

Six young women, undoubtedly the young women who'd gone missing from Dixie's care, were tied together on a long rope, blindfolded and standing in the middle of the room. The first in their line was a tall, willowy girl with white hair that might once have been long, but was now blunt cut and spiked, serving as a goth-like crown atop her head.

Snaking around the women was a sort of small labyrinth of flame made by ropes soaked in something toxic, sending up short, flickering curtains of blue-white fire. The game was immediately obvious and chilling in its cruelty: the girls were expected to work their way out of the maze without getting scorched, calling upon their apparent "psychic abilities" and intense intuition about the movements, thoughts, and experiences of each other to get the job done. From the looks of their worn, emaciated forms crisscrossed with burns, however, their Sight was weakening along with their bodies.

"Sweet mother of Jesus," Nikki hissed beside me.

"We'll get them," I promised her. "There are only six?"

"Six is enough." Nikki peered around the dark room. "And I wasn't lying to Dix back there. If Binion's has these girls out on display, who the hell else do they have? This place is a shithole, but it's got a reputation for high-grade black magic."

"Then keep a lookout. But we have to keep moving." Because Dixie's girls weren't the only lost souls in this den, and perhaps more importantly, they weren't the ones who would give us the answers we were supposedly seeking. The guy at our back pushed us toward another door, this one flanked by two enormous bodyguards, their muscled bodies like something out of a comic book. Thick plugs stretched the guards' earlobes and heavy metal horseshoes hung from their wide noses, and their soulless eyes watched us levelly as we approached.

Their heavily pierced and modded bodies were also completely naked, a fact that was not lost on Nikki. "I do admire their personnel standards here, I'll give you that," she said. The men didn't respond, but I could feel their gazes focus on her. Scowling in stereo, they stood aside at the sharp command of the man behind us.

The door swung wide.

The thick stump of a man at the center of the room was not the most interesting thing in the place, but he was the most important. Even better, I knew him. Sort of.

Son of a bitch.

Jerry Fitz had been one of the few buyers of magical artifacts I'd been told to avoid by many of my earliest mentors in this business. I hadn't realized he'd set up shop in Vegas. I wouldn't have pictured him at Binion's either. The guy had money, and a whole lot of it. What was he doing in the back room of a two-bit demon hole on Fremont Street?

I struggled to remember what I knew of Jerry Fitz. He'd started out life as an oracle of sorts, then had quickly figured out that the big money was in pimping the talent, not putting himself out there on the line day after day, particularly as the Connected community got darker and more dangerous. He picked up a mini harem of psychics drawn to his charisma and money, and when the first one had tried to leave, he'd made such a vivid example of her that no one else had attempted it. After that, it was merely a matter of luring in new talent with money and drugs and protection, keeping them locked down and performing at the rate he needed them to perform, and then going where the money was.

And the money had apparently led him here.

Once again, this was quite a few rungs down on the evolution scale. What was I missing? It was dark, it stank, and the crowd outside had seemed decidedly low-rent. True, he clearly had total dominion here, but

I hadn't heard a word breathed about Fitz in the past few years. For a megalomaniac like him, that was tantamount to forever.

More intriguing, it looked like he was going to be our personal moderator on today's Q&A session. For someone who had a rep for turning over the dirty work to his minions, that was unusual. Was he seeking a particular question to test his process or tip him off to danger? Had he become more OCD over the years? Was he trying to branch out, learn new skills?

I took in his stumpy form. The picture I'd been given of him five years ago when I'd gone after my first artifact had clearly been pre-body mods. Now Fitz had more metal and plastic implanted under his skin than the Terminator, with not terribly attractive results. But he did look scary enough, I supposed. And those mods... Something about those mods made me nervous. The tech on this job was becoming a little intense, like the bright shiny map of the planet in the Magician's French stronghold, and the electronic death helmet that had encased Kreios beneath the abbey.

Magic had always been about low-tech mastery, you and the force of nature, the ephemeral connection between and around all living things. Magic and psychic skills combined with electronics was...an unknown quantity. It went beyond modern technoceuticals and into places like the Stargate experiment of the 1970s by the US Department of Defense during Russia's Cold War push for dominance. Back then, those experiments had failed.

I got the feeling they wouldn't be failing now.

Fitz finally seemed ready to give us his full attention. "Welcome, welcome," he oozed, turning from his high-tech command center, with its knobs and screens and levers. "What is your question? How can I help you achieve the peace you so deserve?" He glanced at Nikki, smiling indulgently at her garish outfit, then switched his gaze to me.

And froze.

Freezing is never good.

"You..." he said wonderingly. In that moment, I made a half-dozen quick realizations. First, Fitz was either batshit crazy or high. His eyes had that glittering frenzy of someone stretched to the breaking point, and everything on him twitched. Second, he didn't look nearly as bad as he should have for someone hopped up on drugs. He was positively spoiled with health, in fact—skin tone rich and flush with blood, hair still on his head, teeth intact. Third, his breath smelled of burnt acid, which might or might not mean anything more than a really bad burrito for lunch.

But it was a final set of insights that were the most troubling. One, he wasn't wearing a weapon. That meant he didn't need one, which didn't make me feel all warm and fuzzy. Two, he was solidly built beneath all the body mods, so he wasn't going to go down easy.

Third, he clearly recognized me. Or thought he did.

I took a step back as Fitz barked out a command in some language that—once again—I couldn't recognize. Clearly, I needed to brush up on my ancient tongues.

But it was too late to consult the Rosetta Stone now. In the space of a breath, two guards were at either side of me, bracing my arms so hard they lifted me off my feet. Another two guards held Nikki—the bouncers from the front door, as it happened, which I didn't know was a good thing or a bad thing. Without being told to do so, they pulled her from the room and back into the chaos of the club, so I decided: good thing.

Meanwhile, my personal set of guards had liberated the gun from my holster as well as my deck of cards, dumping both on the table in front of me, along with my box of Tic Tacs, cell phone, some stray euros, my tourist map of Rome...and a key-fob-sized Magic 8 Ball. I frowned at the last item. Granted, it was a really cute tchotchke to have on hand as a backup to my cards, but it wasn't mine. In fact, I'd never seen the thing before. Where the hell had it come from?

That thought, of course, led me straight to Kreios. Had the Devil planted the toy on me when I wasn't looking? And if so, *why*?

Ignoring both me and my perplexing pocket toy for another moment, Jerry Fitz leaned over the console in front of him. Suddenly, the panels lining the wall slid apart, revealing two stunning young women collapsed on the floor behind a sheet of glass. I surged forward, but the guards held me tight. The two sprawled girls were nearly naked, their hair fanning out around them, but there was no question that they were the twins from Father Jerome's list—and from Dixie's wall of wonders. Both of them sported matching black hair, pale skin, delicate features, long limbs. Both of them appeared dead to the world. Both of them were Greek goddesses in the flesh who moved only when a gong-like chime sounded at a flip of Fitz's fingers.

With an almost ghostly languor, the girls stretched upright, stirring toward wakefulness. Eventually, they pulled themselves to their knees, then their vacant gazes swung toward the glass. Resolve knifed through me. These faces would *not* haunt me, dammit—they would not join the ranks of the missing whose lives I could not save.

"Lost." The whisper slowly built. "All is lost."

The Oracle of Delphi was ready for her close-up.

CHAPTER NINETEEN

Beside me, staring at the plate glass, Fitz fairly bounced with excitement.

"Do you have any idea how long it is between visits from a truly gifted Connected?" he asked, though who he was asking, I wasn't really sure. The two creatures holding me in place weren't talking, and I wasn't much in the mood for twenty questions. "I seek so little in this world. The chance to explore. To learn. To put my creations to the test, refining and improving them until they could take their place among the angels. But I must always wait. Be patient. It is…tedious."

"What are you doing here, Fitz?" Did he truly know who I was, specifically? Somehow, I didn't think so. I didn't think he'd truly looked at my face. He'd just sensed something about me at twenty paces, the same way I could sense the level of magical ability in a person by touch. Either way, whatever he sensed in me now had him chortling to himself.

I wasn't a fan of Fitz chortling.

"It has taken many years to perfect the formula." He fiddled with more controls as I assessed my situation. I couldn't overpower the guards without my gun, and the room wasn't offering much in the way of other great ideas. Fitz had decorated the place in vintage Hugh Hefner, all silk pillows and shag rugs, rosy light and artful porn. Whoever he entertained here on a regular basis was either male or extremely open-minded. Shelves filled with artifacts lined the walls, some of the pieces worth quite a bit to my trained eye, but none of them close enough to matter.

An unearthly moan sounded over the speakers, and my gaze snapped back to the glass wall. The young women in the chamber were now swaying, colorful gas filling the room around them. Fitz turned another dial, smiling as their faces creased in pain. "I call it *Pythene*: methane, ethylene, benzene, and a few other nice additions to make the oracles more animated," he said, watching the girls as if they were his prized pets. "Admittedly, the combination is quite lethal after prolonged exposure. But my newest subjects have proven to be delightfully durable. And, in the end, there are always more voices to add to the song."

His oily glance slid over to me. "Like yours, my dear. I have a knack for sensing talent, I should tell you. Yours is exquisite." His hand shook with his own pleasure, and I squinted at his wrist. A large black metal cuff adorned it, etched with a glyph that looked almost like —

"Speak!" Fitz commanded, watching me, and I jerked my gaze back toward the girls. They now stood pressed up against the glass. Despite myself, I shrank back. Their eyes were dead, their mouths agape. And they were staring at me.

"Chosen," they intoned, and Fitz leered.

"You see? I am never wrong. You've been sent to me like a gift, to further my exploration. To take me closer to the ultimate truth." He turned back to the women. "Why is she here?"

"Finder!" the woman on the right cried out, her hands lifting to her ears.

"Chosen!" the other moaned before lapsing into unintelligible babble.

They both rocked on unsteady feet, their loose shifts slipping off their shoulders, revealing the bodies of girls who were barely teenagers. They pressed their hands against the glass as if straining to get out, their faces tight with pain. "Darkness," they all but sobbed in near tandem, one echoing the other in some sort of twisted overdub. "Death and war and darkness." Revulsion coiled in my stomach at their words, their panicked faces. What must these women be seeing?

Fitz almost giggled. "And so you have come into my place of darkness, on the brink of death and war, to achieve your potential." With another sharp crack of his command, the guards shoved me down to my knees. I was now eye level with my scattered cards.

"Sorry, guys," I muttered, knowing that no matter what happened in this room, I probably wouldn't be keeping hold of them. Half the cards were on the floor, but the one topmost on the tabletop pile was faceup. And I really wasn't happy to see it again.

The Tower.

In a Tarot reading, being dealt the image of an exploding building was very rarely a good thing. Especially when you were currently trapped *inside* a building, with no discernible way out.

"Speak to me." Fitz stood right in front of me now, his bug eyes bulging as he held up something that looked distressingly like a hookah. He pushed the nozzle of the contraption into my mouth as one of the thugs clamped down on my jaw and pinched my nose shut.

Then—with a sharp brutality I wouldn't have

thought he had in him—Fitz shoved his fist into my stomach.

Startled, I blew out a sharp gust of breath, then inhaled before I could resist the primal urge. Only, the gas from the hookah hose now stuck in my mouth was nothing like actual air. I instantly convulsed, going rigid in the guards' grip as Fitz did something with the device that shot more gas into my lungs. My head filled with images and noise, my stomach roiled, and when he finally yanked the hose out of my mouth, I lurched forward, ready to throw up everything I'd eaten for the last six weeks.

Instead, only words spewed out of my mouth, thick and hot.

"Death comes for you," I wheezed and took some satisfaction from how Fitz's face suddenly went from cackling enjoyment to confusion. "Destruction. Loss. Your kingdom— vanquished." I said this last on a gasp, and the effort it took to push the word out grated along my windpipe, as if the word itself had claws.

I swung my gaze to the women behind the glass. Was this what they felt every time they were compelled to speak their prophecy? The pain was raw and fiery, and it didn't dim with the passage of words. Not when more of them kept bubbling up insistently. "Lost. Failed," I wheezed. "Destroyed. Forgotten."

"You haven't been properly prepared," Fitz growled, thrusting the tube at my mouth again despite my efforts to squirm away.

The gas poured into me once more, and my eyes practically rolled back in my head, the images shattering through me those of destruction and pain, fire and noise. Once again, with startling clarity, the black papal seal seared across my memory. I flailed forward, grasping Fitz's wrist to where an identical seal was etched into his cuff. "You are betrayed!" I gasped.

"Get off me!" Fitz threw up his arm, and clearly his mods included some sort of steroidal component, because for a small man he really could pack a punch. I staggered back against the guards, barely coherent as they hauled my body up once more, Fitz beside me the whole time, blasting my face, my eyes with the gas. As I mumbled words that made no sense, I was dragged across the carpet, deadweight in the arms of the two guards. A door opened, and they tossed me to the floor. "Full dose," I heard Fitz call out as the door slammed behind me, and I blearily turned to peer through the glass.

What I saw was a nightmare.

There was no longer just the sleazily posh room of Jerry Fitz and his thugs on the other side of the smeared glass, but the throng of dancing humanity *beyond* it as well, then the worn-down Binion's casino beyond that, people hunched over faded baize-topped tables, acrid smoke heavy in the air.

And I could see farther, to where the Devil reclined in some glassed-in penthouse, sipping from a golden chalice—then off again through streets and deserts and cities and oceans, until I soared far into the East, to the seat of Fitz's master, amid a glorious palace.

Beyond that, as if lying in wait, something alien stirred in the darkness—a blue figure trapped on a field of red. And in the midst of all this, in the center of a great, arched room hung with gilded paintings and glittering treasure, I could see soldiers standing at attention around a black-robed man whose slight stature belied his strength. They all bent over a gleaming black console—as sleek and dark as Fitz's wrist cuff, emblazoned with the same grim seal, minus the dagger that also adorned Fitz's. While gas filled the small chamber and the young women beside me sent up a keening wail, I lurched toward the glass. *They're coming!*

"Speak!" The voice crackled over me, so loud it could be God himself demanding me to share my desperate vision.

"SANCTUS!" I cried, and I could sense Fitz stiffen, though his guards didn't flinch, apparently unaware of the meaning of the name, unaware of anything except the commands of their leader. I pounded against the glass, my words frantic now, panicked. "Death! Destruction! Your kingdom turned to fire!" I shook my head, frustrated at my own confusion. *I need to be more clear!*

"You lie!" Fitz roared back at me, and I felt the tears pool in my eyes, the warm rush of them falling down my cheeks as another burst of gas streamed from the vents. "I have delivered them their Devil and they have paid me for my work. I am one of *them*. I have done all that they asked, an initiate to their cause. I am ready to serve!"

"They *despise* you," I cried, gagging on the gas that filled the space. "You are the filth they must get rid of before what is to come. You will die — you must."

"I have met my obligations!" Fitz strode toward the glass, shoving his finger at me. "No! You are not ready. I sensed the Sight in you, but it's too wild, too broken. You're a shattered toy that no longer serves its master, and I have not put you back together yet. I will, though." His face swelled up with meanness, and he leaned toward the glass, bug-eyed and cruel. "You cannot partake of the Pythene mists if you're not pure of heart, *and you are not prepared!*"

The laughter welled up inside me as I reached

some new level of hysteria, something snapping within me like a too-frayed string. "And you have been *betrayed*," I hissed, my words silken with threat. I crawled along the glass wall, my fingers grasping at its smooth surface. "You have been betrayed, and you will *suffer*, Gerard Fitz, undone by fear and treachery."

"Shut up!" Fitz snapped, but he stumbled back from the glass at whatever he saw in my eyes, grabbing for his console.

"Did you think you could deceive the prince of lies?" I continued, slithering against the glass, tracking his path. "That there would be no price to pay? That pain would not rain down upon you in a storm of fire, engulfing your very soul?"

Fitz's fingers twisted knobs on his console, and a new mixture flooded into the room. Even in my hallucinating state, I recognized a change in the gasses, my body sagging forward as Fitz grinned in unholy triumph. Foggily, blearily, I realized his leering mug would be the last thing I would ever see on this earth.

That was a little depressing.

Right up until the moment his head blew apart.

The glass shattered with the force of the blast, and oxygen rushed into the space as the noxious fumes spilled out, creating a deadly cocktail of gas and fire. The guards, realizing too late the carnage that was about to ensue, still managed to almost reach the door before being blasted through it, and I could hear the screams of the dancing throng in the world beyond.

And then, for a long and horrifying breath…there was nothing but smoke and darkness, and a distant, shimmering blue figure, trapped on a field of red.

Watching me.

"Sara!"

Nikki was at my side, hauling me up as my eyes

blinked open again, one of the body-modded guards at her side. Somewhere, he'd found trousers, I noted through my delirium, and he gathered up the two girls on the floor, one under each arm, then pounded for the door.

I tried to make my feet move, but my legs wouldn't cooperate, slipping and sliding on the scorched carpet. Nikki used her not inconsiderable strength to throw me over her shoulder in an impressive fireman carry, giving me a unique upside-down view of the room. I blinked and stared, trying to make sense of everything, while trying equally hard not to vomit. Girl had paid way too much for those stilettos.

Fitz's chamber wasn't burning nearly as much as it should have been, given the destruction that immediately surrounded the bomb. Unfortunately, the only thing left of Fitz was a few of his hardier modifications—and the smoking wreckage of his exploded wrist cuff. Lying next to it was an equally pulverized…Magic 8 Ball.

I grinned, drunk on vertigo. Let the police figure out what to do with *that*.

The outer room of the demon hole was impressively empty by the time Nikki dragged me through it, her mouth going a mile a minute. "Hans and Franz—whoever they are, I appreciate muscle like that, you know? And no inhibitions about putting it on display? I mean did you see those guys' asses, I'm telling you," she began, stilettos clumping over the now-doused labyrinth of fire, smoke heavy in the air. It seemed like we were going in the wrong direction, and I suddenly felt…not so good. Not so good at all.

"Fortunately, they agreed Dixie's psychics weren't going to be good to *anyone* dead, after I practically promised I'd have their babies. They're going to be so disappointed when they figure out the plumbing doesn't quite connect that way. Such nice shoulders." She sighed. "By the time I got back to you, all hell had literally blown up, and half the planet had fled like rats on fire."

A door opened and closed, and we were in some sort of hallway, lit by dim blue light. Nikki picked up speed as we moved, and I focused on keeping all my insides from becoming my outsides. "But kudos to Fitz's interior decorator, right? The back of Binion's opens up into a maze of underground tunnels that extend out into points all over old Vegas. You can get *anywhere* from *anywhere* down here, I'm thinking. And most importantly, *we* can get out."

"Mmph," I muttered as Nikki finally clattered to a stop. She slipped me off her shoulder, steadying me as I swayed.

"You look like shit, sweet cakes, but the moment we step outside these walls, the Council is gonna be on you like rubber on a duck." She snapped her fingers in front of my eyes until I pushed her hand away.

"Why?" I managed, then squinted as she waved at the high-tech fixtures blinking down at us over the large door.

"Fitz may have been a bastard, but he wasn't cheap. That unit's from Techzilla." She grinned. "Psychic jamming device, top of the line. I suspect the Council will want to get their hands on it, since it clearly blocks their asses too." She waggled her brows at me. "Unless Hans and Franz strip it out of here first, which I sincerely hope they do. You ready for prime time?"

I nodded, and she opened the door. We were in an alley that ran behind the Binion's building, crowded with delivery trucks and a dozen or so half-clad clubbers. Smoke puffed out of some of the doors as they banged open, smelling of sulfur and too-sweet gas. There'd been so much *gas* —

"Up you go, babe." Nikki had a strong arm around me, keeping me steady when I would have slumped to the ground. "I got a feeling we're not out of this yet."

She was right. We hadn't moved ten feet when my vision was obscured by two perfect feet shod in luxury leather sandals. Laughter floated down around my head.

"I have *so* missed this city." I squinted up into sunlight as the Devil stared down, his gaze full of warm admiration. "And all its many charms."

CHAPTER TWENTY

Nikki let me drop to the ground with admirable speed as she stood up, balancing on her high heels. My head swam, and my lungs felt...fouled. Each new breath didn't improve the situation either. It was like I was adding to the contamination by inhaling the hot, dusty air. I shook my head, trying to clear it. No dice.

Kreios offered Nikki a handkerchief to wipe the grit from her face. "You'd better not have been kidding about that invite to your club," she said as she took it. "I've earned a serious VIP suite."

"I will personally see to all your needs." He considered me again as Nikki's gasp devolved into a stuttering cough. "You were hurt worse than I expected," he said, sounding surprised. "But you killed him, I assume?"

"Fitz? He is definitely dead." Nikki wasn't quite willing to give up the floor, and I was more than happy to let her carry on. "Unless he got modded to regenerate himself from bite-size pieces, anyway."

"*We* didn't kill anyone," I rasped. "You're the one who planted that bomb."

He frowned at me, appearing genuinely confused. "Me?" he asked. "the Council doesn't kill mortals. Mortals kill mortals." He looked down at his perfectly manicured fingers, apparently admiring the job of his nail tech. "The fire that was set outside the necropolis exit was not deadly. Painful, perhaps. Not deadly. The men in the abbey — at no time did I lift a hand against any of them. I had you and your associate to thank for that. And here…" He waved at the bombed-out building. "This is an unfortunate accident emanating from the lair of an avowed meth cooker. We are merely lucky that the police and all their earnest young detectives are on their way. Thank heavens more innocent bystanders were not harmed."

"Right." I had no patience for the Council's loopholes right now, or its effed-up code of honor. And, truth to tell, SANCTUS could have been behind that bomb instead of the Devil. Fitz's wrist cuff had been as destroyed as my Magic 8 Ball. Had Kreios planted a bomb or a harmless toy? And did it matter in the end? I was out. The kidnapped psychics were out.

Either way, there was something in Kreios's words that nagged me, something whispering of warning. What was it he'd said? How had he said it, exactly? My vision blurred again as I bent forward, my hands on my knees, overcome with a sudden hacking fit that teetered on the edge of something far worse.

"How much did she ingest?" Kreios asked over my wheezing. I missed Nikki's answer as I spit into the street, pretty sure I should be concerned at the vivid green hue of my bile.

"What *was* that shit?" I muttered. Kreios stepped closer, apparently unmoved by the Technicolor display.

"In addition to the gasses Mr. Fitz no doubt mentioned to you, as he was ever a fan of explaining his experiments in vivid detail, the mixture contains a cocktail of high-end designer hallucinogenics with electromagnetic properties," he supplied.

"Technoceuticals, I believe is the street term. The very latest coming out of southern Asia, where they've somewhat cornered the market on the trade. According to our resources, your host was engaged in some highly lucrative test applications intended to enhance the ability of known high-functioning Connecteds. With the proper combination, and once he managed to hurdle the unfortunately terminal side effects which seemed to accompany all such combinations to date, he could easily go out and turn midrange Connecteds into high-functioning ones, and high-functioning ones into demigods. Or that was the theory."

"Psychopath." Nikki sniffed. But there was a note in her voice that I didn't miss, and I thought of Dixie back at her chapel. She and Dixie were two midrange Connecteds fighting on the side of good. If anyone would benefit from a technoceutical charge-up, why not them?

"Quite," Kreios said, scattering my thoughts again. "Now that the wards are down on his lair, we will send in our analysts, at least once the police have — "

"Police!" I jerked my head up, panic finally cutting through my nausea. That couldn't happen. His words from before suddenly trickled into my mind. *The police and all their earnest young detectives...* No. No, and no, and no.

"Okay, I'm out. Give Armaeus my love." I straightened up painfully, willing my head to stop spinning. "He knows where to reach me."

"So it is the *police* that centers your fear, Sara Wilde," Kreios mused, eyeing me with renewed interest. "Except your fear is far greater than I find useful, as it shrouds your mind from me."

"Hang on a tick," Nikki interrupted the Devil's complaint, peering down the alley. "That's the ride for my girls. I *also* have no interest in dealing with the boys in blue, scrumptious though they may be. So let me get them out of here. We picked up a few stragglers along the way, and I need Dixie to triage." She strode off to where the narrow alley intersected with a main street. A bright pink bus emblazoned with "Chapel of Everlasting Love in the Stars" now idled there. Next to it, two highly pierced guards stood watch over a clutch of young women, along with some adult males and a white-haired couple huddled together on the pavement, and the still-unconscious twins as well. I should go to the girls, I knew, make sure they were all right. I should report in to Father Jerome. I should close the loop and finish the job.

But the sound of sirens pounded through me, igniting me with a wholly unreasonable fear. *Right now, I have to get out of here.* The rest I'd figure out later.

I turned back to Kreios, but he'd already slipped away—no doubt to explore the building for himself before the police poured through it. The alley was finally clearing of smoke, and dizzying heat beat down on me.

I *hated* this city, I decided. Hated everything to do with it. And everything it held. I wanted nothing more than to leave it behind for good.

But as nausea crashed over me again, pinning me in place for another moment, I also couldn't deny what I'd seen while under the influence of Fitz's Pythene gas.

SANCTUS was coming.

Whether they had killed Fitz or the Devil had, I was no longer sure, but their darkness was stretching toward Vegas—was already *in* Vegas, I suspected. No way was Fitz the only dark practitioner on their payroll. I thought of Barnabus back in Italy. Were the

Knights Templar aligning themselves against the Council as well?

And if so, it all came back to why. Clearing out the Connected communities made sense if you were an ultraconservative religious group. But the Knights Templar were as underground as the Connecteds, and their relationship with the Church had been anything but open. The mere fact they still existed, if they truly still existed, opened up an entirely new level of crazy.

Someone needed to bring the Council up to speed, assuming that Kreios hadn't already. Beyond that, Nikki's and Dixie's people needed to be warned. Prepared. How long had Fitz been operating at Binion's, financed by SANCTUS or at least in their good graces? How much had SANCTUS already penetrated the city? If they were about to wage war in Las Vegas, the off-Strip carnies would be the first to fall.

And then there were the girls from Kavala. They were in no shape to be moved out of the city. It wasn't reasonable to ask Father Jerome to come here to oversee their recovery. He had children of his own to find, in addition to his work in the cathedral. He'd want me to stay, get them on their feet, protect them for as long as it took to arrange for their safe transport back to their home village, assuming that was even a viable option anymore. *How long had they been in Fitz's lair? And what had they endured before they'd gotten here?*

I sighed, the familiar urge to run gnawing at me, matched by the equally oppressive obligation to stay. Those were my options: I could leave, disappear. Hole up somewhere until I could inhale without hearing green slime rattle around in my lungs.

Or I could call Armaeus right now.

The first decision at least made some level of sense.

The second involved actually facing the nightmares that had pierced the mists of Fitz's Oracle room. The soldiers of SANCTUS preparing their plans, and then that—that creature behind them, hovering in the darkness. Lying in wait. In my mind's eye, I felt its gaze flicker over me again—and suddenly I knew.

I couldn't leave. Not yet. I had to warn Armaeus that SANCTUS was coming.

I reached into my jacket for my cell phone, the movement feeling more momentous than it should, as if a ripple was shooting out across the universe, ringing some far-off bell.

Then I remembered my phone was back in Fitz's demon hole, blown to bits.

Oh well. Leaving was probably the smarter idea anyway.

I wiped my hand over my face and, limping, headed in the opposite direction of Nikki and her gaggle of exhausted, half-broken psychics. I'd find some place to hide for a few days, catch some sleep, and heal. Then I'd figure out how to meet my obligations without—

I fell back from the curb as a car shot by me too quickly. Vertigo clouded my vision, and I staggered a little to the side, smoke and gorge rising up once more in my throat. The car braked and backed up, and panic shattered through me. With the visionary clarity of the Oracle, I saw myself stumbling to the pavement as the door opened, sickness overtaking me, never even feeling the hands beneath my shoulders, around my waist, barely able to discern the words sliding through my head.

"A decision, once made, cannot be unmade, Miss Wilde."

"No!" I shook my head hard as the limo stopped

beside me. The door didn't open, though, and I didn't fall down.

Forget that. If Armaeus swept me away now, I'd be just as trapped as those girls behind glass. I knew the Magician, and I knew how he worked. If I didn't go to him on my own terms, or at least healthy, I'd be overwhelmed. It'd happened before.

"Miss?"

I turned and squinted into the sunlight. A man was walking up the street to me, his gait so familiar, so self-assured, that for a moment I simply stood there, unsure of where—or who—I even was. I took a step back, more out of self-preservation than anything else, and something changed in the man's body as well. Recognition swept through me in a visceral wave, so electric that the air seemed to explode, circuits popping in my brain, my heart, my joints, my bloodstream.

The detective—and it was a detective; it had to be, from the cheap brown suit to the badge on his belt to the worn, tanned face, messy hair and squinting eyes— froze another moment as well. I felt rather than heard his next question, the word so quiet I could almost believe I'd imagined it. "*Sariah?*"

Oh. Hell. No.

I reached out for the door to the limo and wrenched it open, piling myself inside. "Go, go!" I gasped as the door slammed shut behind me, the pounding steps of a man fading into the background. The driver complied, bending forward to jump out into traffic, revving the engine hard to leave the detective in the dust.

Holy shit. Brody Rooks. Had he truly seen me? His voice had been uncertain, his eyes disbelieving whatever his brain was trying to convince him had just happened. He had to have known it was really me, though, right? *Right?*

No sirens erupted behind us as we zipped along the boulevard, however. And the driver — Armaeus, of course — didn't ask for my destination. Instead, he studied me in the rearview mirror. "You want to tell me what that was all about?"

"Can't you figure it out yourself?"

"No, Miss Wilde, I can't. Which, please let me assure you, I find more tedious than you can possibly imagine."

His unexpected candor threw me for a second, and I hunkered down in the backseat, alternating between attempting to breathe without pain and trying to unscramble my brains. Neither was working out too well.

"Where are we going?" I asked instead, sounding like a thousand-year-old smoker.

"To Prime Luxe."

I frowned at him. "You live in a steakhouse?"

Armaeus didn't dignify that with a response, which was fine by me. I was hunched so low in the limo seat that I felt like I was five years old, seeing Vegas for the first time. Only I wasn't seeing the Vegas that everyone else saw, I knew. We approached the Strip from the north end, and as we passed the Stratosphere, I squinted hard, seeing the barest shimmer of another shadow casino. "Who lives here?"

"No one," Armaeus said curtly. "You should rest. There will be plenty of time for you to explore your new home once you have recovered."

"I'm not staying here." Every time I spoke, I expected the words to come out of my mouth on a puff of smoke, like a cartoon dragon. "There's too many people in this city."

The silence from the front of the car was

noncommittal, but I knew Armaeus was anything but. Which irritated me as well. He didn't know me, not really. He'd used me for a half-dozen jobs, and I was a reliable finder to him, nothing more. He had no right to ask me to stay anywhere I didn't want to stay, and if he threw the whole SANCTUS war at me, I'd call bullshit.

Oh God. SANCTUS.

I struggled upright, the movement hurting more than it had any right to. "You need to know this."

"If it isn't about the man who was following you, it can wait."

"It can't wait." I clenched my hands into fists and pressed them against my belly. Why wasn't I feeling any better? "Jerry Fitz was working with SANCTUS. He had a cuff on his wrist that was imprinted with the same glyph that I saw tatted on that Swiss Guard lookalike. Pope hat and tails, the whole bit. His also had a dagger at the bottom, for what that's worth. He was transmitting to them the whole time I was there. I have no idea what, but when I was…in that room…"

"Rest is the best way you could serve right now, Miss Wilde. Do not make me force you to do so. As you requested, I am asking you nicely first." Armaeus's haughty golden glare raked over me. "But I'm only going to *ask* you once."

CHAPTER TWENTY-ONE

"Fine." I flopped back in my seat, my bones jarring with pain. "I shouldn't hurt this much, by the way. Just sayin'."

"Do you know why you do?"

"Because Jerry Fitz is — was — an asshole? That about covers it, I think."

"There is more to it than that, I suspect." Armaeus cruised past the Wynn Casino. I blinked down the Strip and saw the negative reflections of the half-hidden homes of the Council. The white tower soaring above Treasure Island, the stone fortress that dominated Caesar's Palace. Scandal, the only arcane casino that chose to advertise, flickered above the Flamingo. An elegant castle of fairyland proportions glittered in the harsh sunlight above Bellagio, and a black tower surmounted Paris.

Farther down was the ancient yet somehow techno-modern steel-and-glass monstrosity of what was apparently called Prime Luxe, the Magician's home. It didn't have its name flickering in neon along its towering spires, but with a name like Prime Luxe, I couldn't blame it.

Still, the palace towered over the Luxor Hotel with its gleaming pyramid and golden sphinxes, and I had to smile at the nod to a lifetime that could never be restored. Armaeus had been Egyptian before he had become Arcanan. Some memories were worth keeping alive, apparently.

Up in the front seat, Armaeus was waiting for me to continue. Loudly.

I sighed. "Yeah, well, forgive me for stripping it down for you. Fitz stuffed his Pythene gas tube into my mouth and turned the jets on full. That much hot air did a number on my lungs, not to mention my nervous system."

"Certainly, but that's not the only reason."

"Enlighten me."

"We're here." I looked up and, as always, Armaeus was a master of the understatement. He cut the wheel and sped into the drive of the Luxor like he owned the place. Which he did, after a fashion. The valet-service boys jogged up to us, their Luxor uniforms flickering between the garish gold of the beloved casino and the deep navy of Luxe. Armaeus stopped and glanced back at me. "Can you walk? I can assist —"

"I can walk." The door swung open, and a masculine hand reached out, which I grabbed with perhaps a bit more force than expected. Still, I was half lifted out of the vehicle with admirable grace, and I didn't have the mental strength to figure out how Armaeus had managed to move from the front seat to my car door in a split second, replacing the valet boy. He folded my hand over his arm, snugging me to his body. The contact with him short-circuited my system from the tip of my head to my toes, and, too late, I realized I no longer wore the Tyet around my neck.

Armaeus's chuckle was soft. "I'm not going to accost you when you can barely stand, Miss Wilde."

"Mmph." If anything, my vertigo grew worse, not better, here in the Magician's lair. I squinted and shook my head, trying to reconcile the tone-on-tone overlay between the very real Luxor and the not-quite-as-real Prime Luxe. I hung on to Armaeus shamelessly, and he provided a solidity I hadn't experienced in far too long.

Don't get used to this, I warned myself, but any attempt at intelligence was not really tops on my list right now. Not after what I'd been through over the last few days. Not after what I'd been through over the last ten years. Not after what had happened to me a decade ago, on a sun-blasted day in Memphis, when everything I'd thought I was and everything I thought I'd be had blown up in my face.

Bake my biscuits. Brody Rooks. Of course he'd be called in to investigate the one place in Vegas I most needed him not to be, before I could escape cleanly. Of all the gin joints in all the world…

But it wasn't *that* surprising, I supposed, that he would get the freak-show detail for Vegas. Back in the day, he was the cop who'd made his name working with the kooks in Memphis. Back in the day, he'd been willing to listen to people who didn't merit much more than a snickering reference on cable news.

Back in the day…

I shoved those thoughts away as Armaeus shouldered me closer to him. He punched the button to a bank of elevators that shimmered slightly out of alignment with the other elevators in the Luxor lobby. I peered around, trying to get my bearings, which was impossible with the cases of kitschy Egyptian trinkets all around me and the wildly colored carpet that assaulted the eyes along with all the gold.

The doors swooshed open, and he ushered me inside.

I really did mean to stop leaning on the Magician then, to support myself on one of the four very capable walls surrounding me. But that seemed like an awful lot of work.

"I can help you heal, Miss Wilde, but you must allow me to do that."

"So what are you waiting for," I muttered against his chest. It was a very nice chest. "You got insurance paperwork for me to sign or something?"

"Not exactly. But your mind is closed to me."

"That's kind of the point, isn't it? It being my mind and all."

The slightest trace of irritation laced the Magician's sigh as the elevator slowed, an amber light glowing on the console marked "P." I was pretty sure we weren't heading for the Parking garage. The doors opened, and my suspicion was rewarded with a flood of light from windows on all sides. "You don't have to make this so difficult. I'm not going to attack you when your guard is down."

"Oh, give me a break. That's exactly what you're going to do."

"She's right, of course." The Devil's rich voice floated over us, full of laughter, and the Magician's entire body went rigid. Given my proximity to said body, it was a good reminder of how strong the guy really was. And how hot, for the record.

"Now you decide to show up?" Armaeus refused to let go of me until we reached the main sitting area of the opulent space, a collection of overstuffed couches that were built for giants. Nevertheless, I held off on being deposited on one. The moment I sank into that much luxury, I was going to pass out.

"I don't suppose you have a bathroom somewhere closer than a quarter mile away in this place? I'm pretty sure I still have glass shards in my hair."

Armaeus twitched with irritation. "Of course. We

need to assess your condition anyway."

Before I could comment on how wrong that idea was, a woman emerged from the side of the room. Built like a discus thrower, she was dressed in the same liveried uniform as the valet, but she had the firm, no-nonsense manner of— "Oh, for God's sake, Armaeus," I groaned.

"You have two choices, Miss Wilde." He didn't elaborate on option number two. He didn't need to.

"Gotcha. Nurse Ratched it is."

The woman smiled. "I'll do my utmost to ensure you're not lobotomized while in my care. Sir?" She gestured to Armaeus, who was still holding on to me like I was his prized stuffy. He reluctantly handed me into her arms.

We hadn't cleared the lobby before he started laying into the Devil, once more using the strange language I had heard them speak on the phone. Really, I was going to *have* to look into the Google Translate options for ancient Sumerian.

"You've done quite a number on yourself." The woman exited to a long, quiet corridor, the hushed lighting and plush carpet a balm to my senses. "Your first time in Vegas?"

Despite myself, I laughed. I was leaning harder on her than I wanted to, but she seemed unfazed by my weight. "You get banged-up guests a lot in here?"

"On occasion. My name is Margaret Sells, by the way—Dr. Margaret Sells, if it makes you feel better."

"Sorry."

"My fault for not wearing the white coat. I didn't want to alarm you until I could introduce myself."

"Armaeus call you on the Batphone or something while we were en route?"

I could hear the smile in her voice, though my eyes

had drooped to half slits. "Something like that. I am on retainer with the Luxor. When Mr. Bertrand has a need for me, I'm happy to help. You're the first bomb victim in a while, though." We turned into a room that could have served as anything from a massage parlor to an operating suite, and she eased me over to the sink. "Let's get some of this glass out first, before I examine you."

"You've got the con."

The next several minutes were accompanied by the pinging sounds of shrapnel landing against stainless steel as the woman dictated a laundry list of my injuries into what I assumed was a digital recorder. Either that or she just liked the sound of herself nattering on. Either way, I learned that I suffered several minor contusions and lacerations, a probable slight dislocation of the right shoulder, a left ankle sprain I hadn't even noticed, and probable significant gas poisoning. The green tint to my lips was apparently a key indicator.

By the time we'd gotten to that part, I was sitting on the massage table, blowing into a device that looked impressively like a Breathalyzer. The doctor clucked as she watched the readings. "I've never seen anything like this, and I've been at it awhile," she said. "The makeup of these toxins…"

"Pythene gas," I managed after she took the mask from my face. "Ever hear of it?"

Her gray eyes flicked to mine. "Pythene, no. But I'm guessing it's tied to Pythia, as in the Oracle of Delphi?"

"You know your mythology."

"It's becoming an occupational necessity." She pursed her lips. "I can't prescribe an antidote for this kind of poisoning, though. Deep breathing of purified oxygen will help, but otherwise it's just time." She frowned as she looked into my eyes, and in my peripheral vision, I saw her pick up a slender penlight. With a murmured warning, she shined it in my eyes.

I didn't flinch.

"Your pupils aren't reacting. Has your vision changed since your exposure to the gas?"

I grimaced. "You could say that. But I can see you and the rest of this." I waved tiredly around the room. "Even though the rest of the world can't."

"The transdimensional paradox, yes." Dr. Sells spoke as if I should know what the hell she was talking about. "Our initial perception is that we should be standing in the middle of thin air, but the transdimension, where this building exists, is quite real, if you know where and how to look. And if you have Connected capabilities."

My blinking had nothing to do with her penlight. I reached out and touched the only exposed skin in easy reach, her arm above her plastic glove. Sure enough, there was the slightest zing. "I didn't know."

She smiled. "You'll find minor ability throughout the medical community, I expect. There's a reason why intuition plays such a powerful role in a doctor's success."

"And are you part of the *community* community?" I asked. "As in, here in Vegas?"

The idea appeared to startle her. "You mean, do I interact with the psychics?" She frowned. "I don't have much call to do so."

"Yeah, well." I thought about SANCTUS and the visions I'd seen at Binion's while sucking on that infernal gas. The visions of a war in the heart of Las Vegas, of blood and spirit and fire. "You're about to."

"Miss Wilde."

We both startled like girls caught out gossiping, and mentally I kicked myself. For whatever reason, the Magician couldn't crawl around in my own brain, but that apparently didn't stop him from riffling through Dr. Sells's mind like a deck of cards. I scowled up at him, and Armaeus smiled.

"I see you're feeling better," he observed mildly. He regarded Dr. Sells. "Other than the reaction to the Pythene compound, are there any other concerns you didn't mention in your report?"

The mind of the Magician. Better than a digital recorder any day. Beside me, Dr. Sells shook her head. "She needs rest, and she should avoid eyestrain." That merited me a startled glance from Armaeus, and I pointedly didn't strain my eyes looking at him. "Otherwise, she should be fine in a few days, depending on how her body processes the gas." She considered him. "Have you collected a sample? What I have from her lungs is pretty degraded."

"We'll have three separate samples sent to your lab by this evening," Armaeus said. He flicked his attention between us. "If there's a way for your team to replicate the compound—"

"Team?" That roused me. "You've got a team?"

Dr. Sells reached into her pocket and pulled out a card. "Call me day or night, with whatever you need," she said. "Your recovery is my primary concern." She turned to Armaeus. "She needs rest more than anything."

He nodded, his manner perfectly polite. "She'll get it."

Then his gaze shifted to mine, and his smile turned predatory.

"I'll make sure of it."

CHAPTER TWENTY-TWO

The Devil had evidently bugged out, since the vast sitting area was empty when we moved back through it. "You guys kiss and make up?" I asked, trying to shore up my strength against what I suspected was going to be in my future. A bed, most likely.

A bed and Armaeus, if I wasn't careful.

A bed, Armaeus, and a reaction I was going to regret unless I got a serious handle on things.

Fortunately, Armaeus seemed to be distracted by my question. Distracted and vaguely irritated, both of which worked fine for me.

"Kreios, like the rest of the Council, is not under my control, Miss Wilde," he almost snapped. "While I am the titular leader of the Council, I am not its ruler."

I casually leaned against the edge of the couch, as if my feet were totally steady beneath me, and I just, you know, wanted to take a load off for a second. "So what does being leader get you, then? From what I'm picking up, you don't even have a full Council sitting here now. What is it—the Priestess and the Fool? And Kreios, of course."

"The Empress and Emperor are here as well, as I am sure Kreios told you," Armaeus said coolly. "They are not needed for the daily work of the Council."

I frowned at him. "Not needed? Really? Do you

seriously not give a crap that SANCTUS is planning to drop by for a visit?"

"You don't know that for a fact."

"Yeah, well, let's call it a really strong hunch." I stared out the far window to the sweeping panorama of Las Vegas. "There's a lot of people down there who aren't going to fare too well if SANCTUS decides to clean house, Armaeus. And I don't know who actually is paying attention to the actions of the Council, but if you can't do anything in your own backyard…"

Somehow I had made it off the edge of the couch and onto the cushion while I spoke. I didn't remember doing it. Still, now that I was here, I decided it was an outstanding decision on my part. Couches were much less dangerous than beds. Couches were in living rooms. It was broad daylight. The fact that my words were slurring ever so slightly was completely beside the point.

I flattened my hands on my knees, stretching out my fingers. They hurt. Then again, everything hurt. "So what's the plan?"

Armaeus sat in the chair nearest me, amusement in his golden eyes. "The plan?"

"The fight. SANCTUS. They're coming, and they're probably coming here first. How are you going to stop them?"

"We're not."

"What?" I shook my head. I'd probably misheard him. I was feeling dizzy again, the vertigo returning even though I knew my feet were planted firmly on the ground, my hands gripping my knees, my shoulders tight, my back straight, my chin —

"You need rest, Miss Wilde." Armaeus's voice was suddenly too close. I blinked, startled, and realized he was face-level, which meant he was no longer sitting next to me but kneeling now, leaning in. "How can I convince you to do so?"

"I—" My words broke off quickly as he leaned just that much closer to me, his lips brushing against my mouth. He tasted of cinnamon and sunlight. "Um, that's not helping."

He edged back a fraction of an inch. "You don't have anything to fear from me. I thought we'd established that. There is nothing that I seek to do to you without your tacit permission—other than help you heal."

"Heal." I blinked at him, forcing myself not to look at his sensuous mouth. He could help me, I knew. If I wanted him to. Which I didn't. Instead, I squared my shoulders. "I'm good. I'll go to sleep on my own. I promise."

"It's not been a good day for promises."

Something in his tone made me look up at him sharply. "What's that supposed to mean?"

"I don't recall there being a deviation in my itinerary for you and Kreios, yet I understand that he exposed himself to more danger—and others as well—after you both left the necropolis. That's not the way you were supposed to conduct yourselves."

"Look, I did the job you asked me to do." I didn't know if Armaeus was deliberately pulling my chain, but I couldn't help but bristle. Bristling hurt. "I boosted Kreios from the Vatican and got him here. It's not my fault he decided to take a detour. If you'd told me what exactly was hiding in that box, maybe I would have handled it a bit more carefully. As it was, I could no more stop him from doing what he wanted than I could stop you."

I lifted a hand to tuck a strand of hair behind my ear. That hurt, too. "Besides, you've got bigger problems than Kreios. At least he's *here*. Whether you lead him or rule him or you're just the first guy in line to kick the ball, he's with you. And he's useful. Which is more than I can say about your little Golden Boy back in France. Unlike, I might add, your limo driver."

Armaeus's brows lifted. He hadn't moved from his kneeling position, and I felt his gaze on my face, steady and certain. "You're speaking of Maximillian?"

"Yes, Maximillian. He's the real deal, Armaeus. Dante isn't. You have to know that."

His lips twisted. "I don't need another Bertrand to be the real deal. As I told you before, just because one member of a household has taken a position within the Council, doesn't mean that future generations must share the burden."

"He wants to share the burden, trust me. He can go after Barnabus or figure out his own mad skills."

"Barnabus is being tracked through other channels. Max would do well to remain where he is."

"Oh, bullshit." I waved my hand in front of his face to get him to back off. Instead, he captured my fingers in his, turning my hand around to study my palm as I kept talking. "He's way overdue for an upgrade from limo boy, and… Um, what are you doing?"

"Your hands." Armaeus barely murmured the words. "I thought Dr. Sells attended to them more carefully."

"She attended to them just fine. They're banged up is all. It happens when you — oh."

My words broke off again as Armaeus pursed his lips, then blew a soft sigh across my abraded palms. A chill swept over the skin, instantly sensitizing it, and as I watched, frozen, the edges of the bright red scratches drew together, the skin knitting and smoothing until all that was left was a thin white scar. "Dude, what *is* that? Wolverine Breath?"

Armaeus merely picked up my other hand. I didn't resist—what idiot would? This was way better than Neosporin. I tried not to moan as cold absolution swept over my palm. It was almost as if I could feel my wounds actively healing, stretching over the tears not only in muscle and flesh but in my psyche, repairing the damage caused by everything I'd seen inside Binion's. Nikki's poor lost psychics, the throbbing mob, the loud, soul-sucking music. And something—something else too. Some*one* else.

My mind slipped and stuttered, refusing to take hold. I was floating, adrift in a boundless sea.

"Sara." Armaeus's voice seemed to be coming at me from too far away. Was he in this ocean of sensation with me? My body shifted, becoming unmoored from its axis, but the Magician wouldn't let me fall. He eased me back, steadied me, and his hands were at my face, my chin. Instantly, my headache eased. Even my hair felt better.

I stared at the ceiling, unable to speak, unable to move, lost along the waves of healing, pain dissolving into the endless waters surrounding me. My lips parted, and I heard my own ragged breathing as I went deeper, then deeper still, to a place where there was no more pain, no more sorrow, no more regret. I would have sworn he was healing injuries I didn't realize I had. I'm pretty sure he filled a few cavities while he was at it.

"Sara," Armaeus said again. Then the hands moved from my head and drifted down my body, the energy not quite reaching my skin. "This would be easier if you would allow me to remove your clothes."

That woke me up. "What? No!" My eyes flew open, but Armaeus was right there, his hands at the hem of my shirt, which had slid up when I'd stretched out on the couch. He pressed his hand against my stomach, and I moaned out loud. Dr. Sells had said something about a kidney bruise, but whatever it was, Armaeus found it with the palm of his hand. Waves of soothing cold radiated through me, and I felt my legs loosen right along with my willpower.

"It will take the barest of moments," Armaeus murmured. "We can continue talking if you prefer."

His words were mesmerizing as his fingers slipped up farther under my shirt. Cool air suddenly brushed against my skin, but before I could figure out where it was coming from, Armaeus had curled his fingers over my right shoulder.

"Sweet Christmas." I went rigid with the reaction, his grip the most painful thing I'd experienced today, which was saying a lot. My semi-dislocated shoulder seemed to come apart in five different places before settling back in place, the pain shattering through me in a push-pull with the frozen wonder Armaeus was unleashing. His left hand stroked down my neck and over my collarbone, but even as my back arched off the couch, he slid both hands along the outer edge of my torso, completely missing my chest. I was pretty sure my breasts hadn't been injured, but hey. He didn't know that.

Then he hooked his fingers under the waistband of my leggings.

Instinctively, I grabbed for his wrist, the connection of my hand on his skin practically jolting me off the couch. "I'm good—I'm good."

"I won't harm you, Sara."

"I know you won't, it's just that—"

Armaeus ended my objection with a kiss. As he leaned into me, I could feel one of his hands shoving down my leggings, his broad palm clasping my battered right thigh. The cramping instantly stopped, and I nearly whimpered as his fingers wrapped firmly around my left ankle.

"Better?" Armaeus murmured against my lips, and I tasted the salt of my own tears as he moved to my left leg, healing the long gash with the trailing of his fingers up my leg. That gash extended far north of my knee, however. By the time the edge of the wound was shimmering with cold white fire, I was dealing with an entirely separate issue.

Desire pooled inside my belly as if my core had become liquid, all the frigid healing strength banking as he stoked fire within me. Armaeus may not have an all-access pass to my brain, but he wasn't an idiot. He had to know the reaction he was causing.

I got my answer a second later, as his fingers finally, slowly closed over my breasts.

I nearly passed out.

Armaeus's mouth was by my ear, his chuckle low. "You're not wearing your Tyet. Should I take that as a sign?"

"Lost," I gritted out. I wanted him to stop, but at the same time, I didn't want him to. The danger crested again inside me, the fear of an unknown end with this man—this being—this whatever he was. "It was at Binion's when…everything exploded."

"We'll get it back." But he hadn't moved his hands from my breasts. He kneaded my body as if seeking unseen injuries to heal, and damned if I didn't arch up into him once more, molding myself to his powerful hands. One of those hands snaked around me and supported my back as Armaeus bent his face to my neck, his lips dragging along my pounding pulse. "Slowly… Slowly," he murmured, and even my pulse found that it had to respond to the Magician's command, as my racing heart stuttered to a gallop, then a trot, and the tears started fresh.

"Shhh, Sara," he said, and something about his voice caught at me, something strange and foreign. He'd been calling me Sara, I realized, this entire time. Not Miss Wilde. On purpose? A mistake? Did it matter?

It didn't matter. It couldn't matter. Just as it couldn't matter that Armaeus was standing now and pulling me with him, picking me up as if I weighed nothing.

"You really get off on carrying me around, don't you," I half muttered.

"It's a weakness of mine."

I laughed as he shouldered open another door, registering the chamber as a bedroom, but not Armaeus's bedroom. It had an unlived-in look, as if it was constantly ready for company that might or might not arrive.

He slid me into the sheets with a murmured laugh. "Now, you will sleep, Miss Wilde," he said. "Now, you will finally rest."

He moved away from me and I shuddered with an echo of my former pain, an almost physical ache that was so crisp that I narrowed my eyes at him, instantly mistrustful. "Am I going to regret this?" I asked, already feeling sleep weigh down on me. "What you just did?"

His smile was enigmatic, his words so quiet I almost couldn't make them out.

Almost.

"Not half so much as I am."

Before I could ask him what he meant by that, he was gone.

I lay there for a long time after that, willing myself to surrender to a sleep that wouldn't come. I knew I needed to sleep, to heal. But I felt more than anything else like I was back home again. As in home, home. Before the explosion.

My fingers clutched at the sheets as one by one all the images reasserted themselves in a long dark march of despair. In the weeks leading up to the end, nearly three years after I'd first identified little Maryann's whereabouts in a sensational news story that had led to claims that I was a burgeoning psychic detective, Mom's behavior had gotten more manic.

She'd been chafing at the bit for more notoriety for me, especially since the police had adamantly refused to officially acknowledge my participation in missing persons investigations for fear I'd be targeted. At the end, though, she'd turned petulant. Almost resentful. Like she'd had her hand slapped for reaching into the cookie jar and couldn't understand why. Then she'd announced that *she* was taking up card readings herself, and things had gotten better for a while. She'd been terrible at the cards, but I'd fed her readings before she'd leave to visit her "clients." We had a system. It worked.

Until that last night.

I closed my eyes, willing myself not to cry. Mom had been my responsibility, but I hadn't known that at the time. I hadn't understood. And because I hadn't been diligent enough, careful enough, she was gone.

I'd known something was wrong the next morning too. She'd left a note but not returned. Still, that was common enough. My mother had many, many friends who were more than willing to share a drink with her so late into the night that it was dawn before they stopped. I'd been uneasy, but not worried...until I touched the note itself.

Not thinking, not even breathing, I'd hauled ass out of the house—only to be knocked into a ditch by the force of the blast that had gone up behind me.

After that, I didn't look back.

And I'd never really stopped running.

By the time sleep took me, my face was wet with tears."

CHAPTER TWENTY-THREE

I was drowning in great, rolling seas.

No matter which way I turned or how I flailed, I couldn't escape. I pawed frantically, and the water wouldn't give way. It would shift backward, then flow toward me again, pressing against me, holding me close.

And it smelled like cinnamon.

Wait a minute.

With more effort than I would have thought I was capable of, I dragged open my eyes. I was alone, surrounded by at least seventy-eight pillows, in the middle of a massive bed that wasn't my own. Which was easy enough to determine, because I didn't own a bed.

Around me, the world dipped and rolled dangerously, my sense of vertigo feeling almost familiar. The automatic questions popped into my head. How hurt was I? *Where* was I? And what was I trying to steal?

I lolled over, feigning sleep, in case anyone or anything was watching me. I'd learned over long years — some longer than others — that my first order of business was always my own physical state. None of the rest mattered if I couldn't make my legs move.

I went through the assessment methodically,

buried under the covers as I shifted and tensed and twisted, and the more body mass I covered, the more nervous I became.

Nothing hurt.

Everything felt unspeakably healthy.

That hadn't happened in... That honestly hadn't happened, ever.

Bits and pieces of my last conscious twenty-four hours flowed back to me. The meeting in Paris. The chase. Armaeus. Rome. Kreios. The abbey south of Rome. Vegas. Dixie Quinn. Binion's. Brody —

Nope, not going there.

Either way, the spell was broken. I remembered the rest of it too, all the way up to the watershed I'd sworn I'd never give myself over to again. Oh, well.

More to the point, I was in the middle of Armaeus's lair, and the man hadn't touched me. Not in any real sense. I mean, yes, he'd done the whole laying on of hands to heal me, which wasn't to be discounted, but he hadn't gone any further than that. Was it something I said?

I shifted again in the coverlets. I was wearing garments that were clearly not my own, but a sweep of the gloom-shrouded room revealed a tidy stack of what almost looked like my clothes, only they were way cleaner. Curled up on top of the clothes was the Tyet.

Despite my fantasies of bounding out of the bed, gathering up my stuff, and hitting the road, my progress was markedly less impressive. It took me a full five minutes to reach the end of the bed, let alone flop over it. Still, the drop to the carpeted floor wasn't jarring so much as dizzying. I brought my head up too fast, and the nausea swamped me again.

I looked out over the room, and there were no more

walls, no more windows, no more ceiling or floor. I was suspended over a vast cavern, and the city of Vegas lay sprawled out beneath me, pulsing with pain. While businesses and houses and grand estates spread out like children's toys from the epicenter of the Strip, the heart of the city lay here, as if a gold strike rested directly beneath in the desert bedrock, except the vein was pure magic, not metal. As I watched, that vein raced up toward me — or I toward it, plummeting down toward the crack in the land with no way to stop, no way to turn back, no way to —

"Stop it!" I gritted out. I drove my fingers into my thighs hard enough to bruise, and the pain instantly cleared my brain. My vision returned to normal, the room around me settling into place.

I didn't know what exactly was in that Pythene gas Jerry Fitz was so free with, but man, I needed that shit out of my system. But how did you get an oxygen transplant?

And perhaps more importantly... Why had the Magician left that *one* part of me untouched? Surely while he was performing his oral search and seizure of my various body parts he could have locked lips with me and inhaled or something to suck out the badness. It's not as if that move hadn't been chronicled a dozen times already on the SyFy channel. It was clearly a move.

One he hadn't made.

My feet seemed fairly solid on the carpet now, so I risked movement again. At some point, Armaeus or one of his lackeys had come in to check on me. I wore some sort of thin nightgown and decidedly new underwear, the same brand and style as the ones I'd nearly melted off myself during Armaeus's little foray into playing doctor yesterday. I pulled the gown over my head and left it on the floor as I reached for my more familiar clothing.

I frowned. Other than the boots, the clothes weren't mine. Similar but not quite, just like the underwear. I shrugged, fingering the thin cotton of the tank, the simple bra. The leggings. It shouldn't matter that I was in Armaeus's house, wearing clothes he provided. It shouldn't make me feel weird.

It did, but it shouldn't.

I dressed anyway, buckling on my boots with the first sense of relief I'd experienced in a while. The Tyet was around my neck again, resting against my chest, but it alone among all my belongings felt foreign to me, like it needed to be recalibrated. My eyes were decidedly gritty, and I turned to leave the room— surely there was a bathroom somewhere.

"*Yo. Sara.*"

I was getting tired of people using the psychic network to check in with me, but this voice sounded urgent. Familiar. I blinked, and my vision blurred again. I couldn't breathe. I couldn't see. The world around me dissolved into a rushing kaleidoscope of shapes and colors, the soft muted colors of Armaeus's world changing to the thick concrete shapes of a building I didn't know, white and gray and blue rushing by me, struggling to take form.

"*Sara, dollface, c'mon. If you can hear me, we've got a problem.*"

The forms and figures all coalesced, and I nearly hurled. "Nikki!"

But Nikki didn't answer. I was standing in the room with her, the sense of distortion back as it had been when I'd stood inside Fitz's glass box. I could see what was in front of me, and then what was beyond— the doctors and nurses moving through the corridors, the shuffling patients, the watchful orderlies. All of them shifting and drifting in an endless dance in and out of sterile rooms with blinking monitors.

But here in this room, all I saw was Nikki. Nikki and two empty beds.

As Nikki turned to run out of the room, I could see the past of the young women who had slept in those beds stretch out in front of me like an inviolable thread. The furthest back image was that of laughter and bright skies and girls in pretty dresses with long dark hair flowing in the sunlight. Then there was a pool of water — mirror bright — and something seemed to change. The girls' lives spun more quickly around that pool, they aged faster and they laughed less, but they were ever drawn back to the pool with its flashing brightness as it reflected the sun's glare and pulled them back over and over to its edge. To what they saw within its surface. To what they thought they saw in each other's eyes.

Their eyes. Something about their eyes…

The scenes scrolled too quickly then to count. School, friends, strangers in the distance, always out of reach, but never quite gone. Their parents' faces gradually more careworn, their shoulders drooping. Gifts of gold and whispers of protection. The strangers coming closer. Darkness encroaching on their special, sacred pool of light. Spinning, turning faster. The last day, the lost day, the day they turned the corner and the car was there, the strangers were there, and then —

Panic seized me, clawing up my throat until I gagged.

"Miss Wilde!" This voice was far closer, but I couldn't shake the thrall of the vision. Not when I heard my name again, more loudly, more forceful. Not when I felt the electric shock of the Magician's hands clamping on my arms, trying to ground me. I saw the sisters' violation with eyes that stretched so wide they could see the whole world. I saw them stripped, manhandled. Not raped, thank God. There was at least enough superstition that their virginity was considered necessary to maintain. But abused in other ways. Frightened. Restrained. Separated.

They can't be separated.

Even their captors recognized this quickly enough, and the comatose women were hustled back toward each other, then shipped on a plane, watched like prized treasure but treated like animals. They clung together, alternating weeping and raving, until Jerry Fitz stepped into the room —

"Miss Wilde." I swung my gaze toward Armaeus, staring into his eyes. But I didn't see him, not really. I saw the gilded twin cages that hung high in the rafters of Binion's, lit up with spotlights so Fitz could put the girls on display. I saw their white fingers interlaced across the narrow space between their perches.

I saw the hookah with its puffing steam, and smelled the desperation and fear. The gas helped and it hurt. It helped and it hurt. It wasn't of the gods. It wasn't pure. The things it showed were not for Man to know.

I saw the two women entering on the arms of the bodyguards, and I knew — I knew.

"You have to wake up."

I felt the pull of the Magician's words. I sensed his touch more clearly. The vision began to fracture around the edges — no! It couldn't. I was too close! The woman — me — and her ragged clothes and hard face and lost eyes. Eyes that were too quickly clouded over with the Sight, something wrong with that, something bad —

Another noise assaulted me, but I batted it away. The burst of light and sound made me cringe as if I was reliving the explosion, watching the world shatter into fire and dust. Then there was movement and the sunlight—how long it had been since I'd seen the sunlight! And the cold, concrete place with its rasping white sheets and squeaking wheels and wailing, squawking monitors and so. Much. Noise.

And then she was there.

Quiet, soft hands. Loving hands. Loving voice. A mother's voice.

"Miss Wilde. I have Dr. Sells with me. I know you can hear me. We can't let you stay where you are. You have to come back."

Quiet, soothing hands. Caring hands. Caring voice. A teacher's voice.

"You're going into shock, Sara. You have to break the connection."

Quiet, steady hands. Blessed hands. Blessed voice. A goddess's—

Wait. A goddess?

"Clear!" A blast of electricity came out of nowhere, and I jolted as if I'd experienced a full-body Tase. My skin practically sizzled for a second, and I whipped my head around, my eyes hot, my mouth full of words too impossible to speak.

Vertigo descended on me again, then I was on my knees, gasping and struggling not to retch, my body racked with deep, rolling coughs and my need to vomit so violent and present that I was crying again, crying and shaking and unable to fight off the hands that clasped me. Hands that didn't hurt, hands that didn't pull, hands that—

My head came up. Dr. Sells stared back at me. "Hello, Sara. I'm Dr. Sells. Do you remember me?"

I opened my mouth. I knew where the girls from Kavala had disappeared to. I *knew.*

Her smile faltered, but not in fear or shock, merely concern. "What is it, Sara? You need to sit down now. Why don't we sit down?" Her words twisted and tumbled in my ears. I swung back toward Armaeus. He watched me, leaning up against the doorjamb now, missing nothing, as if I was his own personal hunting dog, his own prized pet. His own little finder to bring to his doorstep trinkets for the Council's pleasure.

"Where is she?" I managed. My voice sounded strained, garbled, the words foreign in my ears.

"Where is who?" To his credit, Armaeus truly did look confused at my question.

Dr. Sells was fussing at my side again, and I wheeled back, batting away her hand with its syringe.

"Get away from me."

"I need to take your blood, Sara." She grabbed my arm and steadied it. "The toxins in your system are not going to dissolve on their own. Until they do, you're going to be at the mercy of those visions you're having, not knowing what's real and what's not. You want to see a video of what just transpired in this room, you're welcome to it. Trust me when I tell you it's not a performance you'd want to repeat down on the street."

That quieted me long enough for her to plunge the needle into my arm. It didn't hurt. The electrical pulses chittering along my skin crackled and popped, but I couldn't feel the pain of a pricking needle. "Why don't I feel that?"

"Your nervous system is currently overloaded. That's the only thing keeping you upright." The Magician's words were almost curious, like a boy enthralled with his latest lab project. I narrowed my eyes at him.

"You shocked the crap out of me. With your hands."

"Who is it you wanted me to take you to, Miss Wilde? You said 'Where is she?' She, who?"

The urgency of my vision came back to me. I wrenched out of Dr. Sell's grasp and stalked toward him. With the cocktail of gas and electricity racing through my system, I suddenly felt invincible. "She, Eshe. The High Priestess. I know she's taken the twins out of the hospital, and that they went with her willingly. Where are they?"

He lifted an eyebrow, patently unimpressed with my show of anger. "You really think a hospital is where those girls most needed to be?"

"Well, they sure as hell don't need to be with her. They think she's a *goddess*, Armaeus. An Apollonite high priestess for real. Jesus."

"I think you're mixing your metaphors."

"This isn't a game. And we're not your pawns." I dropped my hand from my face. "I don't know what it is you're trying to do here, but the girls are not part of it."

"Are you, then?" His words were low, dangerous, and I could instantly sense the peril here, though I didn't fully understand it. "Are you willing to stand in their place, for whatever the Council needs?"

I stilled. "What do you mean?"

"I just watched you." Armaeus was calm, intrigued even. "Based solely on whatever you saw in your mind, you reached back into those girls' memories and pulled out their pasts, their present—things you couldn't possibly have known. You barely had seen the young women yourself before the explosion in Binion's. You certainly hadn't touched them. And yet you were able to pinpoint them, to see what must be seen." He leveled his gaze at me. "That's a very useful talent. And as you're so fond of pointing out, you're already on the payroll. With your additional ability, we won't need the young women."

"They're not yours to 'need' at all, Armaeus."

"Magic is the province of the Council."

"These are human beings, not specimens." I shook my head irritably. "Take me to the goddamned High Priestess. Those girls need to go home, and you need to make sure that 'home' is safe for them."

He shrugged. "As you wish."

"Fine."

He turned on his heel, and I followed. That all...seemed a little too easy.

I should have known that was bad. .

CHAPTER TWENTY-FOUR

The room Armaeus brought me to was definitely part of his complex. I figured we were probably hanging out somewhere over Las Vegas Boulevard, easy for anyone to spot with their transdimension setting turned to "on." If I was planning to spend any significant time in Vegas, I needed to get square with the whole displacement of time and space, but I had bigger fish to fry right now.

I'd been worried that Armaeus would walk me into some kind of Roman temple, given the whole "High Priestess" thing Eshe was working. Thankfully, I'd gotten that wrong.

What I saw was bad enough.

A full-on hospital suite had been set up at the end of a long hallway, the girls ensconced in matching adjustable twin beds, both of them dead to the world. Sure enough, Dr. Sells split away from us and went over to the monitors, and I eyed her with more than a little betrayal. She was supposed to be on my side, based on our very meaningful fifteen minutes together. Where was girl power when you needed it?

On this side of the glass, staring through it, stood the High Priestess herself. Eshe.

I'd seen her only once before, when Armaeus had agreed to meet me in public in Vegas, the first time I'd come to the city. I'd been nervous, on edge. I'd done the research, I knew where people lived.

But I was like the kid cutting school who was absolutely certain that the principal would be able to pick him out of a crowded club. Eshe had shown up, expecting to be introduced to Armaeus's "little courier," and my eternal enmity for the woman had been born.

There was no denying that she was patently stunning, though. It'd been months since I'd seen her, and she still appeared the same: long and lithe, with a waterfall of lustrous black hair tumbling down her back. Even standing in Armaeus's makeshift hospital room, she oozed power and influence, along with a curious sense of entitlement, as if all the world owed her its every adulation. Lean and mysterious, otherworldly and arch, she turned to glance at me with impatient authority, her strappy silver gown's fluttering sleeves revealing gold arm bracelets to go along with the silver and gold wrist cuffs, jeweled rings, diamond pendant necklace, and swooping earrings.

"Kind of overdressed, don't you think?"

"I suppose I should thank you. If these women recover, they'll be the finest oracles to serve me for over five hundred years."

"They weren't on the delivery order." I slanted a look at Armaeus. He didn't seem impressed. "They're not staying."

"Don't be absurd." Eshe turned around and scowled at Armaeus. "We need these women. I need them."

"For what? I thought you didn't interfere with the actions of the mortal realm. What could the visions of two seers possibly tell you that would be of any use to you?"

She kept her gaze on Armaeus. "Is there a reason why she's still talking?"

"Look, duckface—"

"Wake." Armaeus's voice echoed out through the room. Beyond the glass, the women stirred, rousing to consciousness. Eshe caught the movement and whipped back around. "How are their numbers?" she demanded.

"Thready," Dr. Sells said severely. "They should not be here. They should be in a fully functioning facility. With medical specialists." She scowled at her monitors, never glancing in our direction. I didn't know if I liked the woman, but I liked her attitude at the moment, anyway.

"I don't trust those facilities. Too many walls." Eshe's tone had turned petulant. "You should have everything you need here."

"I do, for life support." Dr. Sells flicked her hand across the screen, and the picture changed. "And congratulations, these two young women are going to survive. But I can't even determine the true impact of this Pythene gas on Sara right now, and she only inhaled it for about an hour. These women have been sucking down that concoction for the past several weeks. There's no telling the long-term neurological damage it's inflicted, let alone the state of their pulmonary systems. They should be under observation for weeks to be safe."

"Weeks?" It was my turn to be petulant. "I need to get them back to their family"

"Broken and incapacitated?" Dr. Sells looked at me through the glass. "If you truly feel that their systems in their home countries can outstrip what the Council's money and connections can provide them here, then I suppose that's a wise choice."

Son of a bitch. My opinion of Dr. Sells took a nosedive, but I couldn't fault the woman's logic. I felt Armaeus's smug glance at me. He was behind this, somehow. I couldn't quite believe that he'd orchestrated these women coming here — even I wasn't that paranoid — but he sure as hell would benefit from me being stuck in the city for a while.

"Fine," I muttered. "Then get them out of this hole in the sky and onto the actual earth, so if their parents want to come here, they can. I want them protected, but I don't want them hidden. There's too much of that as it is in the Connected community."

"What — again, why is the courier allowed to speak? The oracles go nowhere but here. If we need these specialists" — Eshe said the word with a flick of her fingers — "then we bring the specialists here. We've done it before."

"Not negotiable."

"And I told you to be silent." Eshe moved with such a languorous grace that a lesser person wouldn't have seen her attack coming. But I'd been working the back alleys of the black market for going on five years now. I knew the difference between someone working the grift and a sorcerer with real talent. Eshe, for all her bad manners, was the latter.

I dropped to the floor.

The wave of power surged over me, lighting up my nerve endings that were still in full-twitch from the Magician's electroshock therapy. The blast slammed into the back wall, getting absorbed harmlessly into whatever substance made up this structure. Somehow I didn't think it was drywall.

I rolled to my feet and danced to the side of another blast, not missing the fact that Armaeus stood aside, watching us both with keen interest but no apparent concern. Screw. That.

I didn't have magical powers, but I had something Eshe didn't, I was willing to bet.

A good right hook.

She rushed me, and I pivoted left, readying my body and tightening my abs as she screamed in frustration, her hand coming up to throw some reinforced spell at me point-blank. I brought my fist up —

And punched through air.

The momentum carried me forward into the arms of a man I swear hadn't been there two seconds before, a man whose embrace I'd already experienced once this day, the lingering effects of which were not completely forgotten. "I've so missed you already, Sara Wilde," Kreios murmured.

He turned me neatly in his arms, caging me so that I faced out.

The Magician stood close to me, too close, his hand on Eshe's shoulder, handling her far less roughly but with the same restraint. "Look at her," he said.

"I will not be —"

"Look at her, Eshe. She has agreed to substitute herself for the oracles. Look at her and tell me she cannot do what you need her to do."

"She can barely be trusted to speak in complete sentences." Eshe flicked a glance at me, then stilled. As usual, I caught on a second too late. By the time I decided to avert my eyes, I couldn't.

"What is this you have brought me?"

Her words were almost exactly what I recalled Kreios saying to Armaeus over the phone in Rome, and the odd phrasing caught at me as I held Eshe's dark-eyed stare. I felt her trying to peer into me, through

225

me, but the twist of her pouty lips told me of her lack of success, before she shrugged off Armaeus. "I can't reach her mind. She's useless to me."

Armaeus let Eshe go willingly. Kreios did not seem to have the same agenda. His arms remained locked around me, pinning me to his muscular form. His chuckle was low, almost intimate, and it caused Eshe to look sharply at him. "I suppose you have something to add? Since you invariably do?"

"You don't need to wrench the visions out of her, Eshe. She will give them to you freely enough."

"I will?" *I will?* The idea of me giving Eshe anything except a hard time was difficult for me to imagine.

"She will." It was Armaeus who spoke now, and his lip curled with annoyance, as if he'd finally noticed Kreios's stranglehold on me. "She won't allow you to touch the women from Kavala. She knows they would go to you willingly, have already gone with you once before. You would not coerce them. You would not need to."

"Of course I wouldn't," Eshe sniffed.

"Accordingly, if she doesn't want the girls to get anywhere near you, she has to offer something in return. Something only she can do." Armaeus shrugged, eyeing me dispassionately. "And so she will."

I struggled against Kreios's hold a moment more before he let me go, though I could feel the energy of his touch even after he'd released me. I rubbed my arms, sensing his smirk, and irritation lashed through me. I should be more upset, I knew. I should be outraged. But Armaeus was right, and Dr. Sells was right, and Father Jerome, who probably didn't even know he was going down for this, was right.

"Fine," I said, staring daggers at Eshe as she boldly met my gaze. "You want me to look something up from your global Rolodex, I can do that. Until the girls are strong enough to leave the city. And that's not going to take months." I scowled at Dr. Sells. "That's going to take weeks. But if my newfound visionary ability suddenly goes poof, there's no bothering the girls. I want your word on that." I wasn't glaring at Eshe when I made this announcement, but Armaeus. He inclined his head gracefully. "Not your nod, your word."

"I give you my word as my bond. You will serve as Eshe's oracle until such time as the women leave Vegas to continue their recovery."

"I'll need her longer than that," she protested.

"Oh, bullshit," I snapped. "By that point, you'll have broken down the gas you've collected from Fitz's stash into its component parts. You can make your own little hallucinogenic cocktail. You won't need to crawl around in anyone else's brain at that point. You can suck down the gas yourself." I grinned at her horrified expression. "C'mon. Rub elbows with the little people, why don'tcha? Could be fun."

"You're revolting." She scowled at Armaeus. "How do we even know she can do what you say she can?"

"Oh, for God's sake." I waved down her theatrics. "What do you want me to see for you? What past or future do you want to view?"

"Tell me what really happened when Kreios was stuck in that abbey."

Behind me, Kreios stiffened. "That's hardly relevant."

"It's eminently relevant," Eshe shot back. "You certainly haven't been forthcoming, and this is information the Council needs to know."

227

"It's no good for another reason," I said, carefully pitching my tone to be nonchalant. Nevertheless, if Kreios wanted his secret kept, it was easy enough for me to do it. And if ever there was someone I wanted to owe me a favor, it was the Devil. "I was there, Eshe. I showed up about ten minutes after Kreios went underground, so I was privy to just about everything that happened to him. Not exactly useful as an oracular test. You're going to have to ask me something else."

"Fine," she snapped "Tell me something about myself that no one in this room could possibly know but me. That will serve."

I stared at her, but only partially in disgust. The other part rushed up too quickly, filling my mouth with words and thoughts and plans and expectations. I shook my head, but the pressure to speak grew almost unbearable. Finally I breathed out a long, ragged sigh. I swung my gaze back around to Eshe, and I could tell by her expression that she was surprised. Maybe a little worried?

Worked for me. "You killed to ensure that you—"

"Stop—that's enough!" Eshe commanded, shock suffusing her face.

"Oh, I wouldn't be so sure," the Devil drawled. "There are so many ways that sentence could end, and all of them completely entertaining. Do go on, Sara."

"And I said no. What she's said is sufficient. I can use her for my research." Eshe folded her hands demurely. "You'll remain with me in my domain until I have need of you."

I bristled. "I'm not your chew toy. I'll work for you the same way I work for Armaeus. On my own hours, and not until you've paid me a retainer fee."

"Unacceptable. Do you have any idea how long I've been without—"

"And do you really want to push me? You've already agreed to leave me alone the moment my senses return to normal. That could happen in the next thirty minutes if you're not careful. And thirty minutes is about all the patience I have for this science experiment right now. So you want a piece of me, then let's go. But I'm out of here after that."

"Out of here." She smirked. "You reek of Armaeus's touch. I don't think he's going to be letting you go anytime soon."

"Not your problem." I didn't miss Armaeus's cold stare at my profile. I couldn't figure him out. He'd just put me back together like Humpty Dumpty after the fall, then extorted me to work in this city for God only knew how long. Not for the first time, I began to suspect he had an end game that I wasn't going to like. Also, not for the first time, the itch to flee became overwhelming.

Flee this man, flee this city, flee this life.

Then my gaze flicked past Eshe's sneer and into the room next door. Once again, I was seeing the oracles of Kavala behind glass, like they were circus animals on display. That would have been their future with Jerry Fitz without question, and my heart twisted into a hard little knot. The girls were fully awake, their faces luminous with youth and frailty. Away from the smoke and filmy costumes, they looked like ordinary girls. Girls with a future. Girls with hope.

Like the little girls and boys whose pictures still haunted me. The ones I couldn't save when I'd been barely more a kid myself.

And they were staring out into the observation room, their eyes filled with wonder, as if they were viewing an actual goddess in their midst. Or a savior. Or the Stay Puft Marshmallow Man.

But now the twins from Kavala weren't looking at Eshe. They were looking at me.

I sighed, then glared again at the High Priestess. "Let's get this done."

"Of course," she purred, putting out her hand to draw me toward her. "This will only hurt a little."

CHAPTER TWENTY-FIVE

I had to hand it to the Council. When they wanted to put on a show, they put it on with style.

Armaeus and I stood in an antechamber, waiting to be ushered into the Council's grand meeting hall. I was edgy, ready to go, since Armaeus had spent the last few hours annoying the crap out of me with delays. First I had to shower, then eat, then sit in a quiet room to "meditate." Read: "fall asleep." He'd finally shown up again, with a new set of clothes that apparently had been ordered up by Sister Fashionista. I was now wearing designer trousers over my boots, and my tank was covered by a shimmery white shirt with long sleeves. I looked like a receptionist at a high-end art gallery. Eshe had wanted me in a toga, but even I had my limits.

In the meantime, Armaeus had provided me with access to his computer. I'd declined his offer of a new phone. The entire point of a burner device was that it wouldn't be LoJacked by the Council, after all. Kind of defeated the purpose for them to make a gift of one to me.

Granted, what I'd seen on his computer *had* satisfied me. Namely, $30,000 being transferred to my bank account. I could find a whole lot of kids for thirty grand.

"Each time you agree to serve as Eshe's oracle, to provide her the answers she seeks, that amount will be transferred, Armaeus said. "You can make your arrangements with your own bank from this terminal as well—"

"I'll do it tonight." I shook my head. "On my own."

He didn't roll his eyes, but he might as well have. "There is very little about you I couldn't find out if I didn't want to, Sara. You really think I don't have an intimate understanding of how much money you have and where you spend it? How do you think I found you in the first place?"

"Boundaries, Armaeus." I waved a hand at him. "You want me to work with your little freak-show harem, you at least give me the illusion that you respect my limits. Otherwise, I'll walk."

"You won't walk." His smug smile couldn't have been curved more perfectly to piss me off. "You have the girls in Las Vegas Medical to protect. The phone calls have already been placed to their family, so you have them to protect as well. And as you pointed out yourself, the city is potentially about to be overrun by curious agents of SANCTUS, wondering how, exactly, Jerry Fitz managed to explode himself while wearing a cuff that bore their symbols. A cuff which, miraculously, survived the blast and made it into police custody."

I scowled at him. "I saw it, Armaeus. There weren't two pieces left of that thing larger than a dime."

"You're correct. But you weren't the only one to see the arm cuff. And Miss Dawes is not so careful with shielding her mind. We were able to create a reasonable facsimile and leave it at the bomb site. Queries are being made through the highest channels at the Vatican, and we've started slight ripples at

Interpol. It isn't much, but it's enough to serve as some well-placed thorns. It won't take SANCTUS long to come investigating."

I stared at him. "You *want* them to come here. I thought you were all about noninterference."

"You mistake the role of the Council in the affairs of magic." Armaeus shook his head. "You'll have the opportunity to correct that error during your extended stay with us."

"Not with you." How many times did I have to make this point? "I'm not floating around in hyperspace while I'm here. I don't care where you stick me. Put me up at a casino, buy me an RV, I don't care. But I'm not staying here." He looked ready to argue, and I held up a hand. "I'm more useful to you out there than I am here, other than when Eshe wants to play Psychic Scavenger Hunt."

"It's not safe."

"You can't keep me here against my will." This too was something else I had figured out in the intervening hours between our little standoff in the hospital room and now. I might not know all the ins and outs of the Council, but I wasn't a complete idiot. That had been a carefully orchestrated scene by Armaeus. Down to the last impossible choice. "You had to get me to *agree* to stay on as your little windows on the world of my own free will. The girls had already agreed to it, and apparently even hallucinating yesses count as yesses in your book. But I hadn't. Why the hangup? What happens if someone says no?"

"We've not had to deal with that for so long, I wouldn't know."

The light, clear sound of a gong interrupted us, and the doors swung open. Without saying another word, Armaeus gestured me inside.

I went.

The great hall of the Council looked a lot like…a conference room. Fancier, of course, with a long center slab of marble instead of particleboard with cherry veneer, and throne-like seats in place of rollaway chairs. But the general effect was the same. Darkness hung heavy on either side of the table, which was illuminated by a bright central light, cast in such a way that everything seemed limned with gold.

"You guys are the best. Someday you're really going to have to tell me who does your decorating."

Eshe stood at the front of the table, and to my surprise, Kreios sat next to her. Sat, or more like sprawled, in one of the opulent chairs. He stared at me as I approached, clearly not a fan of my outfit. He wasn't the only one. Armaeus had been angling for the toga as well. Not going to happen.

Eshe pursed her lips as I approached. "You should be kneeling."

"A lot tougher to walk that way."

"You should—"

"The oracles that Fitz used were cooped up in a glass chamber, and they were able to respond, Eshe." Armaeus's voice was firm. "Miss Wilde can sit or stand. Whatever is her preference."

"I'll stay on my feet." From Eshe's little half smirk, I got the feeling I wouldn't be upright for long, but I was feeling lucky.

"Then we will begin."

Her words made me tense up, and I fixed my eyes on her, suddenly uneasy. With that short sentence, her voice had dropped several octaves, far past bass into something so elemental it seemed like the very murmuring of the rocks and earth. The lights dimmed over the table, and I vaguely had a sense of Armaeus seating himself beside Kreios. The High Priestess's gaze was locked on her hands. Despite myself, I glanced there as well.

And was caught.

A ball of fire had erupted between Eshe's palms, but not like any fire I'd ever seen. It crackled with blue and purple veins, green and gold and red, and it seemed to expand to fill my whole world.

"Are you ready to see and share all that may be seen?" Eshe's words were so quiet, they were almost subvocalized, but I felt myself nodding. Though whatever she asked me next, I couldn't have said.

Because there was the tiny problem of my brain exploding.

Without warning, pain radiated through my system, my body jolting into a tight arch of agony, breath crystallizing in my lungs. I wanted to vomit, but my bile was fire in my throat, burning through my esophagus. My blood vessels seemed to swell to six times their normal size, my pulse racing like traffic fleeing a storm after the roadblocks failed. I twisted away, desperate to escape, to find Armaeus, Kreios, anyone who could help.

Something sounded in my ears again, demanding my attention, and I realized my eyes weren't seeing. I reached up to tear away the obstruction, and pain lacerated my face.

Before me sat a group of men at a table, leaning close. Not just men—women too, all of them robed for surgery. The room didn't look like a surgical suite, though. More like a room in a crappy hotel. Not abandoned, not some sort of crack house, but a tired, beat-down room with cheap polyester comforters and old, faded carpet and tan walls that maybe once had been white.

They had a body stretched out on the table—not a bed, a table, like a portable gurney. A drip was attached to a pole, and the body was white, too white, too small, the legs and ankles protruding to the edge of the table but not quite reaching. A child? A teen? There was no way to tell until a knife slashed and the feet convulsed, and I realized this child was awake! Awake!

Another impossible pressure weighed on my brain, and I moved closer, closer when all I wanted to do was leave. I placed my hand against the shoulder of a man, and he shrugged me off, shivering, but the movement shuffled him to the side, and I saw the small form on the table. Not a child, but not quite a man yet either, judging by the sharp protrusion of his collarbone. His chin jutted up in a paroxysm of pain. Without thinking, I placed my hand on the boy's leg, and his pain became mine, suffusing me with a new wave of sharp horror that buckled me at the knees.

The boy on the table relaxed, and the men around me spoke in words I didn't understand, couldn't understand, but they passed into me and through me as I focused on the boy, sending him all my strength and taking all the pain that I could, watching with dead eyes as I saw the implantation of the device into his chest cavity, low and deep, up against his solar plexus, the center of his energy, I knew. I could feel the boy's power stirring, waking, an eye fluttering open that saw too much. It would see me!

Instantly, I was pulled almost physically from the scene, twisting away, and then I was in another place, another hellhole. There was only one person here. A woman, bound to a wall. I was forced toward her by unseen hands, though I could smell the rankness of her death. She was gone, but only recently, her life spirit still heavy in the air. I lifted her head, brushing her lank hair out from her face, and my stomach turned over again. Her eyes were gouged out, her tongue cut away. The sweat was not yet dry on her face, though. Her captors were close — close.

Pushing against the compulsion to leave this place entirely, I turned and raced through the corridors, slipping between the bars that kept this woman trapped underground. It didn't take me long. The men were hunched over their spoils, like pirates with looted treasure, and they didn't see me come upon them until I was already past. I whirled to face them, my eyes peeling open wide, and they blanched as they walked through me. But I saw their faces. Saw and remembered. Saw and reported.

The next and the next and the next place whirred by like a sickening storm. More violations. More experiments. A lab in the middle of a frozen landscape. A sacrificial ceremony in a swamp. A high-rise bristling with computers where maps of the star systems were overlaid with mathematical equations and ancient texts, while men and women hunched over their screens with a frenzied hope.

Then finally, a familiar face in an unfamiliar place. A face that turned to me, that smiled into the nothingness that was my presence, as if he could almost see me back.

I rushed by, not stopping, not speaking. I hadn't been sent to find Max; he wasn't supposed to be here. Instead I climbed the stairs of the palatial building with its austere, clean lines and moved quickly past guards and tourists, drifting down quieter and quieter corridors until I entered a room that was markedly different from all the others I had seen this day.

It was clean, it was orderly, and it was occupied by a group of businessmen who were wielding pens, not scalpels. There was something off about this group, though, something that breathed as much danger as any of the foul places I'd been before.

Then the doors opened, and I caught my breath. Darkness roiled into the room with an air of authority I had never before experienced, but the man it attended was familiar to me. He'd been the leader of SANCTUS, the figure I'd glimpsed in Binion's lair. But here, in this place, his presence was much stronger, much clearer. It was also not quite human.

In that moment, he looked up, and I felt myself yanked out of the room, out of the building, the same soul-crushing pain grinding against me like a cheese grater until I came all the way back to myself in the chamber, the blessedly dark chamber, with walls and ceiling and floor and table and chairs and —

I slumped, almost hitting the ground before I was caught in a cool, steadying embrace. I smelled of fire and blood.

"That," came the droll voice of the Devil, "was most unexpected."

My eyes flickered open as I was hoisted up again. To my surprise, Armaeus didn't carry me out of the room, which I heartily deserved, in my opinion. Instead, he poured me into one of the enormous chairs around the table. Eshe was seated as well, looking credibly shaken.

"Who are you?" she asked.

I stiffened. "Rich, or I'd better be." I scowled at Armaeus, who regarded me with that maddeningly contemplative stare. "What? What did I do?"

"What you said you would," he said. "You saw, and you shared what you saw."

"She did more than that." I blinked at the High Priestess's tone. For all of her animosity toward me, there was something new lining her words. "Where are you from? Who are your parents?"

"Okeedoke, I think the bonding moment is done, thanks. You guys going to tell me the import of anything I just saw?" At Eshe's new layer of surprise, I rolled my eyes. "Yes, I remember what I see. If that's not usual, let's give the dearly departed Fitz some props. He's improved on the original toxic fumes your little oracles inhaled. Though I gotta tell you, that hurt like a bitch."

"Molecular displacement," Armaeus said. "You literally came apart at the seams to travel the way you did, but retained sentience to report."

"Yeah, well, it stung."

"What you saw was the Connected community eating its own tail, if it matters." Kreios reclined back in his chair, his fingers steepled together. "The experiments have been going on for a long time, but the electronica angle is new. New and dangerous. And possibly exactly what's needed."

"What I saw was not needed, I can pretty much guarantee that."

He conceded that point with a nod. "But the idea was on track. Even doctors had a reason for leeching their patients, back in the day."

"Look…" I sighed. "I need some air. You guys keep talking. I'll be back when I've accounted for all my missing molecules."

"You can't leave." Eshe leaned toward Armaeus, but her tone wasn't petulant anymore. It was worried. "She can't leave."

"Watch me," I said.

CHAPTER TWENTY-SIX

Getting out of the Magician's lair was less exciting than I'd anticipated. Outside the Conference Room of Doom, an elevator bay lay dead ahead, and when I pressed the button, it opened right up, mercifully empty. I rode it down to a bright antechamber clearly announcing itself as the Luxor's front lobby, and wandered over to the bell desk, reviewing my options. I hesitated, keenly aware that I was being watched by two sets of staff members — from the Luxor and from Prime Luxe — both of which appeared to be clued into my appearance. It was like standing in the hotel lobby of *The Shining*.

I didn't have any preset plans. I just had to get out of there. Besides, something about the Council's coldness up in their hallowed heavenly halls had me thinking of Nikki and Dixie again, and the city's Connected community. And the girls from Kavala.

More to the point, if I was going to be stuck in Vegas for a few days, I needed to learn my way around. And where else should I start but the friendly neighborhood Welcome Wagon?

"Hello," I said to the small, faintly European-looking concierge standing there. "I'm trying to get the lay of the land, and I was hoping you could direct me to the Chapel of Everlasting Love in the Stars?"

"Love in the Stars? But of course, mademoiselle. You are a bride-to-be?"

The man's accent seemed legitimately French, and I blinked at him. "No—well, I mean, I need to go to the chapel, but I'm not—"

"It is the most romantic chapel in Las Vegas, you will see! But it is a bit of a distance. You would like a taxi, yes?"

"Yes." I smiled at him. Then I remembered: I had no purse. I had no plastic. I had no phone. I sighed. "Never mind. How far away is it from here?"

As the man peered at the screen, I heard the unmistakable hard stride of a giantess in steel-tipped stilettos. I turned around in time to see Nikki doing a double take as she scanned me from head to foot. She was back in a chauffeur costume, but, given the hour, she'd apparently upgraded to the fully sequined version.

"Whoa, girl. What the hell are you wearing?" She frowned at my art-gallery outfit, her scowl lightening briefly as I pulled off the shirt to reveal my tank underneath. "Well, now you're not just pitiful, you don't match at all."

"Says the woman wearing a sequined chauffeur's outfit."

"Says the woman *rocking* a sequined chauffeur's outfit." She grinned. "C'mon. I've been camped out here in this kitsch palace waiting for you for the last three nights. Sooner or later I knew you'd show up."

Something about her words struck me as wrong, but my brain became wholly occupied with the effort of movement. As we walked the short distance to the car, I could sense the vertigo sneaking up on me. We stopped at a potted plant in the shape of an enormous scarab beetle just as I was feeling the need for something to steady me. I held on to it as Nikki leaned against the valet station and made eyes at the young man standing there. "Please tell me you didn't park my car in the Nairobi desert," she said. "I gotta bounce."

Whether the valet was blinded by her sequins or her smile, he blinked rapidly, then took her ticket and dashed off. Nikki glanced back at me and frowned. "You feeling okay?"

I shrugged. "How are the psychics you recovered from Binion's? Are they safe?"

"Most of them didn't need to be admitted." Nikki pulled out her phone, scanning her messages as she talked. "The ones who did were admitted more for dehydration than for their wounds. It seems that Fitz kept his entertainment nourished enough to function, but ten hours a day in that smoke-filled hole-in-the-wall eventually wears a body down." She scowled, looking up at me again. "Their burns will heal, but some of them will be scarred for life. Shitty way to go for people who already had the cards stacked against them, pardon the pun."

"And their minds?"

One corner of her mouth kicked up in a wry grin. "At least there they've got a bit of an edge. Being an acknowledged Connected as a kid tends to toughen you up mentally, prepare you for the road ahead. It's us poor sons-a-bitches who don't figure it out until later in life that have the harder road. Fortunately, what the psychic network didn't prepare me for, the police academy did."

I blinked, not sure if I heard her correctly. Police academy? True, Nikki could handle a weapon with the best of them, and she had a certain no-nonsense style beneath her flash. But though I didn't know her well, I wouldn't have pegged her for a cop. Especially not as —

She laughed at my confusion. "Oh, I didn't look like this then, dollface. That was before the change. That was before a lot of things. Still, you don't really ever forget the pain, you know?"

Her tone was a little wistful, but before I could respond, her sleek town car cruised up the ramp and slowed to a stop. The starstruck young man leapt out of it as Nikki rounded the front of the vehicle. He handed over the keys — and his card. The latter Nikki tucked into her bra, and I wondered if she still had the Devil's card in there as well, or if her foundation garments were permanently lined with mementos from the streets of Vegas. "I love this town," she sighed happily as she slung herself into the car. She looked at me in the rearview mirror. "Dixie's, I heard you say?"

I shook my head. "Hospital first, since you saved me the trouble of finding you. Armaeus said that they'd moved the Kavala twins to a private room at Las Vegas Medical. I want to double check that for myself, before their parents arrive tomorrow." I drew in a shaky breath that I was sure contained some oxygen in it. "So, that was one heck of a distress call you piped into my brain earlier today. I didn't know you could do that. I got out of there as soon as I could."

Nikki's gaze, momentarily occupied by getting out into traffic on the boulevard, slanted back to me. "Um…'k. But the girls' parents have been here for over a day, sugar."

"What?" I'd seen those girls not five hours ago in the Magician's medical suite. Something wasn't tracking. Then something else clicked in: Nikki's words, about waiting for me for the last three nights… "Ah, how many days has it been since I saw you in Binion's, then?"

"That would be three. You went poof into the Cat in the Hat's limo, and I didn't hear another word out of you. Then the oracle girls disappeared from the hospital. Like, now you see them, now you don't disappeared. Their bodyguard was beside himself. And he's big enough on his own."

"That was all the first day?" My mind balked at trying to parse such simple information.

"Tuesday, yep." Another whiskey-eyed glance. "Any of this ringing a bell?"

"Not so you'd notice."

She shook her head. "I tried to contact you but got no reply. Good to know it worked, though, even if your connection is a little spotty." She grinned. "Then I got a message from one of the Council's couriers that you were safe and healing, that the Kavala twins were fine, and I should focus on getting anything I could out of the young psychics we liberated from Binion's. Their medical care was covered by the Council, by the way. Dixie let that slip."

She blew out a long breath. "Then yesterday, I get *another* call from the hospital, since somehow I've been assigned as the twins' ward. They were back in the hospital, and oh, yes, could I please come down and sign a bunch of paperwork. Which of course I did. The girls woke up midday, but while I'm given to understand they can speak English, they seem to need to be in a trance to do it. So we basically smiled at each other a lot. Their parents don't speak much English either, but I got them to the hospital in one piece. The Magician is putting them up at the Palazzo. Nice digs, but not cheap." She paused. "There are also more guards assigned to the family now. At the hotel and at the hospital. Someone cares about these girls, it seems."

I thought about what the High Priestess had planned for the sisters—what I'd taken on instead. My body felt like it was held together with Krazy Glue and chicken wire. "They're recovering?"

"The hospital is expecting a specialist in tomorrow to start doing a full tox study. They found enough trace remains of the gas to perform a chemical analysis, but not enough, apparently, to reproduce it for further study. I'm pretty sure there were more than enough canisters of that shit stored around Binion's that didn't go boom, though. And I'm not the only one."

That sounded ominous. "Who else is looking—oh." It hit me with the punch of a medicine ball dropping on my stomach. "The police."

"The very same." We turned the corner, heading off the Strip. "After your little disappearing act, the detective on assignment came looking for me. And while I always appreciate his pretty blue eyes and fine ass, I had to go full-on diva meltdown over the remaining girls to keep him off his balance until Dixie took over and I could split." She eyed me again. "He asked if there'd been a woman in the club, maybe someone who'd found the psychics. He called her Sariah Pelter."

Sariah Pelter. I hadn't heard that name in a long time. "What did you tell him?"

"I told him I didn't know what he was talking about, that there were two hundred people in that place, and that it was dark, it stank, and I wasn't doing a census. Then he pulled out a picture."

That did make me sit up straight. Something hard panged in my chest. "A picture? What sort of picture?"

"The sort you got from newspapers back when they still had newspapers. It was beat to shit too, despite the little laminated pocket thing he had it in.

And it was you, dollface, circa age sixteen, not counting your eyes. Those put your birth date more at the creation of the world." We pulled into the parking garage at LVM, and I shuddered as we entered the concrete structure in an actual car vs. via the psychic highway. Traveling by limo hurt way less than traveling by brain waves. Or whatever it was I'd done. Nikki parked and half turned in her seat. "You wanna tell me that little story before I up and say the wrong thing at the wrong time?"

I opened my mouth to speak, but her phone beeped. She glanced down. "Hold that thought, honey," she said. "The girls just flatlined."

We piled out of the limo, Nikki bolting for the elevator for several long steps before she realized I wasn't keeping up. With a curse, she strode back to me, pulling one of my arms over her neck to carry some of my weight. "I thought you were supposed to be healing."

"This is me healing."

I couldn't fully hear Nikki's expletive as we made it to the elevator bay. She practically threw me up against the wall, bracing me as she punched in a button for the fourth floor. Then she scowled at me and also punched one for the fifth.

"They separated the girls?"

"They did not," she said. "Just hedging my bets given your awesome athletic prowess right now. I can't manage everyone collapsing around me at the same time."

"Great," I muttered. I couldn't seem to fill my lungs. I'd started out fine at the car, but within three steps, I'd needed a deep breath of air, and—it wasn't there. Whatever was pumping through my veins was high-test something or other, but it certainly wasn't oxygen.

The elevator pinged open, and Nikki punched it closed again, not moving until we'd hit the fifth floor. "Here we go." She hauled me out of the elevator and down the hallway. Room doors stood open, some with patients, some not. She stepped inside one and deposited me on a chair, then squatted until she was eye-level.

That, apparently, was the wrong thing to do. "What are you on?" She scowled at me, then pulled a phone out of her cleavage. "Burner. No passcode set. Do me a favor and don't set one now, not until you stabilize. Which ain't going to be anytime soon, sweetcakes."

She held out the phone, and I took it, wincing against another chest spasm. "I've got the number, and I'll text you if it's clear," she continued. "When you feel better, *if* you feel better, it's room 425. If you don't feel better, crawl into this nice bed here and tell the nurse I'm one floor down. It's not like they don't already know me in this joint."

I nodded, and Nikki gripped my shoulder, then stood. I couldn't see so well, but I heard her heels clicking down the long corridor. Twenty steps, then a pause, a door slam, and silence.

Stairs, I thought. I could get to the stairs.

I couldn't stay where I was, no matter what Nikki said.

What did the High Priestess do to me?

I closed my eyes and thought back to the events leading up to today's oracular gymnastics. I remembered the girls, the fight. The afternoon of preparation, a meal. Being left alone and nodding off.

Nodding off.

The meal.

I frowned. I'd been tired, yes. But I hadn't been ready to drop into a coma. Had Armaeus drugged me? Worse, was one of the side effects of that drug an even more enhanced capability for astral travel or whatever the hell it was I'd done?

Just whose side was that bastard on, anyway?

I struggled to straighten in my chair—which was a good first step, I thought. At some point, my phone pinged, and I glanced down at it. My eyes blurred with pain almost immediately, so I tucked my phone away. Nikki was supposed to text me when she had the all clear. Well, she'd texted. What she said didn't matter, I just needed to get to her.

I pushed out of the room and sighed, swaying closer to the wall. Walls were good.

Fortunately, the unit was all but empty tonight, and I made my way down the interminably long corridor mostly by breathing through my nose. The place smelled like antiseptic and citrus, which, surprisingly, helped stabilize me. Then again, I'd been in and out of a lot of hospitals, back in the day.

As Sariah Pelter. "C'mon, c'mon," I gritted out. "Not the time."

I made it to the door marked EXIT and pushed it, almost crying with relief as I staggered into the cool white stairwell. I pressed up against the wall and realized from the shock of contact that my skin was fiery hot. "Goddammit, Armaeus," I muttered. "What did you do to me?"

Only silence greeted me. I tried to remember whether or not the Magician had spoken inside my head since I'd entered Binion's. He had, hadn't he? But not since he'd "healed" me. And certainly not once I'd been prepared for the High Priestess's visioning work.

Man, all that had *sucked*. Still, if I hadn't stepped in,

Eshe would have tried to force the girls from Kavala to perform for her, and they clearly weren't up for that kind of crazy. Then again, maybe they wouldn't feel it as strongly as I did. Maybe since they'd been doing it for years, the experience of being blasted apart and then put back together would feel like coming home.

I sort of doubted it.

The trip down the stairs was mercifully brief, since I had gravity on my side. By the time I pushed out onto the floor, I felt more or less steady. A controlled sort of chaos was holding forth at the far end of the hallway. But it didn't look like desperate chaos. More like happy, fluffy chaos. I needed more fluffy in my life.

Besides, that had to be where the girls were being held. I eased out alongside the wall, pausing a moment to rest. Because of the ruckus, no one noticed me. I was feeling better, I told myself. I could totally make it if I stayed pressed up against the wall.

Ten steps down the hallway, I began to rethink my decision.

Twenty steps, and my breathing gave out again.

But it was at step twenty-three that my good luck really took a nosedive.

A firm, no-nonsense palm appeared out of nowhere, pressing into the wall before my eyes. It was attached to a powerful forearm that disappeared beneath the sleeve of a rumpled white shirt rolled up almost to the elbow.

But I didn't get much beyond the hand, honestly, given what was dangling from it.

An LVMPD police detective badge. With a name I had imprinted on my cerebral cortex since the first time I'd heard it when I was twelve years old.

"Hello, Sariah," Brody Rooks said.

CHAPTER TWENTY-SEVEN

Wincing, I flopped around so at least I had the wall at my back, then forced myself to look up. And up still farther. I'd remembered him being tall, intense, and mind-bogglingly hot but…I hadn't expected there to be so much of him.

Then again, I hadn't expected ever to see the man again.

What little shot I'd had at breathing normally was now completely dead.

Standing in front of me was six-foot-something's worth of heart-stoppingly gorgeous detective in a rumpled suit and a three-day beard. His eyes were rimmed with fine lines and ringed with fatigue, his hair looked like he'd been raking his hands through it, his body was as tight and coiled as a lion about to spring. Some of what I saw was new, but most of it was as familiar as my own skin, a million different details pounding at me, filling in a decade of memories.

"Hello, Brody."

He jerked back at the sound of my voice, as if he'd half thought I was a mirage. His hand dropped from the wall. Eyes the color of a winter sky took my measure, the smooth, tight lips and chiseled jaw assaulting the fading sepia-toned image I had carefully preserved in the scrapbook of my mind, inviolate and impenetrable.

I'd left that image behind the moment I'd picked myself up off a hot Memphis back lot ten years ago, the sound of my own annihilation ringing in my ears, the smell of copper and fire rank in my nose. Stumbling, coughing, and half-dead with shock, I'd walked away that morning from everything in my life that had turned to pure evil.

And I'd *run* from the only thing left that was good.

"That was you, I assume," he said coolly. "Four days ago at Binion's?"

I didn't bother answering that one, and his jaw tightened. The subtle movement unlocked a completely unexpected and unwanted flood of heat inside me, valuable at this moment only because it mortified me to the point of movement. I lurched off the wall, swaying, and began trudging down the corridor again.

Brody turned too, not touching me. Which I appreciated. Almost. "What are you doing here?" He didn't ask the second question, and the more obvious one: *What are you doing alive?* I appreciated that too.

"I'm here to make sure the girls are okay. There's no law against that, I assume."

He morphed smoothly into cop mode. "What's your connection to them?"

"Saw them on the street outside that terrible, terrible accident." We reached the knot of people in front of the girls' room. There were fewer of them now. Fewer was good. Apparently sensing that I was in no shape to be stopped, Brody let me keep going. I homed in on Nikki's glitter.

"I'm sorry, ma'am, you can't—"

251

"She's on the approved list." Nikki waved me in, her eyes rounding as she took in my new detective-size shadow. "Hello, Officer Hottie."

My gaze flew to hers, but her bright-green contacts were trained on Brody. Beside me, he sighed. "I thought you said you didn't know her, Nikki."

"I had no idea you meant dollface. But, Sara, look sharp. The girls apparently stopped their cardiac arrest dealio the moment you had your little fainting spell in the parking garage. They woke up crying out for you. We've only barely gotten them calmed down."

Leaving Brody behind, I pressed forward into the room. It had to be one of the nicest hospital rooms I'd ever seen, a double wide with two side-by-side beds and enough monitors to run the space station. "What is all this?"

"Experimental technology wing. Three guesses who underwrites it."

Hello, Sara Wilde. The Devil's haunting murmur knifed through me, but I ignored it, focusing on the twins. Just like in the medical suite at Prime Luxe, they both turned as if they were tethered to the same string and fixed me with a double-barreled stare. Unlike any other medical team I'd ever encountered, the crew surrounding the girls actually stood back as I got close. Either these guys had been prepped on me, or they landed far more squarely on the "research" side of the spectrum than "caregiver." Worked for me.

"What're their names?"

"Jos and Prayim," Nikki supplied. "Translator at your elbow."

At the sound of their names, the girls' hands lifted, reaching for me, their eyes luminous with shared pain. *Ah shit.* "Did they—" I turned to the translator, a small man in linen trousers and a short-sleeved dress shirt.

"Do they know what happened, ah, with me?"

He put the question to them in a melodic language—Greek, I assumed, or some variant close to that. The girls' faces clouded with sadness, their words coming thick and fast.

"They know that you—" The translator frowned. "They are saying you stepped into the mist? For them. They know you were not prepared. They know you're—"

"Okay, that's enough." I was keenly aware of Brody standing behind me, listening. "Tell them I'm fine, that they have to get better, that's the important thing. To heal." I flapped my hand at them. "Or do whatever they need to do. I'll be fine."

The translator spoke again, and the girls' eyes flashed back to me, too big, too haunted. Between them, their parents watched the two girls mournfully. "I don't suppose they've experienced what I'm going through?"

"Actually, they have," Nikki said. "Apparently, they've 'appeared to die' on a number of occasions since birth. Occupational hazard."

"Right." I knew I should leave, but I couldn't help but ask, "Does it get better?"

The translator put the question to the girls, and their smiles sent a warm wash of reassurance through me. Then the short man spoke again. "Not at all," he said. "But the pain is a gift to the goddess, for which they are honored."

Great. "Of course it is."

Nikki eyed me as Brody finally moved forward and grabbed my arm. A jolt of recognition flowed through me. Not the electrical pulse that I experienced with the touch of a Connected, but the rush of familiarity, of long-ago hopes and wishes and stupid emotions that really had no place surging up now, with a flash of heat so strong I wondered if I was going through the change twenty years too early.

"So this is your secret, Sara Wilde."

The voice purred over the heads of everyone in the room, and this time I did stop, turning to scan the room. Aleksander Kreios leaned against the far wall, watching me. No one seemed to notice him except Nikki, however. Nikki and Jos and Prayim, whose eyes grew large, their faces so rapt that even their parents looked over to the far wall, frowning.

"What is it?" Brody hadn't let go of my arm, but he wasn't stupid. His gaze went to the far wall, and he frowned. "What's with the wall?"

With a wink, Kreios winked out, apparently an illusion tuned solely to the Connected channel. The girls blinked and appeared confused again, and Nikki moved forward in a flash of sequins and swagger.

"Time to break up the party and let these girls get some rest. Detective? Sara?"

The research team stood mutely to the side, and I wondered at them again. Where had Armaeus found them? And what was he hoping to gain?

We shuffled out into the corridor, Nikki staunchly by my side.

"Saria—Sara," Brody corrected himself, as soon as we'd cleared the knot of people. "You want to tell me what's going on?"

"Are you here in an official capacity, Detective?" Nikki asked, her voice dripping with Southern charm that was completely fake but somehow worked for her. "Or you want me to give Dixie a call? I bet she's probably in the hospital right now, looking after her other girls."

I blinked. *Dixie?*

Meanwhile, Brody winced. "Nikki, this isn't the time."

"No really, this is perfect." Nikki had her cell phone out, waving it around. It was as bedazzled as her uniform. "Since Sara here clearly *isn't* the person you asked about the other day, and no one *else* knows she could have been that person either, it probably makes sense for us to have your little chat with Sara another day? Not in the middle of a crowd while girlfriend here can barely keep her feet. But there's no need to waste the opportunity for you and Dixie to get together."

It was my turn to stare. Brody wasn't taking that well. His tired face now had two flags of color at the cheeks, and he grimaced. "We're no longer together, Nikki. You know that."

"Hmm. Well, not sure Dix knows that, word to the wise. What is definite fact, however, is that Sara here is about to faint. Let us go freshen up, and we'll be back in a jiff."

"Not happening." Brody turned and glared. "Beat it, Nikki."

"I'm not going—"

"It's fine, really," I said, reaching out to touch her arm. Her strength radiated from her, welcome and sure. "I can talk."

She blew out a long breath. "Fine." She swiveled toward Brody. "You've got three minutes, then we're outtie."

Not giving him a chance to disagree, she turned up the corridor, her booming voice loud enough to wake the dead. "Doctor! I need to talk with the doctor."

Brody half pulled, half carried me to the next open room, pushing me inside it, then stepping in himself. He didn't close the door behind him, but I still felt trapped. Not being a huge fan of being trapped, I welcomed the spurt of anger that cleared away most of my fog. I forced my chin up and braced myself against the wall. I *was* a big fan of walls at the moment.

Brody stood on the balls of his feet, like a predator about to pounce. "Let's start with an easy one, *Sara*," he said, his eyes cop hard again. "What brings you to Vegas? It's a long way from Memphis, don't you think?"

"I could ask you the same question." I shrugged. "I didn't think this kind of town would be your style."

As soon as I said the words, I knew I'd somehow misstepped. In my defense, it'd been a really long day.

"My style?" Brody's words were too careful, too quiet. "Based on what? Your oh-so-thorough assessment of my character when you were seventeen years old? The scene in your rearview mirror as you vanished into thin air?" Sharp brows lifted above his resolute gaze, and his lips twisted. "Tell me, Sara, was it my *style* that made you leave the city without informing the police that you were still alive the morning after your mother was taken? Was it my *style* that caused you to disappear completely, leaving us to assume you'd also been killed—or were kidnapped—by the same thugs who'd gotten to her?"

His words assaulted me, bringing back memories still too fresh after ten years. The explosion, the screaming, the nightmare of pain and rancid fear... I stiffened, turning away from him. "What I did and why I did it is none of your business."

"Wrong answer." Brody moved too quickly for me to evade him. My feint was more like a faint, and his hands locked on my shoulders, catching me up against the wall.

Heat pulsed through me as he shifted his hands to

rest against the wall on either side of my head. Now I really did feel trapped. And intimidated. And overwhelmed by emotions I couldn't even process. Brody Rooks, the star of a million fantasies and a million nightmares, was in front of me now. Real. Alive. *Leaning into me.* I was afraid to even blink as he edged closer yet. His lips were so near, they brushed against mine, and a million jolts of completely non-Connected energy shot through me. I whimpered, my lungs suddenly forgetting how to work.

"Now *this*, Sara, really is my style," he murmured, his lips moving against mine, a hint of a kiss so intense that my bones ached for him to just do it already. "So I suggest you start talking."

No talking, no talking, my body screamed. "I don't have anything to say to you," I whispered.

"Oh, I think you do." He leaned back from me to study my face, and his hips torqued against mine. I might be unable to breathe, but Brody's body was as jacked as mine was, even if his words were still furious. "I think you have about ten years of things to say to me, *Sara*, starting with where the hell you went on the morning of May thirteenth."

I stared at him, memorizing his pupils for something to do while my brain flapped its hands around and bleated. If I could just get him out of this room, I would run. Fast, hard, and for as long as it took to get away. It had worked ten years ago, it'd work now. I couldn't tell him the truth—not then, and definitely not now. Not ever, really. Some things just couldn't be undone. "Can you give me some air, here?" I managed.

He hesitated, glaring at me.

I gaped back, channeling fluster. It wasn't all that hard.

Finally, as if it took him far more effort than it should have, Brody stepped back just far enough to reach into his jacket pocket and pull out a small, weather-beaten notebook, fastened with a thick rubber band and bookmarked with a pen. He opened the little book, sliding the pen free, then glanced back up at me. Once more, the cool, confident cop was on display — the hot, hard predator leashed. I didn't know which Brody was more dangerous. "Okay," he said, pen poised. "Where did you go?"

My lungs finally collapsed again, and with breath came defiance. "How can it possibly matter —"

He moved just a half inch closer to me, stopping my words mid-bitch. "Just answer the damn question, Sara," he said. "It's important."

"I left town. I hitchhiked," I said flatly. "I was picked up at a campground by a woman in an RV. End of story."

"Who was it?"

"Doesn't matter, she's dead now. Natural causes."

He made another notation. "Then what? Where did you go after she gave you a ride?"

"Around." I waved my hand. "We traveled all over the place. There was a bunch of retirees going from campground to campground, seeing the sights. That's where I went. Sorry it's not more exciting."

"For ten years." His gaze on me was level and hard. "You mean to tell me that you've been roaming around with a group of itinerant campers *for ten years.* No job, no school, no credit cards —"

"Last time I checked, none of that was a crime."

"I was looking for you!" he exploded, fury and disbelief raging over his face. "The morning of the explosion, we all thought we'd find you in that rattle trap of a trailer, and there was nothing — nothing!

There were no calls, not one of your classmates knew where you'd gone, there wasn't one scrap of information. I tracked Jane Doe deaths and kidnapping reports for the next three years, expecting either you or what was left of you to show up. When nothing happened, I didn't know if that was good or bad."

So much death. Swirling all around me, so much death. "I wasn't your responsibility," I said stiffly.

"Your mother had been killed on my *watch*, Sara. That makes you my responsibility."

"Your mother...killed." Hearing the words rocked me in a way I couldn't have expected. Something inside me, the last fragile bud of disbelief, curled up and died. I'd known my mother was dead, of course. I'd known it ten years ago. But no one had ever said the words to me. No one had ever—

"Okay, Mr. Hide Your Witness in a Closet, time's up." Nikki had appeared in the doorway, reviewing the scene with the air of a woman ready to take a body down. "Unless you're going to arrest Sara for unlawful saving of everyone's asses, we're done here. You've got other work to do."

Brody growled as I pushed myself off the wall and scrambled to the side. "Not even—"

"Detective." A man in a white coat entered the room as well, waving an official-looking clipboard. "Having all these uniformed officers on-site is not part of our normal protocol. If you could just sign—"

Brody shot out a hand and caught my arm, turning me around to face him. His eyes were hard as flint, a mixture of anger and—something deeper, more primal in his face. "This isn't finished."

Nikki stepped closer. "It's not even begun, Sugar Lips. Now go do your manly business, and let me get Sara over to Dixie's."

He blanched. "That's where she's staying?"

"You know the number!" Nikki clapped her hands on my shoulders, steering me out the door as the doctor pushed his clipboard into Brody's hands.

Whether Brody watched us leave, I couldn't say.

Once again, I didn't look back.

CHAPTER TWENTY-EIGHT

An hour later we were in a whole new world. With donuts.

Nikki had brought me to the Palazzo Casino and, after a brief stop at the front desk, had sent me into the megahotel's rabbit warren of shops and restaurants to secure provisions. My instructions were clear and simple: get donuts, wait about twenty minutes so we wouldn't be seen in the casino together, then head up to the room.

So now here I was, trudging through the Palazzo, the key card and a box of deep-fried goodness in my hands the only things keeping me going. A beefy security guy waved me through to the special bank of guest elevators. I'm not going to lie, I appreciated his extra muscles, though my problems weren't going to be solved by brawn.

I rode up to my floor alone, then shambled down the long, luxurious hallway past several double doors whose numbers I barely registered. My entire world had diminished to four very important digits. 2-0-1-5. I'd get there eventually.

After what seemed like an inordinately long time, the rooms dwindled to single-door dwellings, with doors spaced farther apart. Then, suddenly, Suite 2015 loomed in front of me. I slid my passkey home, somehow absurdly pleased with the green light that flicked on. I shoved the far too heavy door open, walked inside—and stopped short. "You've got to be kidding me."

Suite 2015 glowed in the warm, ambient shimmer of several discreetly placed lamps in the foyer, the light glinting off a white marble-inlaid floor that spilled out in pristine beauty across the foyer, down a short set of steps, and into a sunken living room area. The room was stuffed with every conceivable luxury: a giant flat-screen TV, unreasonably large plush couches, a prissy work desk bristling both with electronics *and* a huge bottle of champagne in a bucket, and…a floor-to-ceiling view of the most extraordinary world I'd ever seen.

Welcome to Fabulous Las Vegas.

Mesmerized, I dropped the donut box on a table and walked toward the window. My eyes filled with the city's bright lights—and its enormous phantom casinos: The pristine white-and-black towers, the fairy-tale castle and its neighboring hulking keep. Above the Flamingo Hotel, Scandal's glass-fronted lightshow had changed to a pulsing neon burst of purple flames.

I leaned against the window frame, my gaze inexorably drawn yet farther south. Because there, of course, was the final casino, crouched like a predator at the edge of the city. Prime Luxe. It was larger than all the rest, more elegant and more barbaric by turns, its glowing metal spires thrusting up in a primitive and powerful cry to the heavens. I wondered if Armaeus was in there somewhere, watching for me, waiting.

Well, he can go screw himself. I was wrung out; feeling worse, not better, with each passing hour since I'd tripped the light fantastic in the Council's conference room and had my Brody showdown. God, that had all *sucked*. Even the parts that still sent my heart racing. Because I knew what I had to do.

I was staying as long as it took to get the girls out of danger, then I was out of Vegas. Permanently.

Even as I thought the words, the white spires of the Prime Luxe turned red — pulsed — then went dark.

I wheeled back from the window as if I'd been slapped. Jerking the curtains closed, I blanked the view of the city.

"You bring the donuts?"

I looked up, and Nikki stood in the doorway to the second bedroom of the suite, her hair in a garish turban and her body ensconced in an enormous kimono.

"Kitchen table." I pointed.

"You're the best. She padded over, and I realized that she was wearing giant poodle slippers. "I left you a change of clothes on your bed from my go bag. We gotta do something about your wardrobe, but not tonight. Tonight is for donuts and champagne. The latter is on the Magician. I'm sure he won't mind."

I smiled as I trudged my way into the bedroom. The thing on the bed looked like one long piece of hot pink satin, but I didn't care. I unbuckled my boots, then skimmed out of my shirt and leggings. Eventually I found a neck hole in the garment and pulled it on. It was some sort of weird caftan, and it smelled like bubblegum lip gloss.

Nikki hadn't wanted me to be left alone tonight, and I hadn't wanted to be left alone either. Nevertheless, I was a little out of my depth. It'd been a long time since I'd had anything approaching a girlfriend. Other than Father Jerome, it'd been a long time since I'd had anything approaching a friend at all.

She barked out a laugh when I went back into the main area. I'd knotted the garment to the side, and it almost cleared the ground. "Dollface, I swear, if I posted that on Facebook, you'd have to fight the boys off with sticks. C'mere. The donuts are top-drawer. The champagne sucks, but what're you gonna do?"

"Any port in a storm." Instead of going with conventional flutes, Nikki served the bubbly in giant glass tumblers. I picked up the bottle and read the label. "I assume this was the most expensive bottle?"

"I figured you needed it more than the sultan of Dubai."

I laughed. I couldn't remember the last time I'd done that, but Nikki grinned at me as I gingerly slid onto the couch. My mental inventory insisted that everything that was supposed to be inside my body remained inside. Even if it all was still a little scrambled.

"So." Nikki leaned back in her chair, her feet stacked one over the other at the ankle, the white fuzzy poodles wagging their pink tongues at me. She hoisted her tumbler, but her eyes were direct. Cop direct. And her manner was no-nonsense. "You want to tell me what's going on between you and Detective Sexy Pants?"

"Why—is he dating Dixie?" The words were out before I could stop them.

"Nope, but not for her lack of trying. That's a complication for another day, though, because he pretty much looked ready to eat you alive at the hospital, and pretty much all in a good way, once he gets over his pout. What'd you do to him?"

I grimaced. "Let him believe I was dead for the last ten years."

"Well, that would put a guy off, I guess."

I picked up my own glass and took a long swig. Nikki had opened up the curtains again while I'd been changing, and the entire swath of the Vegas Strip lay spread out in front of us like a sorcerer's playground. I sensed all the questions coming from Nikki, but I beat her to the punch. Now, this night, I wanted somebody to know.

"Back in the day, I wasn't Sara Wilde. I was Sariah Pelter, or Psychic Teen Sariah." I rolled the glass in my hand. There was no judgment coming from Nikki as I spoke. I suspected she'd been a pretty good cop at some point. "Your comment about knowing your gifts as a kid making it easier? It does and it doesn't. My mom knew what I could do, and she told her friends, who told their friends. I'd read cards for them when they came over to play poker. They all got a great laugh out of it. Eventually, I was maybe about eleven at this point, someone asked me if I could find her lost dog. God love her, she adored that dog." I shook my head, remembering it. "Little Jack Russell terrier, most annoying thing you could ever imagine. But my mom's friend was beside herself with worry." I let my words trail off, remembering the woman's lined face, her florid bottle-red hair, her heavy makeup. And her eyes. Her eyes had been the worst. She'd known from the start.

"Let me guess," Nikki interrupted my thoughts. "You found the dog in a neighbor's backyard."

"Put out in the trash. I didn't predict that part. She guessed when she went home that night and saw the trash cans all lined up along the street. She attacked everyone's garbage like some sort of crazed maniac and found Kiki within twenty minutes. My mom told me that later." I grimaced. Of all the terrible things I'd seen since then, it was that story that gave me the willies. Maybe because that was when everything had started. "It didn't take long after that for word to get around."

"And how long did it take for puppies to become kids?"

I glanced at her sharply, and once again, despite the kimono and turban and the thin film of facial cream, the eyes that stared out at me were dead-on cop.

She kept going. "You said ten years ago was when you were tangled up with Brody. For him to give a shit, he had to be working with you. Not a huge leap to have the community psychic brought in on an investigation, even if she's a kid. Especially if she's a kid." Her eyes narrowed. "Schoolmate of the victim, I bet."

I worked my hands around the glass. "Maryann Williams. She'd been gone three days. I didn't know her, not really. She wasn't in any of my classes. But her mom told someone else's mom, who told my mom and also the police that I probably knew something because I could find anything. And my mom, of course, was more than happy to march me down to the station to prove their stories true."

"She sounds like a prize." Nikki's words were slightly more judgmental now. "But you did your thing, I'm thinking. You found the kid."

"Yeah." I swallowed. "I was too late, though."

Nikki took another drink and considered that. "Bet you weren't after that."

"Not usually." My words were barely a whisper now. "I became sort of obsessed. I would pore over the missing persons reports, amber alerts. My mom kept bringing me to the station. I'd give information to anyone who would listen. They even investigated me as being an accessory once."

"Gotta love the system. They assigned you to

Brody after that?"

"He was new on homicide, and they tossed him into Crimes against Kids or something like that. He got saddled with me before he could say no." I shrugged. "After a while, it just seemed natural, working together."

"And how long before it blew up?"

I looked out the window again. Scandal was lit up in pulsing purple and red. As I watched, it slid to blue, then green. Like a skyscraping lava lamp. "Five years. Then I just—I had to leave the city. For good. And I couldn't leave a trail. I was off the grid for a long time after that. But eventually, I sort of drifted back, I guess."

"We all do." Nikki rolled the champagne around in her glass. "And then, eventually, Brody transferred here, and you never came clean on the fact that you'd been alive all this time." She looked at me somberly. "Cops take that kind of thing personally. We lose too many as it is."

I winced, remembering the almost crazed look in Brody's eyes as he'd searched my face, unwilling to believe at first that I wasn't some hallucination. "I know."

"But that definitely explains why you've always been hell-bent on leaving Vegas almost before you touch down." She stopped moving her glass. "Until this time. Because of those girls."

"I made a deal with the Council." I sensed the slightest touch of Armaeus in my mind, but I ruthlessly shut him out. "Fitz pumped a lot of that Pythene gas into me, and it did something to me. For the time being, I have the same visioning skills that Jos and Prayim do. So they don't have to play Eye of God for the Council. I can."

"How's that working out for you?"

"About as well as it looks."

Nikki pursed her lips, her glass almost empty as she leaned down to scoop up another donut. "There's more to it, isn't there? The girls had one rough patch in the hospital before we could stabilize them, the only time they spoke in English. Said something big and bad was after us all. Hunting us down. And that it was coming here next."

I saw no reason to deny it. "Yeah."

She shook her head. "Well, Vegas *is* a great place to party."

I laughed again despite myself, and Nikki eased the conversation away from all the dark corners and sharp edges that were forming in my mind. At some point, she helped me to my feet, but the pain in my body had dulled from the alcohol and sugar. I stumbled into bed, telling myself that tomorrow, everything would work out. Tomorrow, I'd find out when the girls would be able to return home, assuming that Armaeus could ensure they would be protected. Tomorrow, I was one day closer to getting my own freedom back.

Sleep didn't creep up on me like a whisper in the night — it hit me like a baseball bat. I'd no sooner closed my eyes than my mind unhinged, and I found myself sifting and drifting through a flood of random, unconnected thoughts, sinking deeply into a profoundly subverbal bliss. Gradually, the mind-static firmed and a soft, familiar murmur slid over me, as intimate as a lover's touch.

Exactly that intimate, in fact.

Sweet Christmas, yes. I needed a really good dream right about now. I let the smile curve my lips, pleasure prickling along my skin, warming it, as I arched in response to the pressure on my body. I sighed with completely unfettered appreciation as the mattress beneath me shifted to accommodate the body of a large, delicious-smelling man, knocking my Sleep Number to an absolute 10. Not any delicious-smelling man either, but a beautiful, dangerous, lust-magnet muffin of stud who I wasn't entirely sure was trustworthy, but at this moment, I pretty much didn't care, *because I was dreaming.* And if a girl couldn't throw caution to the wind while she was sacked out for the night, when could she?

Except...except there was decidedly something non-dreamlike about the hand sliding up my thigh, about the soft murmur of breath along skin, the feeling of lips pressing to my hip bone, my rib cage, my shoulder. Despite my brain insisting that waking up was seriously not in my best interests, even if all of this was a dream, I pried my eyes open a slit.

Just in time to get bodychecked into the mattress by a full-frontal bronzed demigod.

"Miss Wilde," the Magician purred. I felt myself sliding back down a rabbit hole of unconsciousness, unable to escape. Then his next words sent me spinning in an entirely different direction. *"It's time for our work to begin.*

WILDE CARD

All that glitters may not be gold...

When an antique gold show comes to Vegas, Tarot reading artifact hunter Sara Wilde's job is simple: to locate and liberate a set of relics rumored to give their bearers access to an ancient, incredible power. No one wants the relics more than Sara's client – the insufferably arrogant, criminally sensual, and endlessly evasive Magician.

But Sara's heist takes a turn for the trickier as the smoky-eyed specter from her past, Detective Brody Rooks, is assigned to investigate a break-in at the gold show, forcing Sara to confront the one man in Vegas she can't bluff.

Sometimes, when the deck is stacked against you...you've got to play the *Wilde Card*.

Want to keep apprised of the latest news of Immortal Vegas, get sneak peaks and free books? Sign up for my newsletter at <u>www.jennstark.com/newsletter</u>!

A NOTE FROM JENN

I've been so grateful for the opportunity to share the world of Immortal Vegas to readers like you, and I welcome your feedback and ideas! If you enjoyed Sara's adventures, I sincerely appreciate any review that you might wish to post online. Reviews help readers find books, so thank you in advance for helping to share the word.

You can reach me online at www.jennstark.com, follow me on Twitter @jennstark, or visit my Facebook page at https://www.facebook.com/authorjennstark. To subscribe to my newsletter and receive news, updates and special giveaways, sign up on this page: http://www.jennstark.com/contact.

The cards that appear at the opening of Getting Wilde were the ones pulled by Sara before her first meeting with her contact at Le Stube. Here are the three basic interpretations a Tarot reader might give to someone pulling these cards:

The Tower

Structures you have come to depend on may be dismantled, or previously held beliefs may be torn apart to make way for a new reality. Change can crash into your life without warning, disrupting your routine or transforming your life. Alternatively, an explosion of significant proportions may rock you, figuratively or literally.

Death

Change is in the air of a transformational kind. Death is all about transition, rebirth and permanent change—the kind that alters you forever. If you don't embrace this change willingly, something will force you into it, but your life will ultimately improve even if all seems lost. Only in very rare circumstances does Death mean actual death.

The Devil

Issues of temptations, burdens, restrictions surround you. Are you holding onto self-imposed limits? Are you a slave to desires you cannot control? Ultimately, this card represents your own fears—you believe you can't control your life, so you are willing to bind yourself to a negative belief system. Once you take charge and work to effect positive change, you will break free.

ACKNOWLEDGMENTS

So many people contributed to the Immortal Vegas series coming to life, from its first incarnation as the Golden Heart-winning manuscript "Black Jack" to today, with the launch of the first full-length novel in the series, Getting Wilde. Thank you to Elizabeth Bemis for your wonderful design work on the novella cover, book formatting, graphics and my site (as well as your limitless patience and treasured friendship). Sincere thanks also go to Gene Mollica for the photography and cover design/illustration for the first three novels in the series, and to Linda Ingmanson for collaborative and above all thorough editorial skills. Any mistakes in the manuscript are, of course, my own. To Kristine, my sincere appreciation for your many (many, many…) reads, blurb help and brainstorming sessions. To Kay, my ongoing gratitude for your encouragement and highly-valuable suggestions every step of the way. To Rachel, for your impromptu story doctoring and publishing mojo, thank heavens you never sleep! You truly can't imagine how much your feedback means to me. Finally, to Geoffrey, my deepest thanks for your vision, insight, and guidance, since the very beginning of this story. It's been a *Wilde* ride.

ABOUT JENN STARK

Jenn Stark is a Golden Heart award-winning author of paranormal romance and urban fantasy. She lives and writes in Ohio. In addition to her work in urban fantasy, she is also author Jennifer McGowan, whose Maids of Honor series of Young Adult Elizabethan spy romances are published by Simon & Schuster, and author Jennifer Chance, whose Rule Breakers series of New Adult contemporary romances are published by Random House/LoveSwept, and whose Gowns & Crowns series of modern royals romances is now available.

Made in the USA
San Bernardino, CA
11 October 2018